PRAISE FOR BRYAN SMITH
AND *HOUSE OF BLOOD*!

"Smith promises unimaginable brutality, bile-inducing fear, and unfathomable despair; and then delivers monumentally!"
—Horror Web

"Bryan Smith is a force to be reckoned with!"
—Douglas Clegg, author of *The Abandoned*

"A feast of good old-fashioned horror. Don't pass this one up!"
—Brian Keene, author of *City of the Dead*

"In the vein of Bentley Little and Edward Lee...sometimes scary, sometimes amusing, *House of Blood* is a quick, enjoyable read suitable for all fans of horror and dark fantasy."
—Michael Laimo, author of *The Demonologist*

"Bryan Smith has a knack for taking the standard horror tale and turning it inside out to show you the dripping viscera at its core."
—Randy Chandler, author of *Bad Juju*

ALIVE AGAIN

Dead eyes snapped open in absolute darkness.

At first there was nothing but the darkness. This void. Then, all at once, consciousness returned, and, with it, awareness. She felt something soft and plush cradling her body. Then her reawakened senses detected confinement. She lifted her hands and they met almost immediate resistance. She kicked her legs out and encountered more resistance.

A coffin, she thought, horror blooming within her regenerated brain. *I'm in a coffin. But…why?*

Then the memories returned. Her last memories. That awful girl. The gun. The bullets puncturing her flesh and taking her life.

I'm dead, she thought.

But now, somehow, she was back.

And there was something else. A smell, a scent marker as individual and damning as a fingerprint left at a crime scene. It was mixed with something else, sex musk, an aroma that awakened something wicked within her. Something that demanded satiation. That girl…her killer…she was nearby. Close enough almost to touch.

Somewhere…above her.

A scream tore out of Hannah's mouth. She was aware of a new feeling now, something she'd never felt in her previous life. A bloodlust. An all-consuming need to have revenge. To kill.

She screamed again.

And then she began to claw frantically at the coffin lid.

Other *Leisure* books by Bryan Smith:

HOUSE OF BLOOD

DEATHBRINGER

BRYAN SMITH

LEISURE BOOKS NEW YORK CITY

This book is dedicated to two survivors:

My wife, Rachael Wise
and
Cherie Smith, my mother.

A LEISURE BOOK®

March 2006

Published by

Dorchester Publishing Co., Inc.
200 Madison Avenue
New York, NY 10016

If you purchased this book without a cover you should be aware that this book is stolen property. It was reported as "unsold and destroyed" to the publisher and neither the author nor the publisher has received any payment for this "stripped book."

Copyright © 2006 by Bryan Smith

All rights reserved. No part of this book may be reproduced or transmitted in any form or by any electronic or mechanical means, including photocopying, recording or by any information storage and retrieval system, without the written permission of the publisher, except where permitted by law.

ISBN 0-8439-5677-1

The name "Leisure Books" and the stylized "L" with design are trademarks of Dorchester Publishing Co., Inc.

Printed in the United States of America.

Visit us on the web at www.dorchesterpub.com.

ACKNOWLEDGMENTS

I'd like to again thank my family for continuing to be a source of strength and encouragement. My brothers Jeff and Eric for being the two coolest siblings anyone could ever hope to have. My nephew, Dylan, for carrying the Smith horror fan legacy into a new generation. My mom and my wife for propping me up during the harder times and cheering me on during the happier times. My great friend Keith Ashley. My grandparents, Dorothy and Oscar May, and Ruby Smith.

Thanks also to authors Douglas Clegg, Brian Keene, and Tom Piccirilli for being so uncommonly cool. And I need to mention the *Deathbringer* first readers: Randy Chandler, Kent Gowran, Paul Legerski, Nick Cato, and Jeff Strand. Thanks, guys—your feedback helped decide between this one and the "other one."

Finally, a Bryan Smith acknowledgments page would not be complete without again thanking all the rock-and-rollers who keep me from going off the rails: Backyard Babies, GNR, Supersuckers, Iggy, Crystal Pistol, the Erotics, the Creeping Cruds, Wednesday 13, the Hellacopters, the Dead Boys, Sleazegrinder and Faster Pussycat.

PROLOGUE

Hannah Starke watched a fly make its slow way up the length of her slim, tanned leg. The little creature moved with the lethargy of a fat birthday boy stuffed full of cake and ice cream. Cake. Wedding cake. Hannah shooed the fly away and returned her attention to the pad of yellow legal paper propped in her lap. Her flowing script already filled some half-dozen pages, which were folded over and tucked beneath the pad's cardboard backing. At the top of this fresh page in neat block letters were the words, GOD-DAMNED WEDDING CAKE!

Hannah heaved a sigh and reached for the pitcher of sweet tea on the small table next to the lounge chair. She tipped some more tea and ice into her nearly empty glass. The tea eased her thirst, but did little to shake the heat induced lethargy that had rendered her incapable of accomplishing anything productive for going on an hour. She knew she should get

1

off her ass and seek the solace of air-conditioning, but the day was so lovely it kept her glued to this spot on the front porch of her husband-to-be's modest ranch house.

Her peripheral vision detected a hint of movement to her far right. She glanced in that direction and smiled at the sight of a girl attired in the uniform of a St. Mary's student. The girl was on the other side of the quiet street, maybe half a block down. The little plaid miniskirt the girl wore showed off shapely legs Hannah was certain made every dirty old man who got a glimpse drool uncontrollably. The girl's long, shiny blond hair flopped about her head in pigtails.

Hannah sipped more tea and leaned back in her chair. She closed her eyes and felt herself edging toward drowsiness. She wished Mike were here to keep her awake and focused on the serious business of planning their wedding.

But Mike was at work. He was a rookie officer in the Dandridge Police Department. She'd met him in his last year at Middle Tennessee State University, where he'd been a criminal justice major. The chemistry between them was instant and intense. During those initial several weeks together, practically all of their spare time was spent engaged in a relentless quest to fuck each other's brains out. It could have turned out to be just another short-lived but torrid relationship, but once that initial heat waned some, the chemistry was still there. They did everything together and it became a given that this was a relationship with the power to endure.

Then came Mike's proposal on classic bended-knee the night of his graduation from MTSU. She joyously accepted the proposal and a date was set for a year hence. The way she saw it, she couldn't imagine wanting to be with anyone other than Mike, so there was no reason to pussyfoot around.

She wanted to be Mrs. Michael O'Bannon.

And so she would be.

But her happiness failed to negate the worry Mike's choice of career had instilled in her. She often wished he'd gone straight back into school after graduation to pursue a law degree. Not because the legal world was potentially many times more lucrative than what a cop could ever hope to make. No, she fretted so because of the danger inherent in a cop's life.

Okay, so Dandridge was a smallish town, with a population of some twelve thousand. Murders were rare occurrences there. And as Mike liked to point out, no Dandridge cop had ever died in the line of duty. Which, okay, was a compelling argument. But neighboring town Brighton, which was similar in size and pace of life, had not so long ago been the scene of a tragic multiple murder. One night some drug-crazed lunatics—who admittedly had ranged far out of their home territory—robbed a fast-food restaurant and brutally murdered the handful of employees still on duty.

If it could happen in Brighton, it could happen in Dandridge.

But Mike would not be swayed, pointing out that the alleged offenders had been apprehended and were no longer a danger to anyone. The odds against anything similar happening again were astronomical. On a purely objective level, Hannah could see the logic in this. But logic and rational thinking mattered little to her when she slept alone at night and agonized over the safety of her intended. She could too easily imagine an intoxicated redneck pulling a gun on Mike and blowing him away after a routine traffic stop.

She shuddered and her eyes snapped open. Anxious to dispel the disturbing image, her gaze fell back to the legal pad and the words GODDAMNED WEDDING CAKE! With a derisive snort, she shook her head. Mike's meddling mother had announced long ago that *she* would make the cake. Not *pay* a baker to make it, but make it *herself*.

The notion made Hannah livid, but because it was the one way in which Mike's mother had offered to help she went along with it. Which she now regretted. With the wedding less than a week away, Marsha O'Bannon showed no signs of making actual preparations to bake the cake. So now Hannah was in the difficult spot of having to decide whether she should pay a baker an extravagant sum to produce a suitable cake on short notice. It would cause a rift in familial relations, no doubt, but it was looking increasingly like she would have no choice.

A lilting voice called out: "Hello, there!"

Hannah looked up from the page and saw the schoolgirl walking across Mike's front lawn en route to the porch. She lugged a heavy book bag and in one hand clutched some laminated cards. The sight of the girl's smiling face vanquished her own frown. She raised a finger, set aside the legal pad, and got to her feet.

"Just one minute while I fetch my checkbook."

The wattage of the schoolgirl's smile amped up considerably. "But you don't even know what I'm selling!" She giggled. "I could be hawking deeds to nonexistent bridges!"

The girl's enthusiasm was infectious. Hannah smiled, too, forgetting for the moment the maddening matter of Mike's passive-aggressive mother and the illusory wedding cake. "Oh, you can't fool me. I went to St. Mary's too, you know. I'll be happy to buy some magazines from you."

The girl shrugged her book bag off her shoulder and dropped it on the porch, where it landed with a heavy thump. She held out a hand. "Awesome. My name's Molly. Molly Nelson. Jeez, you don't know how much I appreciate this . . ." Her brow arched.

Hannah laughed and shook the proffered hand. "Hannah Starke. For now. In a week I'll be Hannah O'Bannon."

The girl's eyes widened. "No! You're getting married?"

Hannah laughed again, with less restraint this time. She liked Molly. The bubbly girl reminded her of a young version of herself. Molly seemed smart and well-adjusted. Hannah knew nothing about her, but she was unable to suppress the instinct to sketch out some imaginary biographical details. She couldn't help it. It was the writer in her. That part of her always wanted to invent histories for every stranger she encountered. Molly, she was willing to bet, was an overachiever. A gifted girl of many talents who'd been raised right by loving parents. She would go on to great success in later life. It was a bio devoid of drama, but Hannah's instincts told her there was nothing for it—this Molly was one of those fortunate ones God (or whomever was really in charge of these things) had decided to bless extravagantly at birth. Probably some of her less fortunate classmates were insanely jealous of her, which was understandable, but Hannah was pretty sure Molly was levelheaded enough not to let it get to her.

She grinned. "I am, indeed. To my college sweetheart. He's a police officer here in Dandridge. Mike O'Bannon. I'm very proud of him."

"Well, you should be. I bet he's a hunk, huh?"

Hannah chuckled. "You know, he really is. But don't say that around him. I wouldn't want his head getting any bigger than it already is."

The sound that emerged from Molly's mouth now was closer to a cackle than a giggle. "Are you sure about that?"

Hannah frowned. "Um . . . what?"

Molly's eyes suddenly widened again and she glanced at the watch strapped to her thin left wrist. There was a glint of sudden panic in her eyes. "Oh, I totally forgot! I have to go pick my little brother up from daycare in fifteen minutes. Oh, darn!"

Hannah's smile returned. "Just a moment. I'll be back with that checkbook."

"Thanks so much!"

Hannah turned and entered the house. She walked through the foyer and dining room and into the kitchen, where her Kate Spade bag was propped against a fruit bowl on an island in the middle of the room. She opened the bag, located her checkbook and a pen, and turned to go back to the porch.

She stopped in her tracks.

Molly stood in the archway that separated the dining room from the kitchen. The book bag dangled from her right hand. It looked considerably lighter now, as if all the books had been removed from it. "I didn't feel like waiting outside. Is that okay with you?"

There was a strange edge to the girl's voice now, a

hint of something feral. Her posture was different, too. She slumped a bit now, with a hip cocked out and her breasts thrust forward. She was still smiling, but there was now something nasty about the expression. Something sinister and malevolent. The transformation so astonished Hannah that it undercut all her better instincts and sealed her fate.

"Molly . . . I told you I'd be out in a minute." She raised the checkbook with a shaking hand, displaying it like a defeated combatant waving a white flag on the field of battle. "See . . . I was . . . going to write you a check."

Molly snickered. "Oh, I'll be taking your money. Whatever cash you have."

She reached into the bag and advanced into the kitchen, swaying her hips in an exaggerated way. The book bag fell away and Hannah gasped at the sight of the revolver in Molly's hands. The schoolgirl aimed the gun point-blank at the center of Hannah's suddenly twitching and flushed face.

Her mouth contorted in a snarl: "On your knees, bitch!"

Hannah's heart slammed in her chest. She fell to her knees without thinking about it, surrendering to the sudden lack of strength in her legs rather than Molly's command. The girl stood before her, pushing the barrel of the gun against her forehead. Holding the revolver in her right hand, she swept the blond wig off her head, revealing a spiky, dyed-black do. Hannah's gaze dropped and for the first time she glimpsed a barbed wire tattoo encircling the girl's left ankle.

How did I not see that before?

How did I not sense there was something wrong with this girl?

7

Oh, Mike, help me, please . . .

"Look at me, bitch!"

Breath catching in her throat, Hannah raised her moisture-obscured gaze. Had she thought she'd detected something feral in that psychotic gaze before? Well, that wasn't nearly close enough. Savage, that was a better word. And this was just fucking crazy. Even facing certain death she was still editing herself.

The thought made her laugh helplessly.

The inappropriate outburst inflamed her assailant, who loosed a scream and clubbed Hannah in the head with the revolver. Pain burst in Hannah's head like a grenade, temporarily blinding and disorienting her. When she could see again, she was flat on her back and Molly—if that was her real name—stood over her, with one foot planted on either side of her prone victim. The barrel of the gun was still aimed straight at Hannah's face.

And all Hannah could think about now was Mike. She imagined Mike coming home to find her bullet-riddled body splayed in a pool of blood on his kitchen floor. She could too easily see his easygoing grin giving way to abject horror, grief, and panic. It made her mad. It made her sad. All their dreams and plans of a perfect life together blown senselessly apart.

She made eye contact with Molly, unwilling now to wilt beneath the strange fury she saw there. "Why are you doing this?"

That cackling sound came again. "Because it's fun. And because they dared me to."

Hannah frowned. "They? But . . ."

Molly's foot shot out and delivered a brutal blow to her crotch. "Shut up!"

8

Hannah wheezed and made a belated attempt to move away from her assailant, scooting backward on the slick kitchen tiles.

Molly laughed and moved with her. "Too late, you stupid cunt."

Hannah found herself whimpering. The sound shamed her, but she couldn't help it. "Please . . . please . . . I'm supposed to be married . . . please . . ."

Molly smirked. "Wedding's off."

Hannah felt the impact of the first bullet before she heard the gunshot. She looked down and saw blood welling between her breasts. *No.* She'd really been shot. She couldn't believe it. This had to be a bad dream. A really bad dream. Not real. But then she felt the pain and knew it was real.

Another bullet nicked her collarbone and she ceased trying to move away.

And now she looked up and saw the barrel of the gun looming in her face.

She had just time enough to say a silent prayer and send a heartfelt thought through the ether to her beloved: *I love you, Mike. Take care, honey.*

In those last flickering moments she felt an odd kind of peace.

Then the next bullet punched a hole through her forehead and she felt nothing at all. Hannah Starke was dead.

CHAPTER ONE

O'Bannon's house looked every bit as dead as the young woman who'd been murdered in it a week earlier. All exterior lighting was off and there was no indication of illumination within. Drapes were drawn shut over all windows not covered by shutters. To Dandridge police officer Kent Gowran they looked like funeral shrouds. This was a place of death, they announced, a place of finality and desolation.

Hard to believe there was anyone alive in there, but he'd observed Mike O'Bannon enter through the front door not two hours ago, his arms cradling cylindrical objects wrapped in paper bags. Purchases from the liquor store, no doubt. Obviously the kid intended to drink himself comatose. Kent figured he'd do the same in his place.

Kent was on unofficial suicide watch tonight, so he'd had ample time to give the matter consideration. He supposed he'd feel like dying if some random maniac came around and did to Lacey or one of their precious daughters what some son of a bitch had done to Mike's girl. But he honestly didn't believe he'd go through with offing himself. Not because he wouldn't have the nerve—as a fifteen year National Guard vet Kent had been called up and deployed many times into severely dangerous areas—but because he felt the voluntary extinguishing of his own life would be a slap in the face to the memory of those he mourned.

He prayed Mike would find the inner strength to come to the same conclusion.

He sighed and reached for the radio handset, meaning to call in someone to relieve him. The small Dandridge force lacked the manpower to have a man outside O'Bannon's house round-the-clock, but the officers had done their best to coordinate an effort among themselves, taking an hour here, two hours there whenever possible, Kent had stayed as long as he could tonight. There was a pile of paperwork to tend to back at the station before he knocked off for the night.

His fingers brushed the handset and slid away as something in his peripheral vision drew his attention. His gaze moved from the house and he peered into the darkness beyond the light of the nearest street-lamp. He squinted and saw nothing at first, and wondered for a moment whether he'd mistaken floating spots in his eyes for external movement.

But then he did see something.

Darkness emerging from darkness.

A tall, dark, lanky figure stepped into the harsh sodium glare. Kent could discern little about the stranger, but what he could detect triggered faint internal alarms. The man—he assumed the figure was male, but gender wasn't something he could attest to with certainty at this point—wore a long black coat. A black hat with a wide brim was perched atop the figure's head and was tilted down, obscuring most of the stranger's face, save for a glimpse of a pale, dramatic chin so pointy it formed a stark V. And over the chin were thin, bloodless lips that might have been smiling.

The stranger creeped him out. It was almost summer for one thing, and the night was heavy with typical Southern summertime humidity. It made no sense at all to be out and about attired in this manner this time of year. Unless, maybe, you were concealing something.

Kent's internal trouble barometer jumped into the red zone a moment later when the stranger turned off the street and began making his way across Mike O'Bannon's lawn. Kent was out of the patrol car in an instant, the need to call in relief forgotten for the moment. Mike O'Bannon had been emphatic about not wanting to see *anyone,* whether it be fellow officers, family, or friends. He wanted some time away from the world and alone with his grief.

And Kent meant to see to it that this interloper honored those wishes.

He pitched his voice way higher than his normal speaking voice, utilizing what Lacey called his "scary cop voice": "Sir, you'd best stop right there."

The man kept walking, heedless of the command. Kent saw him in profile now, getting a better view of the shadowy, pale face. What he saw sent a helpless shudder through him. The face and head of the stranger were angular to an almost freakish degree.

Kent had an odd thought—that the man looked more like a stark and eerie black and white drawing than an actual living creature. Except that was ludicrous, because the stranger was obviously alive and moving. He was flesh and blood, not an otherworldly apparition. Such things weren't real. But something else was real—the chill settling deep within him.

Steeling himself, he moved to intercede before the stranger could reach O'Bannon's front door, legs churning furiously to outpace the other man's unhurried long strides. His right hand dropped and touched the butt of his service pistol. His pulse quickened and his breath came out in great puffs as fear slithered through him like poison gas filling a closed, unventilated room. A reptilian voice in the depths of his mind sounded a desperate alarm, telling him if he ever wished to see Lacey or the girls again he'd turn around and sprint back to the patrol car.

But Kent refused to yield to the siren call of cowardice, and instead did what he'd done on fields of battle in Iraq and Afghanistan—he gritted his teeth and willed himself to face what he knew to be genuine mortal danger. *How* he knew this dark man was as deadly as any enemy combatant he'd faced in the Middle East was a mystery to him, but know it he did, with an implacable certainty he didn't bother to question.

He caught up with the stranger and laid a firm hand on a shoulder that felt like cold tarpaulin draped over a jutting metal frame. The stranger ceased his forward progress and turned to face Kent. Kent blanched at the sight of those thin, bloodless lips visible just below the tilted brim of the black hat.

Lips that were somehow wormlike, barely like anything on any human face he'd ever seen. Lips that now stretched and tilted upward at the corners, forming an awful, leering smile like something out of a lurid horror comic from the 50s. All at once the deep well of bravery he'd managed to tap time and again throughout his life went dry. He wanted to turn and run, get in the patrol car and drive like hell, just drive and drive until the fucking thing ran out of fuel. Because he needed nothing more in the world now than to put as many miles between himself and this . . . abomination as possible.

But he couldn't move. He was a statue. Somehow this thing, which he knew now was neither man nor woman (was, in fact, nothing human at all), had reached into his mind and turned off his motor control the way he'd flip off a light switch. Tears burst from Kent's eyes and his bowels uncorked an eruption of shit that made the seat of his trousers sag.

Kent saw that the thing's right hand gripped a massive book, the kind of oversized tome some people displayed on their living room coffee tables. Even here in the dark Kent sensed something infernal about it, something unnatural and foul. It was bound in thick and cracked ancient black leather and its brittle pages reeked like something long hidden from light and fresh air, like a corpse interred in a tomb a lifetime ago brought back out into the world of living things. Beneath this smell was another, fainter aroma, a scent of smoldering ash. Faint tendrils of smoke leaked from the edges of the book.

The book was as obscene as its bearer, perhaps more so.

A sound issued from those wormlike lips, a dusty, dry, insidious sound, like the laughter of the devil himself.

Kent couldn't begin to fathom the nature of this thing. Perhaps it really was the devil, inexplicably arrived here in Dandridge to incite infernal chaos. Why that should be he didn't know, but Kent was well past the stage of giving a damn about making sense of insanity. He knew he was doomed. He wished only for an end to this suspended state and a final deliverance from this horror.

More of that dry almost-laughter, followed by a quiet voice that touched his face like a cold breeze: "Your wish is my command."

The thing's free hand reached out for Kent, splayed its fingers and open palm on his chest. Kent felt the presence like tendrils of ice pressing through the shirt of his uniform.

And the thing said, "Die."

And so Kent died, his heart stopping abruptly, like a watch that has wound down.

But he remained upright.

The ancient entity retained control of the deceased officer's lower brain functions. He made the corpse turn and walk back toward the patrol car, then get inside and pull the door shut. The creature retreated from the dead man's mind and the dead cop's body slumped behind the car's steering column.

The creature made a sound of satisfaction and turned back to the O'Bannon house.

Then it mounted the steps to the porch and in a moment stood at the front door.

One long, tapered finger extended and touched the doorbell.

The stranger was gone several minutes later when the door opened and a slumped figure appeared in the doorway. The man saw the book, but did not immediately pick it up. He scanned the area outside his house, searching for any sign of the deliverer of this strange nighttime parcel. But there was nothing. Just the soft evening breeze rolling through the leaves of the trees, eliciting a rustling sound that was like the voices of the dead straining to be heard.

The grieving and weary widower breathed a heavy sigh and retrieved the book from the porch. He went inside and the dark and silent house resumed the appearance of a tomb.

CHAPTER TWO

"I can't believe she's dead."

Avery Starke nodded and stared into the diminishing head of his latest beer. This was his fifth pint of the night, and he knew it was far from his last. Poor, sweet Hannah, his baby sister, was gone, robbed from the world by some fiend with a gun, and he could think of nothing better to do than get stinking drunk. He supposed there might be better, more productive ways of processing grief, but fuck it all, this was the one that called to him, the numbing release of booze. Drink enough of it and you could divorce yourself from any real feeling at all. And that would be best, wouldn't it? To not have to feel this awful, penetrating hurt that went down to the bone, that cut as savagely and scarred more permanently than the sharpest blade.

Tom Crawford slammed his own empty pint glass on the bar, making Avery wince—the sound was like a metal spike through the brain. He suppressed the urge to snap at his friend. Probably he shouldn't be out in public like this at all. He should be with the rest of his devastated family, doing his part to help them all get through this. He knew he was failing them. But he couldn't face them. It hurt far too much to look into the grief-stricken eyes of his mother and father. His gentle, loving parents. Such fundamentally good people. Throughout his life the people he met invariably expressed jealousy at the near-perfect level of happiness evident whenever the members of his family gathered for holidays and birthdays. They were like something out of an obnoxiously sweet television sitcom. And now this. Avery snorted. *Well, the fairy tale's over now, folks. Some beast ripped the heart right out of our family—are you happy now?*

"Avery, are you listening to me, man?"

Avery blinked and lifted his gaze from the golden hue of the beer—the head had evaporated in the time between this moment and his last sip. He lifted the mug to his lips, tilted his head back, and chugged until it was empty. Then he slammed the glass on the bar and the impact dislodged it from his grip. The glass rolled off the bar and shattered on the floor.

Tom Crawford sighed. "Maybe I should take you home."

"No."

Stu Smith, the sole bartender on duty at the Rude Dog Bar & Grill tonight, knelt to the floor with a dustpan and shoveled up the glass shards. He dropped them in a trash basket, then disappeared into a back room for a moment. He reappeared with a mop, which he slopped over the floor area behind the bar a few times before returning it to the back room. When he was done, he folded his arms over the bar and leaned in close to Avery.

"Kid, I can't hold that against you. I'd be doing the same damn thing if I were in your shoes. Maybe worse. But your friend here's got a point. You might be better off drowning your sorrows at home. Stay out in this condition, and you may wind up getting into trouble you and your family don't need. Think about that, at least."

Avery felt a brief surge of unreasoning anger, but it was gone before he could speak. There was that little thing to be thankful for, anyway—he still retained enough control over his faculties to refrain from doing anything that would embarrass him to a mortifying degree in the light of day. Best to keep it that way. He sighed and reached into a rear pocket to retrieve his wallet. He fished out some bills and laid them on the counter.

"Yeah, okay. Let's settle up. Set us up with some coffees before we leave, though."

Stu pushed the modest stack of bills back across the bar. "I'll get those coffees, but I'll not take your money tonight, Avery Starke. It's all on the house. And I'd consider it a matter of respect not to give me any lip over it."

Soon Avery and Tom were sipping from two mugs of steaming coffee. The combination of heat and caffeine instantly took the edge off of Avery's buzz, but only felt invigorating for a few moments. Then the darkness was on him again, sweeping into him like a sickness of the soul. He set the coffee mug down and looked at Tom. "Stu's right about not being out like this, I'll give him that. But I'm not ready to cope. I'm not ready to fucking heal."

Tom nodded. "You want ~~oblivion~~."

"Exactly."

Tom shrugged. He set his own mug down. "Shit, Ave, I loved her, too. You know that."

Avery made reluctant eye contact with his oldest and best friend. "I know."

Tom's trembling smile was laden with the weight of bittersweet memories. "She was my great unrequited love. I think I fell for her the first time I saw her, back when you guys moved into the neighborhood. I must have been fourteen, every bit the epitome of the hopelessly gawky adolescent. And she was twelve. But already so beautiful. With all that lovely golden hair and a smile big enough to break your heart."

Tom's shoulders trembled.

Avery looked away. He didn't want to see Tom break down. His great capacity for empathy made bearing witness to his friend's pain unbearable. Watching this could only trigger his own outburst of anguish and misery.

He laid a hand on Tom's shoulder. "Come on, man. Let's go buy us some oblivion."

Tom's voice was very soft: "I don't know."

"I insist." Avery slid off the barstool and stood up. "First stop, Discount Wines and Liquors. Second, Mike O'Bannon's."

Tom stopped shaking and looked Avery in the eye. "Really?"

Avery nodded. "Yeah."

Tom frowned. "Didn't he make it pretty fucking clear he wanted everybody to stay the hell away from him for a while?"

"Yeah, I guess he did." Avery shrugged. "But I

think Mike's the company we need tonight. Not Mom and Dad. Not Annie. Not Paul. Not even the grandparents. The three of us—you, me, and Mike—we'll seek oblivion together."

"What if he won't let us in?"

Avery almost smiled. "We won't take no for an answer."

Stu Smith felt a heaviness in his heart as he watched Avery and his friend leave the bar. They moved with just the hint of a stagger in their steps. They'd not slammed enough of his beers to get truly drunk, but he wasn't naive enough to believe the kids had any intentions tonight other than drinking themselves senseless. Which was understandable. He only prayed they'd be careful.

He took a clean towel and worked on scrubbing dry a rack of pint glasses. While occupied with this task, he scanned the bar and debated whether he should close early tonight. Most of his regular clientele had already departed for the evening. Only five customers remained, three at the bar, and a couple at one of the booths along the wall. Yeah, the hell with it. The dark mood of the kids—who were in their thirties, but he thought of Avery and Tom as kids because he'd known them since they were squalling little rugrats fresh from their mommies' wombs—threatened to infect his own state of mind. Stu had battled depression since returning from Vietnam a third of a century ago, and he knew it was unwise to allow other things to fuel that tendency to let his mind go to places of darkness.

He'd go home, maybe pick up a six-pack of Pabst on the way, and plant himself in front of the widescreen TV he'd bought the year after his Margaret passed away. There he'd watch the goofiest goddamn movies in his video collection—*Abbott and Costello, Monty Python, The Pink Panther*, all the good stuff—deep into the night. He'd find his own, safer brand of oblivion there.

He set the last clean glass back in the rack, untied his apron and set it aside. He stepped out from behind the bar and was moving toward the front door with the intention of turning the CLOSED sign around when the door jangled open and a stranger walked in.

Stu felt something wilt inside him at the sight of the . . . man?

Only the bottom of the stranger's face was visible. A black hat with a wide brim was tilted down over his face. His hands were plunged deep inside the pockets of a long black coat. He was tall and lanky. Disconcertingly so, like a man made out of wire and brittle paper.

Yet this stranger exuded only strength and menace.

Stu's heart jumped in his chest and he felt a bolt of pain flash up his left arm.

And he toppled dead to the floor.

The reaction was immediate. Screams and shouts followed by the panicked scudding of bar stools across the hardwood floor. Two men worked on the dead bartender, frantically attempting to administer CPR.

But it was too late.

Too late for Stu, and too late for the Rude Dog's last customers.

The Deathbringer's mouth stretched wide and emitted that dry, insidious laughter—a sound that increased in pitch until it filled the bar like an air raid siren. The bar's patrons clamped their hands over their ears and sagged screaming to the floor.

The Deathbringer knelt next to the nearest mewling patron and placed a splayed palm between her ample breasts. Her eyes went wide with alarm and she opened her mouth to scream, but the sound never came.

The stranger reached into her mind and silenced her.

His grinning mouth issued a single word: "Die."

The woman's eyes rolled back in her head and she slumped against the bar.

The Deathbringer repeated the process until each of the remaining patrons was also dead. Then, whistling a strange, lilting tune so ancient no one in Dandridge would have recognized it, he left the bar and walked deeper into town.

CHAPTER THREE

Mike O'Bannon stared at the strange black book that now dominated the living room's coffee table. The thing was huge, and clearly old almost beyond measure. It reeked, too, emitting a stench like a burning landfill. The smell reached into him and made him feel tainted, as if he'd been touched by something unspeakably vile. The stench made him gag and his eyes water. Probably he should toss the book out. But he made no move to do so. There was something inexplicably compelling about it. That some faceless stranger had chosen to place this peculiar artifact on his porch troubled him. A book like this, there couldn't be too many of them in existence. Which led him to believe its arrival at his home was not a random event. The realization filled him with an unaccountable foreboding and apprehension. He had a feeling he would open the book and examine its contents before the night was through.

But the prospect of handling the book made his skin crawl. He'd rather hold and caress a snake, and he loathed those creatures.

Mike sat slouched in the old recliner that had been a hand-me-down from his parents a couple years ago when, tired of the neighbor headaches that were so much a part of apartment living, he'd bought this house. It was a modest ranch-style house. Not big, but not too small either. Perfect for his budget in those pre-Hannah bachelor days. And later on, he'd believed it'd be a good place for a new family to begin their journey through life together.

Mike swigged from the bottle of George Dickel.

The phone rang. Again. He grimaced and waited for the answering machine to pick it up. While the requisite four pre-pickup rings resonated in the otherwise silent house like stuttering explosions, Mike played another tiresome game of Guess Who the Worrywart Is This Time. Couldn't be Mom or Dad. They'd each called within the last fifteen minutes, each leaving gut-wrenchingly heartfelt and tearful pleas for him to please, please, please take care of himself. The plaintive, earnest words stabbed his heart, leaving that already tattered organ hanging by a figurative thread. The calls from his friends were no better. Each of them believed they could be his port in the storm, or else they desperately wanted to convey the impression they could be that for him.

The fourth ring gave way to the terse message he'd recorded a year ago: "Here's the beep. You know what to do."

Then a pause. And a sigh. Mike groaned at that sound.

Erin.

He didn't have to hear her voice to know it was her. That sigh communicated everything he needed to know. Sure enough: "Mike, honey, I know you're going through a tough time. A horrible, awful time. I can't imagine how devastating it must be to lose someone the way you lost Hannah." Another sigh. He could sense her fumbling, unsure of what to say. He wished she'd just hang up and leave him alone. "Maybe it's crass of me to get in touch with you at this time. Hell, I know it is. But I can't help it. I need to talk to you. I need to know you're as okay as you can be. Call me any time, Mikey, day or night." She recited her number. "I love you, Mike. I always have." Yet another sigh. Then, finally, the click signaling the severing of the connection.

Mike shook his head. "Goddammit, Erin."

She'd been his last significant relationship prior to Hannah. The one characteristic the two relationships shared was intensity of passion. But their time together had been marred by fights, small and large. They were too rarely on the same page on any issue, and so the relationship's bitter end had been an inevitability. He'd loved Erin, in a way, but there'd been an overwhelming feeling of relief when they went their separate ways.

Life with Hannah had been so much calmer. With the one exception of her misgivings about his chosen profession, they'd been so closely attuned to one another as to almost be of a single mind. In Hannah, Mike believed, he'd at last found his ideal life partner, the person he was meant to share everything with. To grow old with.

So much of what he'd believed had turned out to be false. Fairy tale love and happy endings, for instance. The idyllic serenity and safety of life in small-town America. All so much unmitigated bullshit. Sweet, tempting lies as illusory as a child's fantasies of glory as an astronaut or athlete. His thoughts took on a deeply bitter edge as memories of the lies he'd told Hannah again surfaced to taunt and torture him.

The kind of random, senseless violence so frequently portrayed on television news just doesn't happen in places like Dandridge, he'd told her. He laughed, a dry, sour sound almost like a parody of the cackling of a movie mad scientist. But there was no humor in this laugh. Only undiluted pain and self-hatred. He wondered again what had gone through Hannah's mind in those last moments before she died. Her killer had made her look death in the eye, so she'd had time to think about it. That much had been clear from even the most cursory examination of the scene. The killer shot her twice—once through the chest, and once in the neck—before administering the kill-shot to the forehead.

So there'd been time.

A precious few agonized seconds.

Mike wondered if she'd thought of his casual dismissal of any danger inherent in small-town police work. He wondered whether she'd cursed him and his lies in the seconds before that last bullet punched through her brain. He hoped she had. He deserved her condemnation. Because it was clear to him that Hannah's murder was some kind of fucked-up judgment handed down from the gods, a divine indictment of his own arrogance.

He imagined telling a therapist that and spewed more of that humorless laughter. *It's understandable you feel that way,* he or she would say. *It is common for those left behind to blame themselves, even when it is not rational to do so. Nothing you did, no choice you made, in the time prior to this tragedy could have prevented it.*

His father had said almost precisely those words to him in the moments after the gut-wrenching memorial service. Dad had meant well, he always did, but Mike had not been in a mood to be comforted. He'd succumbed to anger, ranting at his poor father, his voice heavy with sarcasm as he asked the old man how he could possibly know what was going on in his mind.

Yes, it'd been a truly proud moment in the life of Michael O'Bannon. Screaming at his loving father until he was red in the face within earshot of a crowd of mourners. Until that moment he'd always believed he was a good son, that he was becoming the kind of man his dad could be proud of. But all that had turned to rot and gone to hell. Now, he was nothing. His accomplishments less than meaningless. The shame had been instant and all-consuming. All he'd wanted from that moment on was to get away from everyone, lock himself away from the world, and be alone with his misery. So he made a blustery pronouncement about that, too, and finally got the hell out of there.

And now he had what he'd said he wanted.

Solitude.

His only company this evening was George Dickel, who currently was his best friend in the whole rotten fucking world. There was also whomever the Dandridge police force currently had stationed outside his house. Funny thing, that. They were afraid he'd hurt himself somehow. But he would not. Sure, he felt like

29

dying. Death, in a way, would be a welcome relief from this torment. But there was one big drawback to being dead that struck suicide from his current list of options—death would mean no opportunity for vengeance.

And Mike knew one thing above all else: he meant to have vengeance.

He would be the most pitiless of avenging angels.

The furious, engulfing anger he felt every time he thought about Hannah's killer came at him in tidal waves of galvanizing feeling. This time it made him scream and brought him out of his slouch. He surged out of the recliner and flung the Dickel bottle with all his might. It tumbled end over end, trailing brown liquor like a bullet-riddled fighter plane leaking fuel. It smashed against the far wall, knocking a framed picture of Hannah and himself on vacation in the Rockies off its peg. The picture dropped to the floor and landed with a flat sound of breaking glass.

Mike screamed again, and the scream gave way to sobs.

Many minutes passed.

When the sobs subsided and he again had some semblance of control over his body, his gaze went to the foul old book.

"Yes." Mike nodded. "It's time."

He was babbling. Time for what, exactly? Mike had no idea. But he did know he was ready to look at that book. He had no clue why, but the certainty that it was the right thing to do gripped him with a fervor not to be denied.

He reached into one of the crumpled paper bags at his feet and extracted another bottle of Dickel. He broke the seal, spun the cap off the bottle, and imbibed deeply. Then he sat down again, set the bottle on the table next to the book, and drew the book closer to him.

His hands trembled.

His heart stuttered and his breath caught in his throat.

A strange voice, a dry and insidious one that almost seemed external in origin, whispered in his head: *Vengeance.*

Mike nodded again. "Yes. Vengeance. Mine."

He lifted the book's front cover, and a cloud of dust puffed out. He coughed and waved the dust away. Then he read the words on the title page and frowned, puzzled as to their meaning.

INVOCATIONS OF THE REAPER

He turned some more pages, skimmed over the dense text, and felt a building sense of unease as his gaze swept over a number of very lurid and graphic drawings. His hands moved of their own accord, so it seemed, turning hundreds of pages, seeking one special page. The realization that something unnatural was happening came to him belatedly, and he felt a cold finger of fear slide teasingly down his spine.

What have I done? he wondered. *What's happening? Dear God, what the hell is this infernal book?*

His hands ceased moving and the book fell open to a page near the end. The words written here deviated from all the preceding text in that they were written in red ink. In blood, he knew instinctively.

Mike moaned. "Oh, fuck. Oh, God. Oh, fuck me."

He took the book into his arms, cradling it the way a mother cradles a wailing infant, and began to read words written in a language he didn't know.

Outside, and elsewhere in Dandridge, the dead stirred.

And Mike kept reading, while what remained of his sanity crumbled to ash.

CHAPTER FOUR

Hawthorne opened his eyes and watched twin points of bright light bearing down on him, like some great, yellow-eyed beast of prey swooping through the darkness at breakneck speed. He felt the asphalt tremble beneath his feet, heard the bleating of an air horn, and realized that the approaching beast was the manmade kind. He stepped out of the road and stood on the shoulder while the big semi blew by, whipping his longish gray hair about his head as it passed. The force of the air displacement made him stagger backward until his legs touched the metal guardrail. He had a moment of unsteadiness, during which he pictured himself pitching over the guardrail and tumbling into the rocky ravine below, but he managed to right himself.

He heaved a big sigh and sat down with his back against the guardrail and his lanky legs folded beneath him. Another set of lights came out of the night

33

and zipped past him. Then another. Then several in rapid succession. Most of the motorists failed to notice him. A few who did shouted unintelligible taunts.

Hawthorne closed weary eyes and recalled his last memories of those moments before the Mexican shaman had sent him into a trance. Eldritch, his old and feeble mentor, had sent him to the crazy medicine man. "Crazy" was an overused word, but Hawthorne knew crazy when he saw it and this man's mind had been fried long ago, whether from too much peyote or too much firewater he couldn't say. The man's mottled skin resembled that of an embalmed corpse, and there was a jittery wildness in his eyes that would unnerve the bravest of men. One look at him and his cave abode adorned with animal skins and . . . well, some things that might not have been the skins of wild animals, and he'd wanted nothing more but to turn and flee into the night. But this had not been a real option. He avoided looking too closely at the skins, choosing instead to keep his focus on the grim task ahead.

The Rogue . . . the Deathbringer . . .

You must find him, Eldritch had said. *Find him, then kill him.*

But . . . how? he'd asked.

A most inscrutable smile had touched the corners of Eldritch's mouth. *The shaman will show you the way. And he will provide the means.*

And so he had.

Hawthorne groaned and let his eyes flutter open again. His brow furrowed as a bolt of pain streaked through his head, the beginning of the headaches and wooziness common after coming through the far end of a long-distance temporal displacement. He examined the arcane object in his hands and tried to imagine getting close enough to the wayward reaper to actually use it on him.

Nothing he envisioned seemed plausible.

The instrument in his hands, when used properly, would get the job done. He cursed Eldritch for selecting him for this task. It was an important thing, an honor, but surely there were men available more suited for a task of such importance. Then he gave his head an emphatic shake. No. Eldritch was wise beyond measure. And he'd entrusted Hawthorne with a mission.

He got to his feet and glanced up and down the road.

East . . . , said a voice not his own—the voice of a stranger inside his head.

Hawthorne turned and started in that direction . . .

Toward Dandridge, some one hundred miles away.

Toward a rendezvous with the Deathbringer.

CHAPTER FIVE

"What's your name?"

Melinda Preston's nose wrinkled at the stench that wafted from the blubbering man's open mouth. The cemetery groundskeeper was fat and stunk like some of the homeless bums she'd seen on the streets of Chicago. Scraggly men coated with layers of caked-in dirt and filth. Men who hadn't bathed in months, if ever. This guy's stink was every bit as offensive. At least the bums had an excuse. They were scum, waste, subhuman excrement. Society's castoffs. You expected those fuckers to smell bad. But this guy wasn't a city-dwelling homeless piece of shit. He had a job. A right shitty job as jobs went, but a job nonetheless. So this man had no right to be so foul, so completely disgusting.

Melinda flicked her right wrist and the straight razor's shiny blade popped out, glinting in the light cast by the desk lamp in the groundskeeper's shack. The modest room was a tool shed, but it doubled as the man's living quarters. A small cot was wedged into one tight corner of the room and a black and white television with rabbit ear antennas sat on a card table next to it. The surface of the little metal desk was littered with glossy porno mags. Beau and Doug had already pawed through them, snickering at the garish photos of close-up beaver shots, many of them showing the women pulling their pussy lips apart and feigning ecstasy.

Melinda laid the flat of the blade against the trembling man's throat. He swallowed hard and whimpered at the feel of the cold steel on his flesh. Melinda sighed. "I asked you a fucking question." The blade pressed harder against his throat. She turned her hand slightly and the exquisitely sharp edge nicked his flesh, drawing a thin trickle of blood. It wasn't much, but it was apparently enough to scare the crap out of the big pig-man, because now he was mewling like a goddamned baby. "It's time for an answer. What's your name, fucker?"

Beau, standing behind the groundskeeper, shifted uneasily, jostling one of the man's pinned arms. The sudden movement caused the blade to cut deeper and draw a thicker stream of blood. The man's whimpering increased exponentially. "Damn, Melinda, there's the dude's wallet." He nodded at the desk. "You wanna know his name, just open it."

Melinda shot him a glare. "Remind me, Beauregard—did I ask for any goddamn input from you?"

"Uh . . ." His lower lip twitched several times, making him look like an epileptic on the verge of a fit. He was afraid. The knowledge was gratifying. It even sort of turned her on to know Mr. Badass was terrified of her. "It's just that . . . I don't know . . ."

He looked away, unable to hold her gaze.

"Look at me. Now!"

Though he clearly didn't want to do it, Beau made himself look her in the eye again.

She smirked. "You're supposed to be a tough guy, Beau. Right?" The smirk deepened and there was a taunting edge in her voice. "You don't want me thinking you've turned pussy, do you? Lord knows what I might do then."

She laughed.

Then her gaze snapped to the right and she locked eyes with Doug. Pitiful boy. Beau's slavering sidekick since elementary school. He flinched when she looked at him, like a painfully shy kid sitting in the back of the classroom unobserved by the demanding teacher—until now.

"What about you, Douggy?" Her voice changed, dropping to a mocking little girlish register. "Are you afraid, too? Are you and wittle Beauregard a couple of wittle pussies?"

She giggled.

Doug's face flushed red. "No!"

"That's good to know." She looked at Beau now. "Hear that, sweetie? Your little bitch has bigger balls than you. Tell you what. I'll leave it up to you. We can leave right now. Slink back home like a bunch of goddamned dogs with our tails between our legs. Or we can keep this party going."

She smiled sweetly. "Which will it be, dear?"

Beau's handsome features crumpled like cellophane exposed to heat. He looked like a terrified little kid. Which was kind of the truth. She could tell he wanted to abort the torture of the fat groundskeeper and get back home. Back to that sterile, safe world of suburbia where crazy, razor-wielding chicks only existed in late night cable movies. But he was trapped. He couldn't choose that option without condemning himself, and he knew it.

His gaze went to the floor and he mumbled something.

Melinda's furious voice filled the room: "What was that? Look at me!"

Trembling, not making the least attempt to conceal his terror now, he showed her eyes shiny with moisture and said, "We keep the party going."

Melinda laughed. "Gosh, I'm so glad that's settled, guys." The mocking girlish tone returned to her voice. "I was so worried there."

Beau and Doug exchanged nervous glances. Melinda snickered. She could have made something of it, could have kept twisting the psychological screws, and that would surely have been great fun. But she had other things she wanted to do before the night was over.

Her attention shifted back to the groundskeeper, who had regained some measure of self-control while she was occupied with chastizing the boys. She smiled, but there was no warmth in it. "Are you ready to talk to me, pig-man?"

The big man sighed. "I don't reckon it matters. But I'll tell you whatever it is you want to know."

Melinda moved her hand, making the flat of the razor blade glide lightly over the man's throat like a paint brush over a wall. "Your name."

The groundskeeper cleared his throat, wincing as

the slight movement of flesh resulted in another small nick from the blade. "Duane. Duane Crawford."

"Duane. I like that." Melinda said it again, drawing the word out and relishing the feel of it in her mouth. "Duuuu-ayne. That's a good white trash name. I bet you come from a long line of inbred Duanes and Darlas, don't you?"

Duane didn't reply. He didn't wilt beneath the force of Melinda's glare the way he'd done so often already tonight. She saw resignation in his eyes.

He knows, she thought. *He knows I killed that smug bitch, and he knows I'm gonna kill him, too.*

She reached out to him, stroking his cheek with the palm of her free hand. "They put that bitch in the ground today, didn't they, Duane? The one I killed."

She managed not to laugh at the sudden intakes of breath from Beau and Doug. Fear as palpable as the groundkeeper's stink rolled off of them in waves. She looked at them, saw the shock in their eyes. The idiots. So terrified she'd made the admission in the presence of an outsider.

Fools.

She looked at Duane. "You're gonna take us to her grave, redneck." She pressed the flat of the blade harder against his throat. "Unless you want me to open your throat right now. Do you want that, Duane? Because that's a wish I'd be happy to grant."

She almost hoped he'd say yes. Because she'd love to unzip his flesh and watch the blood geyser forth. Blood and death. It was amazing how easily you could acquire a taste for it. To think that only a week and a half ago killing and reveling in a victim's pain and blood weren't things that came to mind when she was looking for fun diversions. Her idea of decadent fun prior to killing Hannah Starke had been to fuck Beau on his sister's bed while Doug watched bound and gagged from the closet.

But murder was ever so much more fun than messing with the heads and twisted libidos of these redneck doofs. And she had them to thank for turning her on to this marvelous new pleasure.

It'd all started two weeks ago when gorgeous and sophisticated Hannah Starke had come into the video store where Melinda worked part-time. Melinda was awestruck by the striking woman and developed an instant crush on her. She got crushes on women sometimes. It was something she didn't talk about. It made her feel strange, like some kind of fucking pervert. Most times she worked hard to crush the confusing feelings. But doing so never occurred to her the day Hannah Starke strutted into her life.

Maximum Video, contrary to what its name implied, was a small operation. It was one of the only remaining mom-and-pop video outlets in Dandridge, as owner Stan Holt liked to tell anyone who'd listen. Because even in a little shithole like Dandridge the bigger chain operations had eaten up most of the rental business. Melinda was one of three teenage part-timers Stan employed to work the night shifts at Maximum. She was also the newest employee, having been on the job exactly one week the day Hannah appeared to her like some golden goddess emerging out of a brilliant sunset.

She attempted to strike up a conversation with Hannah, but the woman mostly ignored her. She seemed to be in a hurry and barely acknowledged any of Melinda's stuttering overtures. The woman's disregard inflamed the shame she felt at being attracted to a woman. Clearly the bitch thought she was better than Melinda, a conclusion emphasized by the way Hannah behaved after paying for her Hugh Grant movie. Melinda managed to summon a smile and wished her a good day, adding a "come back and see us soon" for good measure. But Hannah was in another world. She flipped open a ringing cell phone, spun about with her movie in hand, and exited the store without a word.

Melinda fumed. And later that evening she'd vented her anger at Beau and Doug. Of course, she'd shared with them a modified version of events, inventing more overt insults and leaving out her attraction to the woman. She'd been so consumed with rage the boys had made fun of her. Beau went one step further, saying, "Damn, Mel, maybe you should just kill the cunt."

A joke, sure, but Melinda had seized on it. "You think I won't?"

She remembered Beau's derogatory laughter. He'd never sounded that way when addressing her again. And he'd said, "I dare you."

So she'd done it.

And Beau and Doug had been her scared little underlings ever since. They were skittish in her presence. Good. She liked them this way. They were stupid rednecks. They were beneath her. But it was good to have a couple of strong, burly guys she could manipulate so easily.

She eased the blade away from Duane's throat and stood up.

"Take us to Hannah, pig-man."

Beau and Doug hauled the big groundskeeper to his feet and bustled him out of the shack. Outside, he led them through the rows of graves, stumbling now and then in the dark because they wouldn't let him use his flashlight. At last, they arrived at Hannah Starke's freshly turned grave. Duane identified it by the simple temporary marker slated to eventually be supplanted by a more elaborate headstone.

"On your knees, Duane. Pig-man."

Even here in the darkness, beneath a thin sliver of moon, the madness in Melinda's smile was discernible to everyone present. Duane fell wordlessly to the ground. Then he bowed his head and began to mumble.

Melinda laughed. "Yes, pray. And ask God if He allows pigs in heaven."

At her direction, Beau and Doug forced Duane to his hands and knees. Melinda mounted his massive back and made snorting and snuffling noises. Then she gripped a handful of the groundskeeper's scraggly hair, pulled his head back and stretched out his neck, and drew the sharp edge of the blade across his throat in one vicious slash. Blood erupted from the wound and splashed the fresh grave dirt.

Duane wheezed and gurgled and attempted to get to his feet. But Melinda held fast, riding him like an urban cowgirl on a mechanical bull at a shitkicker bar. Then, his strength failing him, he collapsed onto the grave and shuddered. Melinda disengaged herself from the dead man and turned her gaze up to the moon, reveling in the glory of the kill. The soft moonlight and the cool evening breeze felt good, better than such simple pleasures had ever felt before. Her senses were exquisitely heightened. It was like being high on crank, only better, more pure, more exhilarating.

She told Beau and Doug to drag the carcass off the

grave, and they did so at once. They'd been frightened before, but now they were delirious with terror. They wouldn't dare disobey her now. They were her sheep. Her minions.

She folded the straight razor blade shut, clenched it between her teeth, and began an impromptu striptease, swaying her hips to a tune only she could hear. When her flesh was bare, she laid back on the bloody earth and held forth a beckoning finger.

"Come here, Douggy."

An expression of terrified puzzlement flashed across Doug's face.

Melinda smiled. "Yes, Douggy. You. I think it's time Beau watched from the sidelines, don't you?" Her smile abruptly vanished. "Get over here. Now."

Doug could not disobey the command. She imagined he wanted to turn and run, maybe go to the police and tell them everything, but he could not. He was under her thrall now. So he came to her, trembling like a shy boy at his first school dance.

"Strip."

Doug made a sound that may have been a whimper. But terror wasn't the only feeling burning within him—that much was evident from the bulge at the crotch of his jeans. One by one, his clothes fell away from him.

And then he was on her. And, a moment later, in her.

Melinda made a mad cackling sound and clawed at the loose dirt around her as the rhythm of sex quickened and became frenzied.

She imagined dead Hannah beneath them.

And she smiled, imagining the dead bitch's ghost observing this defilement of her final resting place.

* * *

Dead eyes snapped open in absolute blackness.

At first there was nothing but the darkness. This void. Then, all at once, consciousness returned, and, with it, awareness. She felt something soft and plush cradling her body. Then her reawakened senses detected confinement. She lifted her hands and they met almost immediate resistance. She kicked her legs out and encountered more resistance.

A coffin, she thought, horror blooming within her regenerated brain. *I'm in a coffin. But . . . why?*

Then the memories returned. Her last memories. That awful girl. The gun. The bullets puncturing her flesh and taking her life.

I'm dead, she thought.

But now, somehow, she was back.

And there was something else. A smell, a scent marker as individual and damning as a fingerprint left at a crime scene. It was mixed with something else, sex musk, an aroma that awakened something wicked within her. Something that demanded satiation. That girl . . . her killer . . . she was nearby. Close enough almost to touch.

Somewhere . . . above her.

A scream tore out of Hannah's mouth. She was aware of a new feeling now, something she'd never felt in her previous life. A bloodlust. An all-consuming need to have revenge. To maim and kill.

She screamed again.

And then she began to claw frantically at the coffin lid.

CHAPTER SIX

The patrol car was still stationed outside Mike's dark and silent house. This time Erin Holt peered closely instead of feigning disinterest. She'd driven by her former lover's home three times already tonight, each time taking pains to keep her gaze locked rigidly ahead. She knew her behavior would draw the attention of even the dimmest cop before much longer. But the closer look confirmed her suspicions—the cop was asleep.

Erin's foot tapped the brake and her rattling Neon slowed. She bit her lip, considering whether she should pull up to the curb and just go for it.

She knew how crazy she was being. This was absurd, obsessive behavior. She'd kept her distance from Mike from the beginning of his relationship with Hannah. She'd even been happy for him. So why was she here, circling Mike's house on the eve-

46

ning of the day he'd put the corpse of his intended into the earth?

She didn't know. Not really. She felt a generalized worry, a concern for the well-being of a person who'd once meant a great deal to her. But everyone close to him surely felt that same concern, yet none of them were out prowling around his house. Stalking him, for Christ's sake. Clearly there was something happening here beyond normal concern. For reasons she couldn't fathom, she was sure something very bad might happen to Mike. She didn't believe in premonitions, or anything else supernatural, but she didn't know what else to call it. The way she felt made no rational sense at all.

Okay. So this was crazy. So it was the wrong thing to do by just about any sensible standard of judgment, but clearly it was something she needed to do, otherwise she'd be condemned to circle this block endlessly, until either she lost her mind or the cop at last woke up and took notice of her.

She pulled the Neon into the driveway and cut the lights. She looked at the tomblike house and felt a sense of dread creeping through her. As was her habit in moments of extreme distress, she reached for the crumpled pack of smokes on her dashboard, tapped out a Marlboro Light and wedged it into a corner of her mouth. She lit the cigarette, drew in a calming lungful of smoke, then opened her mouth and let the smoke roll out of her. Smoking had been one of so many points of contention between Mike and herself. He was militantly anti-smoking, and she vowed never to give up the vice. The cigarettes were a comfort, a kind of security blanket, and she was one chick who needed every layer of security available to her.

She drew in more smoke and glanced back at the cop car. Still no signs of life there. She sighed and stabbed the barely-smoked cigarette out in the Neon's overflowing ashtray. Then, slinging her purse over her shoulder, she got out of the car and eased the Neon's door shut. She quickly crossed the yard to the front porch, ascended the steps, and jabbed the doorbell with a quaking forefinger. Her finger glanced off the button and she jabbed at it again, willing the finger to be still. She heard the bell resonate inside the house this time and she drew in a big breath, hoping against hope she could find some unsuspected reservoir of strength within her before Mike could open the door.

Several moments passed and still the door remained shut. She strained her ears, hoping to detect any hint of movement on the other side of that door, but there was nothing. Self-doubt assailed her. She cursed her monumental stupidity. It'd be moronic to wait here even one more moment. Hell, she shouldn't be here in the first place.

She saw herself as she imagined Mike's family would see her in this situation. A scorned former lover preying on their loved one's battered psyche and weakened defenses. The hell of it was she wouldn't be able to blame anyone for thinking that. But there was nothing predatory in her motivations. She loved Mike and was worried sick about him. But that didn't really matter. Not anymore. He'd passed from her life and she didn't belong here.

She was in the process of turning to leave when she at last heard noise from inside the house. She frowned. This wasn't the sound of someone coming to the door. It was a verbal sound. As she listened to it, her already high anxiety level red-lined and she rushed to the door, pressing an ear against it and willing herself not to breathe. She heard only the rapid thudding of her heart. Then the sound came again and there was no mistaking the level of distress in it. At first it was like a moan, the sound of a heavily sedated dying man, and then it became an agonized wail. It was Mike. She knew that instantly. And his voice shifted pitch wildly, alternating from unintelligible, pained bleating to words spoken in what might have been Latin.

Erin slammed her fists on the door, no longer caring whether she was making a spectacle of herself. Hell, she hoped she was doing just that. Mike needed help and he needed it *now*.

"*Mike!* Please open the door, it's Erin! What's going on in there?"

She heard a thud, something heavy falling, like a burlap sack full of potatoes dropped to the ground. Screaming, she seized the doorknob in both hands and shook it, rattling the door in its frame. Locked. She stepped back a moment and tried to think, biting back the burgeoning panic within her. She considered a dash for the police car and a desperate attempt to awaken the sleeping cop. And she thought of the time that'd be wasted by having to explain who she was and why she was here. Mike could be hurt, even, oh, Christ, he could be dying in there. He might need an ambulance. But every second he was in there alone and suffering could be bringing him closer to death.

She tried to recall the interior of the house, which

she hadn't seen in going on two years. Her eyes widened. The kitchen door at the rear of the house, that's where she needed to go. She flew down the porch steps, circled the house, scaled the chain-link fence that demarcated the backyard, and dashed for the rear door.

She saw the door and loosed a cry of triumph.

Upon moving into the house, Mike had talked of replacing the back door, which consisted primarily of a single long pane of glass in a wood frame, calling it a "security hazard." But—thank God!—he'd never done it.

She screeched to a halt near the door and scanned the ground around her for an object heavy enough to do the job. She saw the perfect thing right away, a baseball bat propped against a lounge chair. She gripped the bat the way Mike had taught her in their occasional trips to the mechanical batting cages, planted her feet, and swung with all her might. The fat end of the bat connected and the glass exploded inward. She knocked out most of the remaining shards and stepped into the house.

The moaning was louder now, more plaintive, a lost child sound. A sound that stirred long-dormant protective feelings within her. Whatever was doing that to Mike was about to have a painful rendezvous with Mr. Louisville Slugger.

She entered the kitchen and moved quickly, her left hip glancing painfully off the island, a new addition to the house since her brief residence here. She caught sight of a very dim, flickering light emanating through the archway leading into the living room and ran in that direction.

Coming through the archway, she saw Mike spasming on the floor, his limbs convulsing and his eyes rolled back in his head.

"Oh my God! Mike!"

He was having a fit of some kind, a seizure. But he wasn't epileptic, so what could be doing this to him? The pungent scent of spilled whiskey filled the room. It rolled out of Mike's mouth with the force of a gale, making her rock back on her heels as her eyes watered and turned red. But there was another, even more powerful smell here, something that carried with it a whiff of death, of decay, and of smoldering ash. She scanned the room for anything that might be burning. Because if a fire was about to engulf this place, she needed to miraculously figure out a way to haul all two hundred pounds of Mike O'Bannon the hell out of here.

She saw nothing aflame and, anyway, Mike's fit was only increasing in intensity. She wished she knew more about first aid and CPR. Her knowledge was limited to television images of paramedics frantically pounding on the chests of trauma victims. She felt useless. Her first instinct was to reach into his mouth and do something about his tongue, keep him from swallowing it. But she frowned, thinking she'd maybe read something about that being the wrong the thing to do. Or maybe she was only imagining that, but she couldn't be sure.

A cry of frustration loosed itself from her mouth.

Mike was dying right in front of her and there was nothing she could do about it. Was it alcohol poisoning? Just based on the overwhelming, nauseating booze stench, she could believe it. But maybe it was something else. Maybe he'd taken some kind of poison. Anthrax. Arsenic. Something. In which case she really needed to get on the line with 911, or call Poison Control, something.

She cast her gaze about the room, but there was no sign of a phone. There had to be one nearby—but damned if she could see it. Tears leaking from her eyes now, she looked again at Mike. The force of the convulsions gripping his body had eased. Either the fit was passing or he was almost dead. She gripped his shoulders and leaned close, sobbing as she talked to him: "Mike, baby, it's me, it's Erin, you're gonna be okay, please be okay, please, Mike, please . . ."

Then he was utterly still.

A cry of grief pealed out of her mouth—but then she felt it. His steady breath on her cheek. Her hand went to his throat. She felt a pulse, and she grinned through the tears. "You're alive, oh, baby, you're alive. Thank God. Thank God, Mike."

She looked into his eyes and saw awareness return by slow degrees. A puzzled frown etched itself into his features. "Erin . . . ?"

She sniffled. "Yes, baby, it's me. I'm so sorry, but I was so worried about you."

Then his frown gave way to a fiercer expression, a hard look that pierced her soul. She braced herself to receive the brunt of his rage. But all he said was, "Move, Erin. Now."

She frowned. "What?"

Mike seized her by the shoulders and spun her away from him. She rolled over several times and came to a stop against the sofa. It was then that she looked up and saw a uniformed police officer, probably the one who'd been sleeping on the job. But . . . there was something . . . wrong with him. Something wrong with his face. She realized instinctively what it was. He was dead. His snarling expression made him look like a rabid animal, but there was an emptiness in those eyes so complete it left no room for doubt—he was dead.

How that could be, she didn't know—and right now it didn't matter.

Because at the moment the dead cop was aiming his gun point-blank at Mike's face.

Erin screamed and surged to her feet.

The cop swung his arm around, and the gun spat bullets in her direction.

CHAPTER SEVEN

Iris Atkins paused in her knitting work and cocked an ear in the direction of the kitchen. She was sure she'd heard something. A faint sound, a soft click, like the sound of a door being eased shut. And now there was another sound. A shuffling, as of stealthy feet sliding over the tiled kitchen floor.

Iris calmly set aside her knitting and retrieved her bag from the floor. She shoved her hand inside, her arthritic fingers negotiating the array of makeup items and random junk that clogged the bag's interior, groping until they fastened around the small handle of the lightweight Kel-Tec .32 auto her grandson Luke had bought for her at a gun show. It was the perfect gun for a woman of her age and brittle physique, though Luke had phrased it a bit more diplomatically than that. It was loaded with eight hollowpoint rounds, and she had no doubt that would be more than sufficient to repel this intruder.

The gun came out of the bag and Iris rose shakily to her feet. She went into the stance Luke had demonstrated at the firing range and aimed the .32 at the archway through which any intruder would have to pass in order to enter this room. She wondered what it would be like to shoot a man, how different it must feel from shooting paper silhouettes, and was dismayed to realize she half-hoped it would come to pass.

Dirty rotten son of a bitch, she thought, true outrage beginning to course through her now. *I've heard of sick bastards like you, cowards too meek to take on athletic young women. Well, here's one old bag of bones you won't be sticking your wee little dick in, sonny.*

She waited in that pose for what felt like hours. No new sounds emerged from the kitchen. She began to think maybe she'd just been hearing things, paranoid imaginings conjured from the confused depths of her deteriorating mind. The notion stirred self-directed anger. She'd been conscious of her faculties slipping for some time and it frightened her. She'd always had a sharp mind, but now it was failing her, and she couldn't abide the prospect of turning into one of those nursing home vegetables she'd always felt such pity for.

Her gaze locked on the gun now. Something crumbled inside her. Tears stung her eyes. There were times when she was certain the only living creature she'd shoot with this thing would be herself. And she would, too, if things got much worse for her. She'd do it while she was still able, before the issue of choice in such matters was removed from her forever.

So occupied was she by this grim line of thinking

that the presence of the stranger didn't register right away. Then everything came back into focus and she gasped. Her finger twitched on the .32's trigger, discharging a bullet that passed through the middle of the strange, black-clad man.

He smiled, an expression that sent a strong shudder through her body.

Those lips . . .

His mouth shimmered and distorted, looking like two thick black nightcrawlers, or, more accurately, *depictions* of nightcrawlers manipulated by the invisible pen of an animator. They stretched and quivered, forming a grin like something from a nightmare. The grin revealed rows of sharp, glistening teeth.

The stranger moved a step in her direction.

This time Iris made a conscious decision to shoot the . . . well, whatever he, or it, was. The bullet punched through his long black coat, passed through him, and lodged in the wall behind him in a puff of plaster. The stranger kept coming at her in his unhurried way, grinning all the while.

Iris's trigger finger squeezed off round after round, until the gun was empty. Every round was on-target. Still, the thing came at her, apparently unaffected by a hail of gunfire that should have assured him a place on a slab in the county morgue.

Iris couldn't move. Here was something inexplicable, an apparition like nothing she could recall from the Bible. This thing wasn't the devil, who was a fallen angel forever consigned to hell. No, this was something beyond the knowledge hammered into her during the religious instruction of her youth.

This thing, this . . . creature, was worse than the devil. Because it was right here, and more real than Satan had ever seemed. And it was reaching for her.

The tips of its fingers were like icicles poking at her collarbone. Then the cold, cold hand slipped around her thin neck and squeezed until the supply of oxygen to her brain was cut off. Then, chuckling softly, the Deathbringer released the old woman.

Iris regained consciousness only a few moments later. Her eyes blinked open and she scanned her living room for any sign of the strange intruder. When she saw that he was gone, she sat up and touched her throat, which still felt tender from where he'd choked her. She remained sitting there for a time while she performed a quick physical inventory. She could tell right away that she hadn't been raped. Nor had she suffered any wounds other than the bruises to her throat.

But something was wrong.

She frowned, fretting over it for a time.

Then she screamed.

And she thought: *I'm dead!*

CHAPTER EIGHT

Avery Starke heard the muffled screams emanating from Iris's house as soon as he cut the Mustang's ignition and the Grateful Dead's "Friend of the Devil" ceased pouring forth from the car's top end speakers.

"Do you hear that?"

Tom Crawford groaned. He was slumped against the passengers side door, barely conscious. Bloodshot eyes fluttered open. "Wha . . . ?"

Avery threw open the driver's side door and surged out of the car. He stood silent and alert in the driveway, waiting to hear the sound again so he could pinpoint its location. The next anguished outburst left no doubt that the sound was coming from the old lady's house. At that same moment Tom at last emerged from the Mustang, hauling himself up and out by gripping the top of the door. The maneuver caused the door to swing backward and nearly propel him back into the car. But Tom managed to stay up-right and pushed himself away from the car.

He staggered in Avery's direction. "The fuck's go-ing on, man? Weren't we going to Mike's place?"

Iris Atkins screamed again, louder than before.

Tom blinked. "Oh."

Avery said, "Get inside and call nine-one-one. I'm going over there."

Avery sprinted across his lawn and the narrow res-idential street. He crossed Iris's lawn in a heartbeat and hurried up the front porch steps. He tested the front door. It was locked. Iris lived in one of the old-est houses in the neighborhood, and because she was barely scraping by on her deceased husband's pen-sion, little had been done to upgrade the house. The front door was a brittle old thing that, unlocked, would yield to a mild breeze. When Iris screamed yet another time, Avery didn't hesitate—he kicked the door open, rocking the top half of it off its hinges.

He dashed into the house, following a sound that had degenerated into mewling. Through the foyer and past a staircase he ran, then turned a corner and saw light through an archway. An instant later he was in Iris's living room and she was staring up at him from a sitting position on the floor. Her wrinkled face was contorted in a mixture of pain and terror.

He knelt next to her and laid a hand on her frail shoulder. "Ms. Atkins, are you okay? What's wrong? Do you need a doctor?"

His queries came out in a panicked rush. At a cur-sory glance, he couldn't detect anything physically wrong with her. She didn't appear to have broken anything in a fall, and she looked too alert to have suffered a stroke or heart attack. Still, something clearly wasn't right. That wild look in her wide eyes unnerved him. It was the look of a lunatic, of a person completely unhinged by some inexplicable trauma.

His hand went to her elbow and he rocked back on his heels, preparing to help her to her feet. "Come on, Ms. Atkins, let's get you over to the sofa so you can lie down. Help is on the way, so don't you worry."

But Avery froze when strange, lilting laughter began to trill out of her mouth. Her thin lips tilted upward in a grin so craven it sent a bolt of fear through Avery. He'd known the old woman most of his thirty-five years and this expression was unlike anything he'd ever seen from her. It was almost as if old Ms. Atkins had been possessed by a demon. Thinking that made Avery feel foolish, but the impression refused to go away.

He cleared his throat and tried one more time. "Ms. Atkins, just come with me. Lie down over here on the sofa and tell me what happened."

He started to come out of his squatting position, intending to pull Ms. Atkins to her feet, regardless of whether she wanted to or not. He had a thought that maybe the right thing to do would be to leave her where she was and let the professionals determine the next step, but everything about this situation was so weird and confusing that he was going with his first impulse.

She started to rise with him.

It was then that it happened, that everything changed forever.

Iris Atkins surged to her feet, opening her mouth wide and hissing like a snake. Then, utilizing a strength that stunned Avery, she pulled his right arm to her mouth, twisted it so that the meatier underside was facing her, and sank her teeth into the ample flesh. The pain was instantaneous and severe, streaking through Avery like a lightning bolt. A thick stream of blood welled around the old woman's slavering lips, poured down his arm, and dripped in a thin line to the carpeted floor.

Avery screamed.

He gripped a handful of gray hair at the back of her head and gave it a vicious tug—but the hair came off in his hand. A fucking wig. The crazy old bat was fucking bald. Little tufts of white hair stuck out from her veiny scalp like twigs dotting a blasted nuclear war landscape. She slobbered and worked at his arm like a pig at a trough, making snorting and smacking sounds that turned his stomach.

There was no sense to be made of the bizarre and horrific turn of events, and therefore no sense in reasoning with the old woman, who'd clearly lost whatever remained of her mind. He drove a knee hard up into her stomach, dislodging her mouth and driving the air from her lungs in a surprised whoosh. She stumbled backward but remained upright. That knee to the belly maneuver would've driven many an able young man to his knees, but for Granny Ghoul here it apparently was little more than a mild setback.

And now here came that hair-raising laughter again. She sounded more like a demented schoolgirl than a rabid old lady. He flashed back to his idea of demon possession and it no longer seemed so far-fetched.

He began to backpedal away from her.

She matched him step for step, grinning at him, his blood smeared around her mouth like the remnants of a cherry pie spread about the mouth of a ravenous child.

Then he heard Tom's voice behind him: "Called nine-one-one. Number was fucking busy. Can you believe that? I figured we could just—"

Tom fell silent when he came up beside Avery and saw Iris Atkins.

The mad gleam in her eyes intensified at the sight of the new arrival. She held out a beckoning finger and spoke for the first time: "Come . . . to . . . mommy . . . boys . . ."

A fresh burst of mad laughter followed.

Tom glanced at Avery. "Goddamn. Christ, Ave, she's a fucking zombie."

Avery clamped a hand around his wound, wishing for a way to stem the blood flow. "She's not a zombie." He grimaced as a fresh wave of pain washed over him. "There's something wrong with her. She's sick. Something . . . toxic . . . I don't know what . . . got into her system."

Iris threw her head back and laughed heartily at this. Then her head snapped forward and she came at Avery like a terrier chasing down a tennis ball. Avery screeched and fell backward, tripping over a wrinkle in the carpet. He hit the floor hard and everything went gray for a moment. When he came to again, Iris's mouth was digging at his throat. He wrenched his head away from flesh-seeking teeth and tried to push her off of him, but she was too strong. He couldn't fathom the brittle old woman's incongruous strength. He knew he wouldn't be able to hold her at bay much longer. Sooner or later those gnashing teeth would find his flesh and tear his throat out.

He heard a sound of retreating feet and knew Tom

had left him to fend for himself. Couldn't really blame the guy. But in a moment he heard the sound again, growing louder, the sound of someone approaching.

Then another, altogether different sound resonated in his ears—a sound like someone ringing a gong. Iris pitched sideways, rolling off of him and landing flat on her back. Avery looked up and saw Tom standing over him, his hands gripping the handle of a large pot. Avery opened his mouth to mutter thanks, but Tom was in motion again, sidestepping to the left and raising the pot high over his head. Avery turned his head in that direction and was startled to see Iris sitting upright—still grinning, still doing an ace impression of an animated corpse, a bag of bones possessed and manipulated by some devil.

Tom brought the pot down in a vicious arc, driving it hard into the top of Iris's head. She toppled backward and he shifted position, straddling her and lifting the pot yet again. It fell again and smashed into her face, crushing her nose and cheekbones. The pot went up again and came down again. Then up again and down again. Over and over, until Iris's face was an unrecognizable pulp. When she was no longer moving, Tom, breathless, tossed the pot aside and fell away from the corpse.

Avery scrambled to his feet and paced the living room in a frantic way, moving in the herky-jerky manner of a man wired on cocaine. He didn't feel the least bit drunk now. He shook his head and laughed without humor. "Oh, man, this is pretty fucked up right here. What the hell's wrong with that crazy old hag?"

Tom's voice, heavy with exhaustion, came out in a near-monotone: "I told you. She's a zombie."

"There's no such thing as zombies, buddy. We've already covered that."

Tom rolled his eyes. "Right. I forgot. I dunno, then. Maybe she just got really ticked off when she learned the Old Fogies Channel would no longer be carrying Lawrence Welk reruns."

Avery grunted. "Funny. Listen, we're gonna need to figure out what to do here. Do we call nine-one-one again? Or do we wipe out any trace of our being here and get the fuck out?"

Tom sat up. "I'm gonna have to vote for the latter, Ave. Don't know about you, but I don't feel like going up on a murder charge. And I'm telling you right now, there's no way the cops'll buy our fucked-up story."

Avery nodded. He couldn't see any other viable alternative. And he couldn't feel bad about anything that had happened. He'd come into Iris's home with the best of intentions. To be her rescuer. He didn't need any trouble with the police, not after all his family had been through in the last week or so.

"Okay. Fine. That's what we'll do." He indicated the killing tool with a nod. "We'll want to take the pot with us. Drop it in a Dumpster somewhere. Or Percy Priest Lake."

Tom held out a hand. "Good idea. Help me up?"

Avery was extending a hand to his friend when Iris popped up again like a bloody goddamned jack-in-the-box. Her battered and crumpled visage rendered that indefatigable grin more horrific than before. Avery's eyes went wide and his body felt paralyzed with shock.

Christ, bitch! his beleaguered mind screamed. *Die already!*

This time she seemed to almost fly off the floor. Tom had a moment to frown at the look of terror in his friend's eyes, but he never had a chance to realize what was coming. Iris seized a handful of his hair and yanked his head hard to the right. There was an awful crunch of bone and Avery knew Tom's neck had been snapped. Iris's mouth closed over Tom's exposed neck and wrenched at the flesh like a hungry dog tearing into a bloody piece of steak. She jerked her head back, tearing out a huge chunk of flesh. Blood arced out of the wound like water from a hose, splashing Avery in the face and drenching the front of his shirt.

Avery stumbled backward.

Iris looked at him through her pulped eyes and laughed.

Avery's paralysis ended abruptly. There was nothing he could do for his friend. And he could imagine no way to put Iris out of commission. He fled the house, running full-out for the Mustang across the street. He glanced back once and saw Iris emerge through the front door of her house. She came down the steps in a hurry and seemed to almost glide across the front lawn.

The Mustang's door stood open, the way he'd left it upon hearing Iris's screams a few minutes earlier. He dove in and reached into his pockets, digging for his keys. He glanced in the rearview mirror and saw Iris drawing nearer at an impossible rate. She'd reached the street by the time he got the keys out of his pocket. His jittery, fumbling fingers found the car key and jabbed it at the ignition unsuccessfully a few times before it finally slipped smoothly into place. He turned the key and the Mustang roared to life.

Another check of the rearview mirror showed Iris several feet directly behind the car.

There was just one thing to do.

Avery jammed the gas pedal to the floor, put the car in reverse, and sent it hurtling backward. There was a satisfyingly loud *thump*. The cars wheels bounced over the prone form of the old woman. Then Avery stomped on the brake pedal, clicked on the headlights, and waited to see if she'd get up yet again.

Some moments passed. He listened to the idling of the Mustang's throaty engine. He listened to the wild beating of his heart. Still, Iris stayed flat on the ground. Then he heard another sound, something approaching from the rear. And Avery had to suppress a groan. Because he was pretty sure he knew what was coming. It made no sense. It flew in the face of rationality.

He looked in the rearview mirror and saw Tom stumbling across Iris's lawn. It was dark, so he couldn't be sure, but he could swear the expression on his old friend's face was identical to Iris's mad grin.

His gaze flicked back to the driveway ahead of him and he saw that Iris was indeed getting back to her feet.

Avery sighed. "Oh, fuck this."

He put the car in gear and again pushed the gas pedal to the floor. The Mustang shot down the street like a bullet, mercifully carrying Avery away from the panorama of weirdness and death. He drove hell-bent-for-leather for maybe five minutes, crossing all the way to the far side of town, finally parking his car outside the main Dandridge cemetery.

It was only then that the enormity of what had happened hit him.

His best friend of more than a quarter century was dead. He guessed. Kind of. He sagged in his seat, leaning forward and letting his head fall against the steering wheel. Moments later he felt a salty tang in his mouth and realized he was crying.

Crying for Tom.

Crying yet again for poor Hannah.

Crying for the loss of the world he'd known.

CHAPTER NINE

Car after car zoomed by on the highway. Not one of them slowed at the sight of Hawthorne standing by the road's shoulder with his thumb in the air. It was disappointing, but he wasn't surprised by the indifference of passing motorists. Were he one of them, say a comfortable and clean-shaven professional in a nice suit, maybe driving a Jaguar or a Porsche, he probably wouldn't stop for a grungy old guy who looked like a first generation hippie burnout, either.

Regardless, if some kind soul didn't stop to offer a ride soon, he'd have to resort to more mercenary tactics. There were certain spells one could utilize. A sort of psychic field could be thrown up, an ephemeral net to catch persons whose minds had already been rendered susceptible to invasion by road hypnosis, that trancelike state induced by traversing so many miles of gray, featureless roadway.

For now, though, he kept his thumb out and maintained his slow backward amble along the road's shoulder. Things were happening in the little town to the east. Things that weren't meant to happen. He felt this the way a person standing hip-deep in a body of water feels the waves when a large object splashes into the water nearby.

People were already dying in Dandridge. Scores of them. The rogue reaper was killing at will, instigating a pattern that, left unchecked, would ultimately result in the global extinction of the human race.

A new pair of headlights appeared in the darkness. These were at a higher elevation than most. A truck. Hawthorne opted not to throw up the psychic net, though it was clearly time to do so. There was just too much potential for disaster if something went wrong and the driver lost control of his barreling beast of a vehicle. So Hawthorne edged closer to the guardrail, preparing to grip it in order to avoid being buffeted by the backblow of the passing semi.

As it turned out, this was an unnecessary precaution. The truck slowed to a crawl as it neared him. The truck and its dusty gray trailer rolled by him, then pulled over to the shoulder. Hawthorne, perplexed, stared at the rear of the trailer, wondering why on earth the driver of a commercial concern, presumably a man on a tight schedule, would stop for him.

The air horn sounded, a single loud *blat* that rattled him and set him in motion. As he neared the cab, the passenger-side door swung open and he got a brief glimpse of a hairy, beefy arm, around the thick wrist of which was strapped an ostentatious gold wristwatch. The hand vanished, slipping back into the cab like a snake returning to a cave, and Hawthorne hesitated a moment, a nanosecond during which he steeled himself to resist any potential threat the driver might present.

He stepped up into the cab and pulled the door shut.

The driver moved the gearshift and the truck pulled away from the shoulder.

Hawthorne risked a nervous glance at the driver. He was a big man, tall, well over six feet, with a prodigious beer belly that hung over the waist of too-tight jeans. He wore a black cowboy hat and a denim vest over a ratty white T-shirt. A cassette tape of Johnny Cash songs was playing on the stereo. Hawthorne didn't bother attempting conversation, because it was clear to him the man was in a kind of trance that had nothing to do with road hypnosis.

This was more of Eldritch's work. The old man had planned ahead, anticipating the difficulties his agent would encounter. Hawthorne said a silent thanks to his old mentor. Temporal displacement was an inexact art, even for one as skilled as the shaman who'd sent him through that warp in the time-space continuum. He'd been lucky to come out the other end of it as near to his destiny as he had.

He settled back in his seat and closed his eyes. More than ninety miles remained between here and Dandridge and this might well be his last opportunity for rest prior to the coming confrontation with the Deathbringer, a battle that could well result in his own death. He didn't want to die. But his death would be an acceptable sacrifice if it occurred in the process of defeating the rogue.

As consciousness ebbed, he slipped a hand into a jacket pocket. His fingers closed round the object given him by the shaman. Its cold solidity against his flesh comforted him.

Hawthorne slept, then dreamed of images so horrific they jolted him out of sleep. Panting, he sat up straight and stared ahead, unblinking, watching as mile after dark mile unfolded along this gray slash in the flesh of the world.

CHAPTER TEN

Melinda craned her neck to get a look at Beau. Doug's shoulder pushed into her throat as he continued to rut away. He was having his second go at her already, having come in little more than a minute the first time around. Beau had taunted the boy, making snide comments about his stamina and the size of his dick. In truth, as Melinda could easily tell from the feel of his stiff member pushing into her over and over, Doug was probably somewhat bigger than Beau. She filed the bit of information away for now, intending to pierce what remained of Beau's once outsized ego with it later.

Frustrated by the brevity of an otherwise enjoyably rough and frantic fuck, her initial impulse had been to shove Doug aside and allow Beau, a more skilled lover (relatively speaking, of course), to have a shot at her. But the asshole's big mouth put an end to that. The way he teased his "friend" seemed a reflection on the choice she'd made, so she'd rolled Doug off of her and onto his back. She'd then gone to work on his deflating dick with an oral skill she doubted even the most jaded old whore could match.

Sure enough, within just a few minutes Doug Jr. was standing erect again. So now they were fucking on top of Hannah's grave again, and it was lasting significantly longer this time, Doug no longer in the grip of the raging urgency typical of the adolescent libido. This was more the way it always was with Mr. McIntyre, her biology teacher, or with Mr. Simmons, her neighbor and also a husband and father of three.

Now she was gratified to see the look of hurt petulance etched deeply into Beau's features. He stood several feet away, slouched with his hands in his pockets, looking amusingly like one of the geek boys he liked to torment at Dandridge High. The thought made her laugh. The incongruous mirth did something to Doug. His rhythm slowed and he began, slowly, to wilt inside her. Probably the idiot thought her laughter was directed at him. On impulse, she bit his shoulder. Hard. Blood seeped into her mouth and Doug screeched, getting to his knees and scrambling away from her. His panicked flight provoked more laughter from her. She put a hand to her mouth, then pulled it away and saw a swirl of red on pale flesh.

She licked the blood off her hand.

Then her gaze went to Beau, her expression a mocking leer. His petulant look gave way to an expression of horror. Probably the two murders had already convinced him his girlfriend was off her rocker. Yet there'd been a kind of remove from that. The victims had been strangers. The violent attack on Doug

73

woke him up to the possibility that what had been done to Hannah and the gravedigger could just as easily happen to him, which was a dangerous way for him to be thinking. It was time to nip this fire in the bud before it could blaze out of control.

She held out a beckoning finger. "Your turn, Beau. I just wanted to play with the geek. Bust his cherry. Mercy fuck kind of thing, you know. I'm assuming he was a virgin." She rolled her eyes. "What else could he be, the way he uncorked inside me in about a god-damn minute."

Beau came out of his slouch. A touch of his former swagger returned. He smiled. "Yeah. Course he was. I've known this little snot all his life. Closest he ever came to getting any was when he stole that old sex doll from my uncle Hank's attic."

Doug's face went a blazing shade of scarlet. Obviously this was one taunt that wasn't fiction. Doug shot an angry, hurt look Beau's way, and Melinda knew this was one of those deep, dark secrets the old friends had sworn never to reveal to anyone else. And she was unsurprised when Doug's furious, quavering voice supplied another revelation: "You go to hell, you goddamned asshole! You fucked it, too."

Melinda couldn't help it. She fell flat on her back as her body convulsed with helpless laughter. Oh, this was wonderful! These redneck cretins could be so entertaining. She'd lived in Chicago most of her life and had often wondered what people who lived out in the sticks were really like. Surely, she thought, they could be nothing like the caricatures on TV. Then came the day when, seemingly out of the blue, her worthless, crack-addicted whore of a mother had sent her packing. This was on her sixteenth birthday.

Mommie dearest sent her baby girl to Tennessee to live with cousins. Really boring salt-of-the-earth type people.

And it'd turned out that life in the South bore little resemblance to what was portrayed on television. The pace of life was as slow as she'd expected it would be in a pissant town like Dandridge, but life here wasn't primitive. The people didn't live in shacks. They didn't walk around barefoot all the time. Most of them seemed to have most of their teeth. They even had cable television and Internet access. In a way, this had been somewhat of a letdown. She'd looked forward to feeling superior to the hicks, had envisioned regaling a bunch of awestruck bumpkins with tales of life in the big city. By and large, however, the bumpkins had been unimpressed.

She began to feel small and insignificant again, like she'd felt when she'd been in school in Chicago. She'd imagined the boys here would be sent into frenzies of desire by her goth slut look. Turned out, though, the look wasn't as exotic in these parts as she'd imagined. Several other Dandridge High girls had a similar look and vibe. Worse, most others seemed of the opinion that the look was passé, a relic of an earlier time.

Well, fuck them. Melinda was what she was. Nothing would shame her more than changing to suit the tastes of the hayseeds. She grew bitter over the course of the following year, consoling herself with fantasies of murder and revenge. Then a great thing happened. She met Beau, and his sidekick, Doug. Dumb as rocks, they were what she'd imagined the general population here would be like. They were big boys, horny boys, and even in the beginning, when

Beau had still been their ringleader, they'd been so easy to manipulate.

Her laughter finally ebbed and she stared up at the sour-faced rednecks. She'd stung them both this time. An expression somewhere between a smile and a smirk twitched at the corners of her mouth. There was one sure way to perk these morons up again.

Sex, of course. Particularly a kinky new wrinkle. And somehow she just knew they'd go for it. Her voice dropped to a lower, more seductive register. "Hey, boys, I just thought of something fun. I want you both on me at the same time."

Even in the murky light of the moon, she could almost see their pupils dilate. Could almost hear their heart rates speed up. They shifted nervously and shot timid glances at each other. And Beau wordlessly reached for his zipper tab. He'd gotten the zipper halfway down when Doug surprised them both by saying, "Fuck this."

Melinda frowned. She watched the geek gather up his clothes and begin putting them on, slipping first into his jeans and then pulling his Creeping Cruds T-shirt on over his head. He sat on the ground and pulled on his shoes, his hands a blur of motion as they raced to tie the laces.

Then he was on his feet again and sneering at both of them. "I've had it with you, Melinda. All you ever do is mess with our heads. It's like you think we're . . . toys, or something, the way you play with us." He snorted. "Yeah, you thought I was ignorant, didn't ya? A dumb redneck. Well, fuck you. I'm outta here."

He turned to leave.

He'd gone a few feet when Melinda said, "Stop him, Beau. Now."

Her voice was devoid now of any mirth. The flat, cold edge that had been there during her sadistic interrogation of the groundskeeper was back. Hearing it served the purpose of reminding Beau that this crazy bitch was not to be trifled with.

It was a voice that could not be disobeyed. Ever.

So he turned from her unforgiving glare and went after Doug. Soon the two boys were just shadowy shapes in the darkness. She heard the sounds of a scuffle. There was much grunting and pushing and shoving. Finally, one boy managed to land a solid blow. A meaty sound followed by a cry of pain. Then the shapes fell to the ground. One had clearly gained the advantage over the other. A hand rose and fell in the darkness, rose and fell, again and again, landing blow after resounding blow.

Melinda smiled.

She could tell from the tenor of the subjugated one's cries that the outcome was the one she desired. This was confirmed in a few moments when the boys returned to Hannah's grave, Doug stumbling ahead of Beau, who kept the boy moving by driving the heel of a hand into his back.

Doug, defeated, fell to his knees in front of Melinda. He looked at her through eyes Beau's fists had nearly reduced to pulp. "I'm sorry, Mel. I was just . . . I dunno . . ."

Melinda put a soothing hand to his cheek. "It's okay, baby. Mommy forgives you."

Doug sobbed. He let his head sag into Melinda's palm. "I'm so fucking *sorry.*"

He sniffled.

Melinda flicked the wrist of her other hand and the straight razor's blade popped out. Doug was so caught up in his misery that he never saw it coming. She brought the blade around in a perfect arc that opened a deep gash in his throat. For the space of maybe a nanosecond, the gaping slit looked like a second, smiling mouth, one that mocked the sounds of pain emerging from the other. Then the gash opened wider and blood jetted from the severed jugular vein. Doug clamped a hand over the wound and staggered to his feet. He tried to say something, but only spluttered blood.

He stumbled away from Hannah's grave, moving in the direction of the far-off groundskeeper's shack. Melinda snickered at the pathetic attempt at flight. Even a guy as dense as Doug had to know he was fucked. He didn't get very far anyway, falling to his knees again after maybe a dozen feet. He pitched forward onto his stomach and didn't attempt to get up again. He twitched a few times, then was still.

He was dead. Good. Melinda smiled. One less stupid fucker to worry about. Her gaze went now to Beau's ashen countenance. She detected waves of grief and anguish emanating from her sole remaining partner in crime. She knew she'd have to kill him tonight, too. She regretted that she'd be without the playthings that'd so entertained her these last months, but eliminating Beau, the last living person with knowledge of her deeds, was the sensible thing to do.

Her voice took on the girlish tone she knew turned him on: "Beauregard."

Beau looked at her. His eyes were wide and bloodshot. He was crying. What a little bitch. Melinda just managed to suppress a snort of laughter. His lower lip twitched and he looked like he was on the verge of blubbering.

Melinda sneered. "Be a man, Beau. He had to die. You know that. He was trying to leave us. Leave the gang. He might've gone to the police and told them everything. And you don't want that, baby. You'd be in every bit as much trouble as me." She didn't know this for a fact, but she had no doubt the simpleton would buy it. "You're the only one I ever cared about anyway. Come to me, Beau. Take your clothes off. Do me the way that limp-dick son of a bitch couldn't."

Beau didn't respond right away.

He fidgeted. He bit his lower lip and glanced at his dead friend. At last, he said, "I don't know. Did you have to kill him, Mel? I coulda beaten him up some more. I coulda made sure he didn't say anything. I know I coulda. . . ."

Melinda shrugged. "It's all a lotta blood under the bridge now, baby." That made him flinch. Melinda was astonished at how good it felt just to frighten him. She didn't get quite the rush from it that she got from killing, but it was nice. "You know the score, Beau. We're in this together. For good. Now get over here."

He felt it again—that undeniable imperative in her voice—she could see that. With great reluctance, he shuffled a few steps in her direction.

She held up a hand to halt him. "Clothes off, Beau. Now."

With trembling hands, Beau obeyed, removing first his shirt and then his jeans. While he was occupied with the process of taking off his shoes, Melinda went into action. She came at him in a rush, snarling like something rabid, spittle spraying from the corners of her clenched mouth. She saw the beautiful terror in his wide eyes in the moment before she dragged the blade across his belly, and she relished it.

The razor slipped through his abdomen with ease, drawing a long, straight line from one side of his belly to the other. Before he could react, Melinda placed the blade behind one of his legs and yanked up hard, like a woman trying to pull-start a lawnmower. Beau screamed and flopped backward onto the ground. Melinda shifted position, getting the blade into place behind her wailing boyfriend's other leg. She repeated the procedure, drawing the blade through calf muscle and then his hamstring. It was a disabling tactic she'd learned from one of the forensics shows she watched on cable TV.

She then pushed and maneuvered Beau until he was lying flat on his back on Hannah's grave. He was still alive, whimpering and mewling like a baby, his guts spilling out on the ground in a steaming pile.

Just the way she wanted it.

It was an experiment. All the other kills had been quick. She wanted to see how it felt to take her time murdering a human being. Wanted to see if the agonized pleading and begging could be as delicious as she imagined. Melinda had a happy thought: *Guess I'm a serial killer, now.*

She knew that female mass murderers were rare, and the possibility of the fame and notoriety her exploits might one day garner her were enough to assuage the fear she felt at being caught. She imagined herself as the subject of a lurid A&E documentary and smiled.

She found the tight, black vinyl short-shorts she'd peeled off before fucking Doug and wriggled into them. She sat on the ground and rolled the fishnet stockings she'd discarded in her striptease back up over her slender legs, noticing with distaste that they each had a long run in them. She then stepped into her heels and looked for her baby-doll Marilyn Manson shirt.

A muffled sound from the vicinity of Hannah's grave distracted her—something odd she sensed didn't emanate from Beau himself. She turned to face the grave again and took a tentative step toward it, frowning and cocking her head at an angle. Beau was still clinging to life, but his breathing was very shallow and he wasn't moving. The only sound emerging from him was a low, continuous moan. He had a gore-smeared hand over his stomach, where he'd tried to shove some of the spilled rope of intestine back through the hole in his belly.

Then he did move.

Or rather *something* moved him, because his body hadn't shifted of its own accord. He pitched slightly sideways on the freshly turned earth, like a listless shipwreck survivor tossed about on rough seas.

Melinda's frown deepened. Something *beneath* Beau's body was jostling him. Her first thought was of some animal, some big rodent, burrowing through the fresh earth. She discarded this idea when whatever it was gave her dying lover a violent shove, forcing him onto his side. The shove caused the gash in his belly to open wider and his moan soared to a higher register.

Melinda moved a few steps closer, squatted, and studied the dirt beneath which the bitch had been interred. A good bit of it had been displaced in a concentrated area. Melinda knelt closer, realized what she was seeing was a small hole, and had just a moment to puzzle over that when a pale fist punched through the hole. Melinda gasped and fell backward onto her ass.

Unable, at first, to process the reality of what she was seeing, her mind reeled at the impossible sight of a wrist and then a slim arm slithering up through the hole. She just stared at the bizarre spectacle in silent disbelief until a second hand exploded through the earth close to the first one. The two arms looked like surreal grave markers drawn on the canvas of some acid-tripping artist. The arms clawed at the ground now, and a bigger shape began to emerge through the earth.

A head.

And then shoulders. Followed in short order by a clearly female torso. Dirt rolled off funeral clothes like water spilling over a cliff side. The woman gave her head a hard shake and dirt and wood splinters tumbled off limp blonde hair. Melinda felt something large and implacable lodge in her throat when the woman's eyes found her in the darkness.

The first sound the woman made was a creaky laugh.

Followed by a single word: "Molly."

Melinda squealed. "Hannah!"

Terror crashed down on her like a wall falling on a construction worker. This couldn't be. She was dead, the bitch. Killed by a bullet to the head. Her first thought was that she was hallucinating, that she'd lost her mind. Was such a thing really impossible, given the way she'd enthusiastically embraced a new life of murder and torture? Surely these were classic signs of a mind that has come unhinged.

But, no. She wasn't crazy. She felt that as clearly as she felt the ground beneath her ass. As implausible as it seemed, Hannah Starke was rising from her grave, reanimated via some means Melinda couldn't fathom. And, really, did it matter *how* so crazy a thing had come to pass? Hell, no, all that mattered was that it *was* happening, and that if she wanted to live beyond the next few moments, she'd better get her sweet ass in gear and make tracks out of this place.

Hannah wriggled farther out of the grave. Soon she was on her hands and knees and was crawling toward Melinda. Hannah showed her a smile caked with dirt. Her breath reeked of decay and chemicals.

Melinda screamed.

She scrambled backward and got to her feet. Upright now, she backpedaled, keeping her gaze on Hannah, whose movements were stiff and slow. But the resurrected woman seemed to rapidly gain strength and mobility, and she was on her feet within seconds.

Hannah laughed again, a fuller, throatier sound this time. Melinda peered closely at her and could see a slight indentation in her forehead where the bullet had entered. The hole had been patched by a mortician, but not as expertly as Melinda might have expected—it was clear that the dent in her head wasn't natural.

Hannah said, "You look . . . different, Molly. Uglier."

Melinda realized she was unconsciously shaking her head back and forth and willed herself to stop. "No. No, no, no. This makes no sense. I blew your brains out, bitch. How can you walk? How can you talk?"

Hannah shrugged and moved another step closer. "I guess it's just a miracle. Maybe God brought me back to kill you." She giggled. "That's what I'm about to do, you know. I'm going to tear you apart. Gonna crack your fucking skull open and have your brains for dinner. Come here, girl."

Melinda shook her head. She'd had her fill of this bizarre spectacle. "No, fuck this, and fuck you. Sayonara, cunt."

She turned to run, but stopped cold at the sight of Doug on his feet again, standing less than six feet from her. Another resurrected dead person. He grinned, showing her teeth coated with coagulating blood. He tried to say something, but the wound to his throat made the sound an unintelligible gargle.

Panic gripped Melinda. She experienced a moment of supreme frustration. And claustrophobia. She felt trapped. Then she felt Hannah's fetid breath on the back of her neck and decided it was time to cut and run, regardless of the odds. She made a fake to her right, throwing Doug off-stride, then cut back to the left and flew past his outstretched arms.

She raced through the dark cemetery, heedless of the unseen obstacles in her way. Twice small grave markers tripped her up and sent her tumbling to the ground. Each time she was on her feet again in an instant. She could hear the footfalls of her pursuers the whole way. They moved slowly at first, then faster and faster, gaining still more strength and moving at a pace that nearly matched Melinda's run.

Melinda tried to keep her cool. They had closed the gap some, but she knew she had enough of a head start to get free of this place as long as she made no mistakes. She sprinted past the groundskeeper's shack and saw Beau's car. Her immediate impulse was to dive behind the wheel and pull the door shut. But that would be suicidal. Beau's keys were still with him.

Her only chance to survive was to continue to the cemetery's perimeter, where she could try to scale the gate and get away from this land of nightmares come to life.

By the time the gate came into view, she was nearly out of breath. The air came out of her in great gasps and she felt weak in the knees. There was a car parked outside of the gate. A Mustang. As she drew nearer, she could hear its engine idling. She fell against the gate, huffing and puffing as she held onto two thick iron slats.

She heard footsteps close behind her.

And more of Hannah's creepy, taunting laughter.

Melinda found a fresh well of strength, raised a hand above her head, and began to haul herself up.

CHAPTER ELEVEN

Erin wasn't sure whether it was pure luck or an act of God, and she didn't care. All that mattered was that every bullet fired from the policeman's gun missed her. She supposed being a reanimated corpse perhaps affected his ability to aim with precision. His finger was still squeezing the empty gun's trigger. A look of dumb confusion colored his otherwise slack expression. Awareness dawned in the dead cop's dull eyes, and he popped the gun's empty magazine out.

He was in the process of feeding fresh rounds into it when Mike went into action. From his position on the floor, he pivoted and kicked at the backs of the man's knees, causing him to fold up and topple backward. Mike rolled out of the way, missing getting crushed by the dead man's ample weight by a margin of just a few inches. He grabbed at the gun and wrenched it out of the man's loose grasp.

Then he was on his feet and backing away from his

dead former comrade. The cop rocked side to side and groped pathetically at the ground, as if unsure of how to go about getting himself upright again.

With the heel of his hand, Mike slammed the half-filled magazine of the Glock home and handed the weapon to Erin, who took it with a look of disdain and held it away from her, like a new mommy handling her baby's soiled diaper for the first time. Mike's hand closed over her hand, forcing her fingers to close around the butt of the gun. He then guided her other hand into place and threaded a forefinger through the trigger guard.

Erin briefly forgot the incredulous fear that had gripped her since the outset of this bizarre turn of events. She shuddered as something within her thrilled to the long-missed touch of the man who'd once stirred such passion in her. She wanted to fall into his arms, turn into his embrace, and let her mouth go to his. But then Mike moved away and the feeling passed.

Reality snapped back into focus. The man on the floor was still ineffectually striving to get upright again. "Mike . . . what the hell is happening? That man . . . he's dead, isn't he?"

Mike nodded. "I think so, yes."

Her brow knitted in puzzlement. "But how can that be?"

Mike's gaze went to the big black book she'd spotted upon entering the room. He looked at her. "I think it's something to do with that book. I'll explain what I can soon, but right now I want you to watch this guy for me while I fetch something from the shed out back. If he gets up, start shooting. The safety's off, so be careful. Don't aim it unless you're ready to blow him away."

Erin's mouth dropped open in surprise and her eyes went wide with alarm. "Oh, Mike, no." She was shaking her head now. "You can't be serious. You can't be leaving me alone with this . . ." Her face contorted as she struggled to say the absurd word. She sighed. "This zombie."

Mike's expression remained implacable. She saw in his eyes that he meant to make her hold the fort down here while he slipped out to do this errand, whatever the hell it was. Beyond that, he was unreadable. He seemed unsurprised by her sudden and unannounced intrusion into his home, but she hadn't the slightest impression of what he thought of it.

"It's got to be this way, Erin. Zombie or not, I don't want this guy getting away. And I can't send you to retrieve what I need from the shed, because it's cluttered and dark in there and you'd never find what I need, at least not nearly soon enough. I won't be but a minute or so." He sighed, and some of the gruffness seemed to seep out of him. "If you panic for any reason, if you get spooked, come out back and find me right away. Okay?"

Still frowning, Erin gave a reluctant nod. "Okay." She managed a weak smile. "You're as unflappable as ever. Don't you even want to know why I'm here?"

As usual, Mike's face betrayed nothing of his feelings, but he did touch her arm, a gesture of reassurance. "I already know."

Then he was gone.

Leaving her alone with the homicidal dead man. Her gaze went to his face, which no longer seemed as dull and empty of intelligence. He met her gaze and smiled. A shiver ran through her at the sight of that smile, a disturbing expression full of malicious desire and dark intent.

Erin swallowed hard and fought a powerful impulse to go after Mike now.

Then the dead man laughed and the impulse grew stronger.

Mike stepped through the ruined back door and crossed the yard to the little shed. He unlatched the plywood door and stepped inside, reaching up to pull a cord that caused a bare 30 watt bulb to sputter to life and cast dim illumination. He found the things he needed and retrieved them, pulled the light cord again, and left the shed without bothering to close or lock the door. Potential theft of tools was not high on his list of concerns tonight.

There was so much to process, so much madness to figure out. His grief for Hannah still loomed large, though he'd been forced by circumstance to shunt those feelings aside for now. The grief lurked like a slavering beast hulking in the shadows, ready to devour him at the earliest opportunity. But he would not let it sway him from doing what he had to do.

Then there was Erin. Under different circumstances—those not involving the sudden appearance of a reanimated friend bent on killing him, say—her presence might have irked him. She was a piece of his discarded past. She didn't belong here, not in this house in which he'd known such sublime happiness with Hannah. In fairness, however, he wasn't surprised she'd shown up. Though tempestuous, theirs had been a romance marked by an intensity of feeling he hadn't ever felt with anyone else, not even Hannah. The drawback had been that this intensity was split evenly between episodes of passion and burning rage. Whereas with Hannah, he'd known primarily peace. Even when they fought, which they did on occasion, there'd always been an underlying sense of respect for each other that made it easy to smooth things over and come to an understanding.

But towering far above these human concerns, at least for now, was the matter of what to do about the apparently genuine supernatural forces that had stormed into his shattered life like a hurricane-force gale. His instinct was to avoid examining the facts too closely, fearful that what remained of his sanity would slip away like sand through his fingers. But the harsh reality was that he didn't have that luxury. He had to get his brain in gear, had to put his trained policeman's analytical mind to work and figure out a proper course of action.

In that spirit, he initiated a precise march through the facts as he knew them. A week and a half prior to tonight a person or persons unknown entered his home and murdered Hannah. On the evening following her memorial service, another stranger, maybe the killer, maybe not, paid a visit to his home. This time a malign book of the occult was left on his porch. *Invocations of the Reaper*. Upon opening the book, Mike felt helplessly compelled to turn to the end of the book and read a passage written in blood. Then everything went gray for a while. When he came out of it, Erin was there. And, standing over her, Officer Kent Gowran, pointing a gun at the back of her head.

Mike reached the patio adjacent to the kitchen.

The timing of the book's arrival had to be significant. That such a bizarre artifact should just happen to show up on the evening of Hannah's memorial service was too weird to be mere coincidence. The murder and the book were connected in some way, albeit perhaps not directly. And the idea that delivery of the book was the work of a twisted practical joker was absurd. Unless said practical joker was some weird dark sorcerer wandering the streets of Dandridge and performing random magical acts designed to incite chaos, and, well, that was clearly not—

His train of thought was derailed by an explosion of violence within his home. A scream. A shrill cry of distress. Erin. Followed in less than a heartbeat by a gunshot. Then another and another, in rapid succession.

"Erin!"

Mike ran through the ruined door, skidded on some glass shards, and just managed to stay upright by flailing and gripping the edge of the counter. In his effort to avoid a spill, he dropped one of the objects he'd retrieved from the shed. While he knelt to pick it up, two more booming gunshots rang out in the living room.

He sprinted through the kitchen and through the archway into the living room, nearly colliding with Erin as she continued backing away from a newly mobile Kent Gowran. He laid a hand on her shoulder and she shrieked at the touch, instinctively whirling on him and aiming the Glock at his chest.

Mike saw her finger squeezing the trigger, a process begun in the unthinking instant before she realized who was in the line of fire. He experienced an odd sense of disappointment when the gun clicked empty. Or maybe not so odd. The one thing he wanted above all others was to see Hannah again. Just because he wouldn't resort to suicide didn't mean he wouldn't welcome death. The bullet that didn't come could have been his ticket to the next world and a reunion with Hannah.

Erin shrieked and dropped the gun. "Mike! Oh my God . . ."

Mike gave himself the equivalent of a mental slap. He had a crisis to deal with and a person to protect, and he'd better damn well keep his self-pitying head out of the fucking clouds.

He seized Erin by her bicep and pulled her out of the way, maneuvering her into a shielded position behind him.

The two items he'd retrieved from the shed were a long length of thick rope and an axe. He shrugged a shoulder and the rope slid to the floor. He gripped the axe handle in both hands and held it low, like a baseball slugger warming up at the plate.

Kent, or rather this living dead thing that had once been Kent, grinned. Saliva dribbled from both corners of his mouth. The front of his uniform was dotted with bullet holes. Erin, as he recalled now from trips with her to the shooting range, was a very good shot. Blood leaked from the wounds, staining the blue fabric a darker color. Mike could detect no evidence of the extra bulk that would indicate a flak jacket beneath the shirt. The Kent thing had absorbed the full force of several rounds and was still ambulatory; indeed, it seemed utterly unaffected by the wounds.

Kent's mouth moved. His voice sounded muffled and distant, like words issuing from the opposite end of a transatlantic phone call. "Mike, you're not about to do anything foolish with that axe, are you? I'm your colleague, man. Your comrade in arms. Your amigo. You wouldn't do a bud that way, would you?"

Dead Kent shared one characteristic with the former living one, then—a fondness for wisecracks. Only in this case it seemed forced. An echo of something that was gone. Mike was sure this was only an imitation of the jovial veteran cop. The reality of this new Kent was plain to see in eyes turned fiercely feral.

Mike's grip tightened around the axe handle. "Stay back, Kent."

A sound like a mockery of genuine laughter coughed out of the dead cop's mouth. "I don't think so, rookie. Hey, rook, I'll let ya in on a secret or two. Me and the other guys on the force, we've hated your stinking guts since day one. You don't have what it takes to be a real cop. You're a pussy. A good for nothing do-gooder. Another thing. That dead bitch of yours? Me and some of the other fellas took turns poking her dried-up dead cooze at the county morgue. Yep, filled that bitch up with some lotion and went to *town*. Man, she was one hell of a lay, even just lying there like that." The leering grin widened, and he chuckled. "But I don't have to tell *you* that, do I?"

Snarling, Mike raised the axe and sprang forward. He planted his feet and swung the axe like Babe Ruth aiming for the fences. Kent, still grinning, held up a hand to ward off the blow, but the blade clipped off his fingers and sent the severed digits tumbling to the floor. The blade punched through his neck, nearly decapitating him in a single blow. Mike wrenched the blade loose, swung again, and finished the job, sending the head spinning through the air. It landed stump up on the coffee table, then fell sideways.

Kent's body, however, was still upright. The headless corpse came at him and grasping hands reached for him.

Mike moved backward a step. "Oh, for fuck's sake."

Erin screamed. "Mike!"

He glanced her way and saw she was pointing at the coffee table. He looked and saw that Kent's severed head was still sentient. It was grinning and its mouth was moving, emitting a strangled sound that might have been laughter.

Mike sighed. "If I didn't know better, I'd swear some sick joker dosed my iced tea with acid at the memorial service."

Erin shook her head. "If you're tripping, so am I. There's a talking head over there. Mike, this is insane. What's going on?"

"Not sure. Something really weird and fucked-up."

"Yeah, that I figured out, thanks. But what's causing it?"

"Let's deal with that in a minute. Business to take care of first."

He stepped forward and swung the axe again, this time driving the blade deep into the flesh just above Gowran's right knee. A hissing sound of a particularly anguished sort issued from the head. Mike tore the blade free of the mangled flesh and bone and swung it again, his jaw set and muscles tense as he strove to deliver the most devastating blow yet. And it worked—the lower half of the dead cop's leg came away from his body and fell to the floor. What remained of the former Kent Gowran's body wobbled on one leg for a moment, even attempted a hop, and then toppled backward, landing with a great crash on the coffee table before tumbling to the floor.

Erin made a sound of disgust and covered her face. "Oh. Oh my God."

Mike looked at her. "I'm not done yet. Turn around if you don't want to see it."

She shot a troubled glance at him over the tops of her knuckles and shook her head. "No." She dropped her hands. "I'm not hiding from any of this."

Mike nodded.

He went to the corpse, which was trying to get up again. Mike drove the heel of a boot into the small of its back and it collapsed again. Then he went to work, not allowing himself the luxury of hesitation. Hesitation would entail thinking. And he didn't want to think too closely about the hideous thing he needed to do. The axe rose and fell, rose and fell, and several minutes later each of the corpse's limbs had been hacked off. One of the arms, the one with its fingers still intact, required special attention when it tried to crawl toward Erin. He lopped its fingers off, then chopped it in half at the elbow.

Mike let out a big breath. He looked at Erin. "Do me a favor and fetch some trash bags from the kitchen. The heavy duty black ones. They're still in the same place we kept them when you lived here."

Erin shuddered. Then she drew in a calming breath. "Okay."

She turned and walked in the direction of the kitchen.

All at once, Mike felt consumed with a weariness that was bone-deep. He dropped the axe and fell into the recliner. His tired gaze went first to the infernal book, which still seemed to call to him—only now its voice was more like a whisper than a command.

Then he looked at the head on the coffee table.

When it saw Mike looking at it, it grinned.

Shuddering, Mike reached for the bottle of George Dickel and drank deeply.

CHAPTER TWELVE

The Deathbringer sat with his legs crossed on a bench in Dandridge's recreational park. He leaned backward, with his elbows propped lazily atop the back of the bench. To a passing observer, he could be just another Dandridge citizen enjoying a quiet evening beneath the stars. A closer look, of course, would reveal attire not suited to the season, as well as a troubling sketchiness, a vagueness of substance and form. An even closer look, say at the bit of face visible beneath the sloping brim of his hat, would induce heart-squeezing terror. Not that it would matter by that point—those who got that close were invariably within the last few moments of their lives.

Ah, death. Sweet death . . .

For almost longer than he could remember, it had been his role in the scheme of things to deliver an extinguishing touch to those whose time on earth had come to an end. At one point, many centuries ago, he'd been an ordinary man. A man with a wife and a family. Until the time when, desperate to provide for his starving children, he'd found himself drawn into the world of the Reapers.

He'd been tricked, allowed to believe he was being granted admission to an exclusive club along the lines of the masons, something he could use to pursue more lucrative business opportunities. But this organization, as it turned out, was far more ancient than either the Masons or the Illuminati. In fact, theirs was the oldest professional organization of any sort.

They were the Reapers.

The Deathbringers. A coalition of men imbued with the power to end life. Theirs was a sacred mission, they were told. They were agents of God, or so new Reapers tended to assume. The force that bestowed their powers was so omnipotent, and so ancient, that it may as well have been God, regardless of the truth of its nature. Whatever the case, the Reapers had served this force, this "God," since the birth of the human race. And because they so feared God's wrath, not once in the history of the Reapers had any of their number dared to deviate from the organization's code of ethics, the Strictures of the Reaper.

Until now.

The financial reward for signing on had been enough to see to it that his family would live out the rest of their days in luxury, and that was a comfort. Enough so that he was able for a long time to suppress the rage he felt at being tricked. Until the time a month earlier when something had given way within him, a protective barrier that had lasted hundreds of years, leaving him suddenly overwhelmed with weariness and anger—and with a burning desire to rebel.

It began with his discovery of the forbidden book of invocations. A tome of legend most believed didn't really exist. This book was said to have been a collaborative effort between an unknown number of disenchanted Reapers, would-be renegades who yearned to return to their mortal forms and live out their lives as normal men. The only way to do this, or so the stories went, would be to find a way to confront and defeat the force that had empowered them. To kill God Himself, as some nervous gossips had it. To that end, these malcontents worked over a period of centuries to compile a volume of the most powerful dark magic in existence.

That book was *Invocations of the Reaper.*

The Deathbringer discovered the book in the remote mountain home of one of the oldest living Reapers, a man who'd been old when the pyramids were built in Egypt. A man who, as he later learned in reading the tome, was one of the primary authors of *Invocations of the Reaper.* The old Reaper's home was in the Deathbringer's geographical territory and he'd been drawn to the ancient dwelling in the same manner he was any time his presence was required in the moment of death—by a distinct aural signal detectable only to the ears of a Reaper. As usual, he had no awareness of the victim's identity prior to seeing him. When he'd entered the man's home and identified him by the black aura enveloping him, he'd been astonished to learn the man was one of his own, a

Reaper. And not just any newly minted Reaper, either. Nor some century-old youngster. This Reaper's remarkably advanced age and great power had been apparent immediately.

He'd smiled at the Deathbringer's arrival. "Come to turn out the lights, eh?"

To which the Deathbringer had said nothing. He'd hoped he was projecting an air of implacable resolve—in truth, he'd been too astonished to say anything.

And the old Reaper had sighed and said, "So be it. You should know I've been expecting you. You see, I've been planning this a long time. When you have seen me through to the other side, you may wish to return here and investigate my dwelling. There are certain . . . artifacts you may find of interest. Perhaps you'll make better use of them than I ever dared." He sighed again. "Or, as I rather expect, you'll be frightened to even handle them, and will immediately report their existence to the High Council."

By this point, the Deathbringer was intrigued enough that he felt compelled to speak. "You speak of The Book?"

To which the old Reaper's only reply was another cryptic smile.

And at that point their conversation was finished, because by then the Reaper had committed suicide, in the only manner available to such as themselves. Frowning, the Deathbringer had gone to the pile of rumpled black clothing formerly worn by the vanished Reaper. He picked up the clothes and shook them. A pile of brittle old bone fragments clattered to the floor. Among them was another object. The

Deathbringer knelt and picked it up, holding it close for examination.

It was the old Reaper's Black Amulet, the mystical stone given to all Reapers at the time of their initiation. The stone did not bestow their powers. That was "God's Gift," the abilities granted them by the governing force of the universe. Rather, it protected Reapers from the ravages of aging. The Deathbringer had one hanging around his own throat.

The Deathbringer was rarely frightened, or even truly disturbed, by anything. Immortality and the power to remove the lives of others with a touch tended to numb one's sensibilities. But what the old Reaper had done *did* disturb him. Though suicide via this method was known to be possible, no Reaper had ever done it. Until now, anyway. Removal of the Black Amulet violated the Strictures of the Reaper, which was bad enough, but the act also had the effect of condemning the perpetrator to hell. And though this couldn't be verified as fact, it was said that eternity in hell for a Reaper was a much worse fate, by a thousand-fold, than it was for an ordinary human.

Why? the Deathbringer wondered. *Why did you do it?*

It was an instant obsession. He *had* to know the old Reaper's motivations. What was it he was facing in life that could lead him to willingly consign himself to an eternity of misery in hell? And so he'd searched the crumbling old cottage, turning up The Book in short order. Despite a nearly overwhelming sense of incredulity, he'd known what it was the moment he caught sight of its cracked and decaying black cover.

But the old Reaper had been wrong. The Death-bringer took the forbidden book with him, reading much of it later that night in a single long sitting in the comfort of his own isolated home. The words of the renegade Reapers had a galvanizing effect on him. He felt swept up in the spirit of revolt that sang in this stunning prose. Especially compelling to him was the confirmation of the wildest of the old rumors, that the renegades had *really* been after an overthrow of the ruling power, nothing less than a revolt against God.

All through the long night, the Deathbringer shook his head in awed admiration. Ultimately, however, he came to feel a kind of contempt for the renegades. He resolved that night to succeed where his cowardly predecessors had failed. He'd come to Dandridge, this tiny town at the edge of his territory, to begin his rebellion against the ruling power, against God, to bring an end to the old ways, and an end to humanity's status as the supreme life form on this planet. Only eradication of the ruling power's finest creation could bring about the confrontation he desired, and this process was already well under way. Soon it would rage out of control, sweeping the planet with chaos and disorder, with total death.

The Deathbringer smiled, thinking of the newly resurrected Prime and reveling in the glory to come.

He spied a mother and small child walking hand in hand down a winding path that would lead them past this bench.

His smile broadened, and he thought, *Come Mother, come Child, come on down and meet your destiny . . .*

He stood.

And grinned at the sudden look of terror in the mother's eyes as he reached for her and drew her and her child into his growing army of the dead.

CHAPTER THIRTEEN

Avery had a dim awareness of something happening to the rear of where the Mustang sat idling outside the cemetery. A rattle of metal. And grunting, sounds of considerable physical exertion. Probably it was some security guard or groundskeeper come to chase him off the property, thinking he was a prowling juvenile with bad intentions. A would-be vandal, perhaps.

Then there was another sound.

A thump, as of a large object falling from a great height before striking the ground. Then a click-click-click of heels heading his way. Next came a furious pounding on the rolled-up passenger-side window.

Annoyed, Avery opened his eyes, lifted his head from the steering wheel, and blinked away the last of his tears. Then he frowned, because there was a topless young girl standing outside his car and peering through the window. She was terrified. Moreover, her

104

jittery movements conveyed a sense of frantic urgency. She kept glancing back at the cemetery.

Avery sighed and thumbed the power window button. "It's fucking unlocked, genius."

The girl yanked the door open and fell inside, slamming the door shut as soon as her feet were clear. She twisted in the seat and the full force of the panic gripping her hit Avery for the first time as he looked into her wild, darting eyes.

She gripped a handful of his shirt, twisted it in her hand, and leaned close. "Drive! Get *out* of here! Now!"

Avery's brow furrowed. "What . . . ?"

Her voice rose to the level of a scream now: "Dead people are chasing me! *Dead* fucking people, asshole! Drive or die!"

Avery gripped her wrist and pried her hand away from his shirt. "Dead people, huh? No shit. A lot of that going around tonight. What the hell's going on?"

There was another sound to the rear of the car. The cemetery gate rattling again. The girl shrieked. Avery was turning his head to get a look when the girl's hand flashed in his peripheral vision and he heard a sharp *smack* that turned out to be the flat of her hand whipping across his face.

He put a hand to his stinging cheek. "Damn, girl."

The rattling behind them grew louder. The girl again seized a handful of his shirt. "That's them, motherfucker. They're coming for me, for *us*. If you don't stop sitting there like a retard, we'll be as dead as they are in a minute."

Avery flashed on an image of a reanimated Tom Crawford shambling out of the Atkins place. The very real, and apparently very imminent, possibility of winding up like that sobered him, obliterating, for the moment, his monumental grief with the force of a wrecking ball.

He put the Mustang in gear and slammed the gas pedal to the floorboard, causing the car to leap away from the cemetery and the danger closing in on them. He sped down Blakemore Boulevard some forty-five miles per hour in excess of the posted speed limit, slowing down enough to make a hairpin left turn onto Dawson, which would take them into the heart of Dandridge.

Avery began to decelerate after another quarter mile. He checked his mirrors for signs of flashing cop lights, but there was nothing. He was glad for that. Not because he cared about getting a ticket, but because he didn't relish the prospect of having to tell a cop his tale of zombies and death. And that wasn't even factoring in the presence of a partially nude, and presumably underaged, girl in his car.

Speaking of . . . he couldn't help noticing how attractive she was, albeit in an extremely punked-out way. Ripped-up fishnets, black heels—a surprise, actually; he would've expected Doc Martens or something similar—and super-tight black vinyl short-shorts made her look like something out of a Sid Vicious wet dream. And her skin was pale and creamy smooth. Her medium-sized breasts were pert and a stiff pink nipple jutted from each. He felt a surge of obscenely inappropriate horniness, which he stifled by forcing his brain to show a highlight reel of all the awful things that had happened since the murder of his sister. It was the equivalent of thinking about baseball or toxic landfills during sex to ward off premature ejaculation.

"What were you doing in the cemetery anyway, girl?"

The girl snorted. "What do you think? You see many hot chicks running around half-naked in the middle of the night? I was in there having sex with my boyfriend. I was getting dressed when one of those . . . things came out of the ground and . . . and . . . k-k-killed my Beau. . . ."

She started to blubber. But something about the sounds emerging from her throat struck Avery as false. He didn't doubt that something terrifying had happened in the cemetery, but he sensed her grief was less than sincere. She'd cut and run when the shit hit the fan and evidently she felt some guilt over that. Which was understandable. And probably the guy had been some schmuck who'd tried to impress the punk chick by sneaking her into the cemetery for a grope among the tombstones—in other words, not anyone the girl would have real feelings for, other than lust.

He sighed. "I'm . . . sorry for your loss. I've lost some pretty important people myself just lately, and I know how it feels. But here's what we're gonna do."

A long moment elapsed in silence. The Mustang continued down Dawson, encountering little traffic moving in either direction. Dandridge lacked the sense of a town under siege, which Avery had half been expecting.

The girl grunted. "Well?"

Avery blinked. He looked at her. "What?"

She rolled her eyes. "You were about to say what we're gonna do?"

Avery nodded. "Oh. Yeah. That's right. Sorry, got distracted."

The girl shot a pointed look at the empty road ahead of them, then looked at him. "By what? By all that . . . ," she waved a hand vaguely, "that nothing?" She smiled. Then she turned in her seat so that her perky breasts were thrust upward and the nipples pointed at him like two miniature pink cannons. "Or were you thinking about how easy it would be to pull off somewhere and have your way with me?"

Avery scowled. "What? No! What kind of guy do you think I am?"

There was a gleam in her eyes now, a spark of mischief. "I think you're like every other guy who ever lived. You all want it. And you want it all the time."

Avery shook his head. "Knock it off. Let's not go there, okay? I'm a grown-up. And I'm one of the good guys. I don't pull shit like that. Got it?"

She shrugged, but the spark of mischief still flared brightly. "Whatever."

Avery cleared his throat. "We're going to the sheriff. That's what we're going to do." He nodded, agreeing with himself. "It's time to get the authorities in on this."

The girl uttered a single syllable as emphatic as any he'd ever heard: "No."

He frowned. "Why not?

The mischievous flirt of a moment ago vanished. She turned away from him and folded her arms beneath her breasts. She now had the air of a spoiled child grimly determined to have her way.

"You can drop me off here or anywhere."

Avery sighed. "There some good reason you don't want to talk to the cops? Something you're not telling me, maybe?"

She turned a cold gaze on him. It was the look of a predator, or just that of a cool and calculating person with something to hide. Whatever the case, the suspicion she regarded him with was unmistakable. A fresh feeling of dread took root within him. He wasn't afraid of the girl. She was clearly unarmed and was slightly built enough that he could break her over his knee if need be, yet there was something about her, some vague hint of menace lurking beneath the surface, that made him uneasy.

She startled him by laying a hand on his knee. "There's a lot I'm not telling you. You should be afraid of me." She gave his knee a squeeze and moved her hand farther up his thigh. "*Very* afraid."

Avery swallowed hard and glanced down at the pale hand as it continued its slow but inexorable path toward his crotch. His penis swelled slightly and there was a moment during which he knew he was close to letting her take this further than was cool. But his sense of self-respect managed, at last, to assert itself, and he moved her hand away.

He looked at her, his expression as sober as it had been since Hannah's memorial service, an event that already seemed to have taken place in another life, in another world—a world uninhabited by resurrected dead people and barely dressed teen punk temptresses—even though it'd only been several hours ago.

"You're gonna have to knock it off with the games, girl."

He applied pressure to the brake and slowed the

Mustang to a crawl. He pulled onto the road's shoulder and put the car in park.

"Why did you stop?" The girl frowned. But the expression shifted, became something halfway between a smile and a leer. "Ooooh. I get it. You want me to get in back. Look, I'll let you do it, but you're kinda old. Maybe you should give me some money first."

"Get out."

Now she was frowning again. "What?"

Avery laughed. "Are you deaf, girl? I told you to get out of my car. I'd like to be rid of you in about five seconds, okay?"

For the second time since her panicked intrusion into his life, the girl appeared genuinely frightened. Her face crumpled and her eyes glistened with moisture. "No, please. I'm sorry. I shouldn't act all trashy, I know. I just feel like I owe you something, you know?" She sniffled. A tear leaked from her left eye and etched a wet trail down her face. "I shoulda known better. Shoulda known you were classier than that."

Then the waterworks erupted big-time and she covered her face with her hands.

Avery sighed.

Women. No matter their place on the social scale, they always had one absolutely undeniable trump card to play. And that was the option to descend into hysterical tears to alter the course of things when they weren't going their way. It worked for all of them, even this girl, this misplaced urban gutter punk. He knew thinking it made him a bad guy. He even knew it was an unfair generalization.

Still, the girl was clearly attempting to manipulate him. It was galling. And there was not a damn thing he could do about it. A less gallant or unforgiving soul might yet toss her out, but he couldn't and he knew it.

"Can I at least take you home?"

She sniffled and looked at him through her tears. "Sure." Her voice was very small, the sound of someone lost and helpless. More obvious manipulation. More horseshit he had no defense against. "I guess that'd be okay."

"Okay, listen—"

He was cut off by the abrupt intrusion of a high-pitched and clipped tone to the rear of the car. He frowned and glanced in the rearview mirror, groaning at the sight of flashing blue lights atop a Dandridge police car.

The girl said, "Oh, shit."

Avery looked at her and felt something twist in his stomach as he imagined the cop leaning in to get a good look at the topless teenage girl in his passenger seat. And he knew without having to look that there was nothing in the back with which she could cover up. His brow furrowed as his mind groped frantically for ways to explain the underage girl's presence in his car as well as her state of partial undress.

The girl met his gaze. "Your car's still running."

"What about it?"

One corner of her mouth tilted up, a smirk bordering on a smile. "Wait until the pig gets out of his car, then burn rubber."

Avery barked nervous laughter. "What, you think this is *The Dukes of Hazzard*?" He rolled his eyes. "Get serious. And 'pig'? You sound like you've read *Helter Skelter* one too many times."

She didn't crack a smile as she said, "It's one of my favorite books."

"I bet it is." Avery sighed. "But look, this is twenty-first century Tennessee. Not late sixties California. We're not acid freaks. We're not killers. Also, by now our friendly neighborhood police officer has filed my license number. I make a break for it now and every cop and state trooper in the area will be on my ass in a matter of minutes."

That strange smirking smile returned. "You're no fun."

Avery opened his mouth to retort, but the words died on his tongue when he heard the patrol car's door open and thunk shut. This was followed by the distinct sound of booted feet crunching shoulder gravel.

Avery stage-whispered at the girl, "Be cool."

She smiled. "I'm always cool."

Avery turned from her and stared rigidly straight ahead, a position he maintained until he sensed the presence of the cop outside his door. Summoning the most faux-sincere smile he could muster, he turned and looked into the barrel of a gun pointed point-blank at his face.

"Officer . . ."

A gravelly voice snarled at him: "Get out of the car."

"But . . . have I done—"

The voice was louder this time, like a percussive explosion in the night. "Get out of the car, mother-fucker! Now, before I blow your fucking head off!"

Avery reached a shaking hand toward the door handle. His heart raced like an out of control rail car about to jump the tracks. Fear ruined his fine motor control, causing his trembling hand to glance off the handle a time or two before finally seizing hold of it. He'd never known fear like this, not even during the surreal horrors of fighting off reanimated corpses. With that there'd been a kind of disconnect, a reflexive product of his mind's inability to accept the reality of the situation. But an angry cop aiming a gun at his face and screaming at him—there was something almost *too* real about that.

He managed to get the door open and emerged from the car on legs that felt weak and withered, like feeble old man's legs. It was all he could do not to fall in a trembling, pathetic heap to the pavement—which was where he wound up anyway in a moment, when the cop curled a hand into a fist and fired it like a cannonball into his midsection. He toppled backward, struck the Mustang's door, then pitched forward and landed on his hands and knees, the shoulder gravel tearing holes in his jeans and abrading his palms.

He felt sick, like he might throw up, but this concern was displaced by a host of others when he felt the cop crouching over him and wrapping an arm around his midsection. His mind reeled. Whatever this guy was up to, it didn't have anything to do with performing his duties as a police officer. Then he felt the guy's open mouth sliding over his neck, felt his teeth pushing at his flesh, and knew it was time to fight back. He tried to drive an elbow into the cop's side, but the bigger, stronger man had him pinned too well.

Panic surging through his veins like icy fire, his gaze went to something shiny in the road. It was the cop's gun, maybe five feet away. For whatever unfathomable insane reason, the man had abandoned the firearm in favor of this physical assault. Avery grimaced at the sensation of the man's teeth pushing into his skin and tried to calculate how he might get to that gun before this sick fuck could finish doing whatever it was he meant to do to him.

But then he heard something hit the ground to his right and a moment later saw slim legs encased in ripped fishnets entering his field of vision. Christ, he'd almost forgotten the crazy punk chick in the midst of this struggle. He saw her pick up the gun and walk unhurriedly back to where he was still pinned down by the lunatic cop. She moved to his left, planted her feet, and unleashed a kick that drilled a heel into the cop's ear. The cop howled and staggered to his feet, falling against the Mustang.

Avery fell flat on the pavement, panting, grateful for the narrow rescue. The punk girl was a bit on the wild side, but hey, that was just part of being a kid. She'd gone up considerably in his estimation and—

A huge sound, an explosion of some sort, seemed to rip apart the night.

It was followed by another explosion.

And another.

Belatedly, Avery realized the punk girl was shooting the policeman. Avery groaned again and turned onto his side in time to watch the cop tumble to the ground. Then the girl was standing over him and aiming the gun at his head. She pulled the trigger several more times and Avery, scarcely able to believe what he was seeing, watched the muzzle flashes in fascination. By the time the gun clicked empty the place where the cop's brain had been was a ruined, bloody mess.

Avery sat up. He looked at the dead cop a long moment before shaking his head, then he looked at the girl. "Well, that's it, then. You and I are going to jail forever. That's if we're lucky. That's if some pissed off cops don't torture and kill us first."

"Not gonna happen."

Avery blinked. "What?"

Now the girl shook her head. "How dense are you? When was the last time a cop tried to eat you? He was one of *them*."

Awareness, at last, dawned within Avery. "Oh."

"He pulled you over to kill you." She chuckled. "I think you can stop worrying about your license being on file. But we better get out of here before more of them come."

She held a hand out to him.

"Get up."

Avery looked at her hand and briefly considered just staying where he was. Maybe he would've been better off if the cop had killed him and turned him into one of those walking dead things. Surely that would have been easier than fighting to survive in a world gone off its fucking rocker.

But he sighed and took her hand.

She hauled him to his feet and they got back inside the Mustang.

He looked at her. "I've got an idea. You can take it or leave it. I don't have a clue how to start dealing with this crazy shit, but I know someone who might. He'll at least have an idea how to put up a proper fight."

"Who are you talking about?"

"My—" Avery caught himself before he could say "brother-in-law," because, of course, that never came to pass. "My . . . friend. His name's Mike."

The girl shrugged. "Whatever. I sure don't feel like going home now, I know that. And I know this: we better get out of here before somebody else comes along."

On that count, Avery was in full agreement with her. He put the Mustang in gear and pulled back onto the road, leaving the dead cop and his flashing beacon of a car behind.

CHAPTER FOURTEEN

It was very strange to be up and walking around again, when Hannah knew full well she should still be beneath the ground, where her dead, decaying flesh should be consigned to that eternal darkness. But some force, some magic she couldn't begin to comprehend, had plucked her essence, her soul, out of the ether, restoring it to a body that, strangely, felt stronger than it ever had in life.

And that wasn't the only curious thing, not by far. Though the final bullet fired by Molly, according to the bitch herself, had blown her brains out, her thought processes seemed to be functioning as smoothly as ever. And she remembered everything of her former life. Her love of Mike O'Bannon. The wedding she'd looked forward to, had poured her heart and soul into. Her dreams of success as a writer. She retained all the human feelings and desires she'd had in those last moments prior to when

Molly had walked across her lawn in that damnable disguise.

With one important exception.

One that made her feel like something less than human. Like something feral, a predatory, conscienceless animal. She was pretty fucking sure the pre-death Hannah had never felt anything like this glorious blood lust. The need to feel warm, pumping gore in her mouth made her shudder, the desire for it was so exquisite, so close to sexual there was almost no difference. It gripped her like a junkie's desperate need for a fix. The urge to kill, to maim and torture, rendered nearly all other considerations unimportant. This was a generalized need, not merely a desire for revenge on Molly. Though that would be nice, too. She felt like a machine, a primitive device programmed with just one grim function, an imperative she had no choice but to obey.

Standing now outside the cemetery gate, she wondered what her next move should be. She felt torn between heading into town and turning in the opposite direction to head for home.

She imagined how Mike might react to her *rebirth* and was slightly dismayed at her conflicting feelings. One part of her relished seeing the expressions of astonishment and terror that would no doubt flicker across his face in those first moments. This part of her looked forward to ripping his throat out, was in fact turned on by the idea. The thing that surprised her was that a not insignificant part of her was horrified at the notion of doing anything to harm him.

She frowned.

Strange.

She wasn't quite human anymore. That was an understatement of cosmic proportions. She was some kind of . . . monster now. Yet her love of Mike still felt very real. It was a hell of a conundrum. She didn't think it'd keep her from killing him, but maybe she could try not to damage his body too severely. She knew she wasn't the only resurrected person wandering around tonight. Molly's idiot friend, the one who'd helped chase the bitch through the cemetery, being a good case in point. So it stood to reason Mike could die and come back, too.

It was something to think about, anyway.

Her gaze had been fixed on the empty road heading into town, the direction in which Molly's goddamned rescuer had sped off in some roaring souped-up sports car. But now it swung in the other direction and she studied the dead boy standing befuddled in the street. There was a big, gaping gash across his throat, where Molly had evidently opened him up with something. Coagulating blood covered his shirtless torso.

"I don't guess you can talk, can you?"

He looked at her and opened his mouth, but the only sound that emerged was a rasping exhalation of air.

Hannah sighed. "Lot of goddamn help you're gonna be."

She remained mired in indecision until she heard a rising noise emanating from the east. She looked that way and saw dim twin points of light appear in the darkness. She watched them grow larger and realized the dead boy would be of use after all. He made things easy for her by turning in the direction of the approaching car. It was a simple thing to walk up behind him and shove him into the middle of the road as the shiny red sports car came hurtling by the cemetery.

The dead boy staggered, struggling to remain upright, looking up in time to make eye contact with the Corvette's horrified driver. Then there was a thump of impact and a sound of limbs shattering as the body rolled up onto the hood, then pitched sideways and fell to the asphalt as the car fishtailed and screeched to a halt. The driver's side door flew open and the agitated driver shot out of the car and went to the broken body in the street.

Hannah smiled.

The Corvette's engine was idling. It'd be so easy to get in the car and drive away, but there was the matter of the lust consuming her with which she had to deal. The Corvette's driver, a middle-aged man in khaki pants and a blue button-up shirt, looked up and saw her coming his way.

He had close-cropped brown hair tinged with gray and blue eyes that looked big behind his wire-rimmed glasses. "Hey, lady, you stay right there, I saw what you did and I'm calling the cops." He removed a cell phone from a belt clip and clicked a button. "What are you, some kind of psycho? I saw you push this poor boy in front of my car."

Hannah moved fast, too fast for him to react. She curled unnaturally strong fingers around the hand holding the cell phone and squeezed until she heard the crunch of bones and cell phone yielding beneath the pressure. The man screamed and tried to tear his hand away, but Hannah held fast to him. She pulled him into an embrace that was a mockery of a lover's clinch, wrapping her arms around him and hooking a leg behind him. Then her mouth went to his throat, and he was screaming again as her teeth began to puncture his flesh. The scream became a whimper and he tried to writhe out of the embrace, but Hannah's mouth was locked on the wound in his throat. She slurped the lovely blood and feasted on his flesh. As the man's strength inevitably ebbed, she eased him to the road and continued to feed until she was sated.

Then, for fun, she twisted his head around until it popped off in her hands. She carried it with her to the Corvette and set it on the dashboard. She admired the trophy for a moment as she licked blood from her fingers.

Then she put the car in gear and drove away from the cemetery.

CHAPTER FIFTEEN

Mike dropped the grinning head into the trash bag and pulled the yellow cinch tie taut before looping it into a knot. Then he set the bag containing head and limbs next to the one with the torso stuffed into it.

His living room was a wreck. It looked as if the Manson family had partied here overnight. Big patches of carpet were stained a deep bloodred. There were bullet holes in the wall. The inlaid glass panels of the coffee table's surface had been shattered and the pieces lay glittering on the floor.

Erin touched his shoulder.

Mike's first instinct was to flinch away, but a deeper need overrode his lingering irritation at her presence—the human need for an ally in a time of conflict and stress. He sighed and turned to face her.

He saw something familiar flare in her eyes, a faint spark of the old passion. Seeing it now simultaneously repulsed and comforted him. The repulsion was in response to a belated recognition that, on some level, he felt what she evidently was feeling. Hannah had been in the ground less than a day. Regardless of how remote the feeling was, it was obscene to entertain any notion of rekindling what he once had with Erin. The comfort was knowing he was in the presence of someone who genuinely cared about him. And with the world gone insane, that mattered.

Erin indicated the bags with a nod. "What are we going to do with . . . that?" Disgust creased her face. The look intensified as she considered their grisly contents. Then she looked Mike in the eye again. "The police will never believe our version of what happened here, you know that."

Mike sighed. "Maybe not." He let his gaze sweep slowly over the living room, taking in the paintings and pieces of furniture selected by Hannah during her time here. The van Gogh print he'd bought for her at a fair in particular tugged at his heart. There was so much of her and their history together here. It didn't make doing what he knew had to be done any easier, but there was no real choice.

He looked at Erin. "I'm thinking there's a chance this isn't an isolated incident. Call it a hunch, because I've got no evidence of that yet. In that case, the police will be involved in trying to contain whatever's happening and no one will think we murdered Gowran in cold blood." He grunted and shook his head. "But we can't act based on suppositions. We have to assume the worst. If Gowran doesn't check in soon or show up at the station, somebody will be dispatched to check on him. And we can't be here when that happens."

Erin frowned. "But . . . we can't just run, can we? They'll come in here and see all this . . . ," she indicated the evidence of carnage with a sweep of a hand, "and they'll jump to some pretty obvious conclusions."

Mike nodded. "I know. That's why we have to burn this place to the ground."

Erin gasped.

"Just listen to me. I know it sounds extreme, but it's the only way." He sighed and glanced at Erin's discarded purse. He knew there would be cigarettes in it—there was a faint whiff of tobacco on her breath. It was one of the things they used to fight about, her smoking, but now he found himself craving one for the first time since his brief flirtation with teen delinquency years ago.

Erin followed his gaze. "Why are you looking at my purse?"

"You still smoke, right?"

Her brow furrowed in puzzlement. "Yeeeeah," she said, dragging out the single syllable out of sheer confusion. "Why?"

"Goddammit, Erin, just give me a cigarette."

She blinked. Then she laughed. "Your wish, my command." She shook her head, then retrieved the purse from the floor. "I think somebody knocked me on the head and I'm hallucinating a world turned inside out."

"Welcome to the club. I've been feeling like somebody whacked me upside the head with a two-by-four a couple dozen times ever since . . ."

Mike looked at the floor.

Erin cleared her throat. "Yeah."

And there was no real need to say anything else on that subject. The world had seemed off-kilter, almost terminally so at times, since Hannah's senseless murder, and Mike knew Erin wouldn't push him to talk about it. Whatever her faults were—and there'd been a time when he'd believed they were legion—she was sensitive enough to know he'd only talk about that grim business when he was ready.

She tapped a cigarette from a crumpled pack and passed to him. Mike wedged it into a corner of his mouth, reflexively renewing a habit he'd left behind at fifteen. She lit it for him with her disposable lighter and he drew in a lungful of poison. He knew it was a dumb thing to do, at least from a health perspective, but inhaling and exhaling the smoke did have the effect of calming him and allowing him to focus.

He started pacing the room, intermittently puffing on the cigarette as he spoke. "There's too much physical evidence here. More than we could hope to clean up or eliminate. So we have to burn this place." He removed the half-smoked cigarette from his mouth and studied it, his face crinkled in a contemplative way. Then he flicked it away. It lay smoldering among the broken glass shards. "It's got to look like an accident, like I got drunk and careless. While the place is going up, you and I will take separate vehicles to a to-be-determined location. You'll go in your car and I'll take Gowran's patrol car." His gaze went to the garbage bags. "I'll take his . . . remains in the patrol car. I know a way I can dispose of them that'll leave virtually no trace. It's a rotten shame and I feel heartsick for his family, but we have no choice. Once that's done, we'll abandon the patrol car and go to your place. With any luck, it should look like Gowran met an undeterminable fate unconnected with anything that went on here tonight."

Erin rubbed her eyes and sighed. "Jesus, it sounds complicated." She looked at him. "There's so much that could go wrong."

Mike shrugged. "Yeah, but I don't see how we have a choice. We'll allow people to believe I went to you tonight seeking solace from my grief." He frowned. "Ah . . . and now that I think of it, we'll have to swing back by here first so I can get my car."

Erin shook her head. "Yet another complication."

A contemplative silence ensued. Mike was busy considering yet another variation on his plan when Erin moved away from him and knelt over. *Invocations of the Reaper*. When he saw her hand reaching for the cover, he moved fast, gripping her by the shoulder and pulling her away from the occult artifact.

She grunted. "What the hell, Mike?"

"I don't think you should touch that."

"And why not?"

He breathed an exasperated sigh. "Jesus, Erin, you remember what happened to me when I opened it, right? What makes you think that won't happen again?"

Her shoulders sagged as some of the feistiness went out of her. "Oh. Right. Good point." But her gaze fell again to the book. "But that thing's our only clue as to what's going on—don't we *have* to look at it?"

Mike stroked his chin. "Hmm. Maybe there's a way to handle it without actually handling it."

"What do you mean?"

"Maybe the book needs a physical conduit to do what it did to me, an interaction of flesh with whatever brand of hoodoo permeates the book itself.

Maybe what we need to do is examine the book without establishing that physical link."

"How do you propose to do that? Know any magic of your own, Mike? Some page-flipping spells, perhaps?"

Mike grunted. "I don't think that'll be necessary. There's a box of latex gloves somewhere in the house. I could wear those and turn the pages with, I don't know . . . tweezers, maybe."

Erin laughed and shook her head. "That's ridiculous."

"You have a better idea?"

Erin sighed and shook another cigarette out of the pack. She lit up, inhaled, and blew a big cloud of smoke into the middle of the already muggy room. "No, I don't suppose I do. Except—have you thought of checking the Internet?"

"What on earth for?"

She shrugged. "You never know what you'll find on the Web. Pull up your search engine of choice and enter 'Invocations of the Reaper.' That's an old fucking book, Mike. And a powerful one. Somebody out there's got to know something about it."

Mike thought about it. It wasn't a bad idea, though he doubted it would yield useful results. "All right. But I don't think we'll find anything. I just have this feeling that no one with knowledge of that book will have a Web site. I picture them living in remote locales, mysterious occult monks clad in black cloaks hiding away in ancient churches made of crumbling adobe."

Erin smirked. "That's quite the vivid imagination you've got there, Mike."

"Hannah was a writer. And a damn good one. It rubbed off on me."

Erin sighed. "Yeah. So let's go fire up your computer before we descend into another uncomfortable silence."

Mike nodded. "Okay."

He led her out of the living room, through the foyer and past the staircase, then through another archway and the dining room. He opened a closed door and they entered the room that had been Hannah's writing office.

The feeling that gripped Mike in that moment was like a cold hand closing around his heart. He hadn't set foot inside Hannah's office since the day of her death. Being in this room was almost like being in her presence again. The computer was on and a window full of text filled the screen. One of her stories, of course. Mike leaned over the desk, fingered the wireless mouse and clicked the X to close the window. A box popped up, asking whether he wanted to save changes made to the file. With a heavy sigh, he chose "Yes" and the window disappeared.

Erin laid a tentative hand between his shoulder blades. "You okay?"

Mike swallowed hard and cleared his throat. "Yeah."

"Liar."

He nodded. "We have to do this."

He sat in the comfortable leather chair that had been his gift to Hannah when she'd taken the big step of moving in with him. Her old writing chair had been a creaky fold-up thing she'd had since high school, and she'd been thrilled to finally throw it out.

Sitting in the place where she'd spent so much of her time conjuring fanciful scenarios and dreaming her big dreams overwhelmed him for a moment. Tears sprang to his eyes and he feared he was close to breaking down.

Erin squeezed his shoulder. "It's okay."

She leaned over him and pried the mouse from his hand. She clicked on an icon and a browser window opened. Then her hands went to the keyboard and typed the book's name into the search engine. She tapped the enter button and a page full of results appeared within moments.

Mike saw the words "Results for 'Invocations of the Reaper'" and sat forward in the chair, his curiosity dispersing the surge of grief. He reclaimed the mouse from Erin and scrolled through a host of results that looked related to fantasy role-playing games. At the bottom of the page was a link to what appeared to be a religious site. The words "Invocations of the Reaper" were highlighted in bold in a text excerpt. The link was www.guardians.org. He clicked it and a very low-tech site loaded. At the center of a white background were two words: "Guardians" and "Vigilance."

Erin made a petulant sound. "What the hell?"

"I don't know."

Mike moved the cursor over the words and discovered a clickable link. It led to a page filled with dense text, which turned out to be a very stiffly written history of an organization called The Guardians. Much of it was cryptic, enough so that Mike suspected a lot of it was written in a kind of code. However, there were two specific mentions of *Invocations of the*

Reaper. There was nothing about the nature of the book, nor of its origin, but the mentions were couched in strident warnings. The book was not to be opened, or even touched, at risk of loss of life and/or sanity. Discovery of any copy of the book, said the final sentences, should be reported immediately to The Guardians. There was an e-mail link at the end. Mike clicked it and a blank email opened.

He hesitated. He turned and looked at Erin, who was still leaning over him. "Is this for real, you think? Could this really be about the same book?"

Erin shrugged. "I don't see how it could be anything else."

Mike frowned. "Yeah. I guess. But . . . we don't know anything about these people. They could be good guys, or they could be bad guys."

Erin stood up straight, turned, and leaned against the desk. "Mike, they're the only lead we've got."

He couldn't deny the truth of her words. He didn't like putting their fates in the hands of these faceless people, people who were less than strangers. But there was nothing else to do. So he typed "Invocations of the Reaper, please help!" in the subject header and typed a brief summary of events into the body of the email. He concluded with his phone number, then clicked "Send" and the email vanished into the cyber-ether.

He leaned back in the chair and steepled his hands. He looked at Erin and smiled wearily. "All I can say now is I hope these Guardian fuckers check their e-mail on a regular basis. If they can take a break between periods of self-flagellation, that is."

Erin's gaze flicked between Mike's face and the

computer monitor. "They're online. I doubt they're as medieval as you imagine."

"We can only hope."

Mike's gaze went to a framed picture to the left of the monitor. It was a picture of him and Hannah taken at Niagara Falls the previous autumn. A kind fellow vacationer had snapped the photo for them while they stood against a railing and a backdrop of tumbling water. Hannah was in shorts and a halter top. Her hair was in a ponytail and her big smile looked radiant enough to warm the north pole.

Mike propelled himself out of the chair and spun away from the desk. "Let's get out of here."

He heard Erin sigh and follow him out of the room.

As he was moving through the foyer on his way back to the living room, he saw headlights appear through a window. He came to an abrupt halt and heard a grunt of surprise from Erin behind him.

"Mike, what is it?"

A cold finger of fear tickled his spine as he watched the lights grow larger and move up his driveway.

"Someone's here."

CHAPTER SIXTEEN

Carlton Hotchkiss popped the tab on a tall can of Busch and took several big swallows before returning his attention to the gravely injured woman lying on the trash-strewn bed of his pickup truck. He looked her up and down and felt Carl Jr. twitch in his pants. He grabbed her by the ankles and hauled her out of the truck. She fell against him like a sack of potatoes, almost pure dead weight, but he shoved her away and she collapsed to the ground.

Carlton kicked her flat stomach with the tip of a steel-toed boot and laughed at the moan this elicited. He'd have to watch that compulsion to beat on her or she'd be dead before he could get any use out of her. And the idea of necrophilia didn't hold much attraction for him. It'd happened once and he'd been haunted by bad dreams about it ever since. He hadn't meant to fuck a dead chick, but the last crack whore dumb enough to get a room with him had checked out while Carl Jr. had been in the middle of giving her a good banging. He'd known it, too, and it had creeped him out at the time. He wasn't so much of a sick bastard in some ways. But, hell, he'd been right in the middle of getting his freak on and had seen no reason not to finish the job.

Not this time, though. If this skinny skank decided to die on him before he could get his rocks off, he'd stop right then and there, toss her dead ass in the grass, and get on home. He'd had enough nightmares of reanimated crack whores coming after him to tear off his ding-a-ling to last a lifetime.

He knelt over the girl and reached for the snap on her denim cut-offs. And it was at that moment that a voice like a puff of refrigerated air spoke in his ear.

"Kill her."

"I intend to, bubba, in a minute or two. But—" He frowned. "Hey . . ."

He whirled around and stood in a crouch, whipping a hunting knife from a sheath attached to his belt. He steeled himself to plunge the big blade into the heart of whoever had been dumb enough to wander into his campsite, but there was no one there. He spun around, scanning the small clearing for any hint of a human presence. But there was nothing.

He stood erect and scratched his head gently with the tip of the knife. He frowned. "Hearin' things again. Goin' crazy, I guess."

Carlton's gaze went back to the girl, who'd gathered enough strength to start crawling for the line of trees beyond the pickup truck. He hurried over to her and pinned her with a knee to the small of her back. Then he slipped the hunting knife beneath the flimsy fabric of her halter top and split it down the middle with one flick of his wrist. He grunted, liking the way her thin, pointy shoulders looked in the milky moonlight. He moved his knee and flipped her over, pulling the ruined halter top away at the same time to expose her smallish breasts. She moaned again and her eyelids blinked slowly. Her mouth opened to issue a plea, but of course he wasn't listening.

He was reaching to cup one of her breasts when he heard the voice in his ear again: *"Kill her."*

Carlton froze. He stared down at the girl, who was now whimpering as she moved closer to total consciousness. She was pretty for being such an obvious skank. He'd snatched her outside a redneck dive bar on the outskirts of Dandridge. Her name was Elise. Funny. He usually tried not to think of their names. They were just skanks. Things. He had more regard for the life of a hound dog than he did for one of these . . . things.

He listened to the beating of his heart a while.

Waited to hear the disembodied voice again.

Because he was certain of one thing—that wasn't his meth-addled brain talking to him like it sometimes did. No, this voice was real, and was clearly external in origin. At last, steeling himself for what he was afraid he'd see, he turned his head to scan the clearing again. And it was as he suspected.

There was no one there. That he could see.

He looked again at the skank. At Elise. She was almost fully awake now. With a sigh of regret, he plunged the long hunting knife into the soft flesh just beneath her sternum, driving the blade all the way through her. She gasped and her body lurched, and

Carlton moved to pin her down again. He slammed the knife down a few more times and watched the life shake out of her.

He wiped the blood off the blade in the grass, then got to his feet.

"All right, you chickenshit motherfucker. She's dead. A waste of a fine piece of ass, too. Show yourself, boy, so I can make you pay for that."

For a time there was no sound other than the usual insect and wildlife noises. Then a long shadow, a deep patch of darkness somehow darker than the night itself, emerged through the line of trees. Carlton felt something like a black snake crawl up from the pit of his stomach and lodge in his throat. It took him a moment to realize the feeling was unadulterated fear. The hand holding the hunting knife began to shake. The dark shape came away from the line of trees and revealed itself to be no shadow at all. It was a man. Or something like a man. Carlton made a sound remarkably like the whimpering he'd heard from Elise in the moments before her death. He wasn't a guy who scared easily, but instinct overrode his usual bravado. Instinct told him this creature was only superficially human.

He moved back a step, brandishing the knife with his trembling hand. "St-stay b-back! I'll gut you, fucker, I swear, if you don't stay where you are!"

But the shape kept coming. It was wearing a long coat. A black duster, looked like. And black boots, and a wide-brimmed black hat tilted low over its face. Visible beneath the tilted brim was an angular slice of alabaster chin and long, thin pink lips like worms, a horrible wedge of grinning mouth.

Carlton's voice emerged in a strangled cry as he staggered backward: "Stop! Who the fuck are you?"

The grinning mouth opened wide to emit dry laughter, a sound like air rasping through a dust-clogged vent. And the voice that followed the laughter was worse, a creaky sound that made Carlton think of rusty nails being pulled out of ancient, rotting timber: "I'm not a stranger to you, Carlton. You've introduced me to several of your—things." More of that creepy, creaky laughter emerged from the thing's leering mouth. "Most recently to dear, departed *Eliiissse . . . .*"

The girl's name emerged as an insinuating hiss and somehow troubled Carlton more than any of the numerous other troubling elements of this supremely fucked-up and weird-as-sin development. And just then the heel of his boot connected with the girl's corpse, yanking a reflexive shriek from his fear-constricted throat. The knife tumbled from his quaking hand. Then he felt something that ripped his sanity to shreds, because it just couldn't be—one of the girl's small, delicate hands was touching his leg, was, in fact, gripping his ankle with a strength that by all rights ought to be beyond the capability of someone as completely fucking *dead* as she was.

Another whimper escaped his throat as he simultaneously kept an eye on the approaching creature and reached to retrieve the hunting knife—but the knife was gone. His eyes went wide with panic for a moment, then he struggled to free himself from the re-animated skank's unnaturally strong grip.

But it was too late.

She surged up off the ground and drove the blade

136

of the hunting knife into his crotch. Cold metal punched through his scrotum as the knife rammed in to the hilt. Carlton screamed and tried to wrench away but the girl had her arms around him and was holding him in place. She pulled the blade out and a thick stream of blood poured out of the wound, making it look like he was pissing blood. Carlton screamed again at the immense pain, a sound that gave way to a cry of surprise as the world was yanked out from under him. He landed hard, flat on his back and got a good look at the rejuvenated girl. Her eyes were wild and her lips were tugged into an expression somewhere between a grin and a feral snarl. And she was strong, stronger than anyone he'd ever tussled with before. She was undeniable. He couldn't resist her at all, not even when she cut away the denim crotch of his jeans and held the cold blade to his wilted organ.

She sliced Carl Jr. off and Carlton managed one more strangled scream.

Then he saw the knife flash in the moonlight before it descended one more time and plunged through his throat.

The world went away for a moment. There was nothing, just awareness of some kind of empty existence in a featureless void.

Then his eyes snapped open and he was back in the world.

He got to his feet and saw that the dead skank was standing near the one he knew now was the Deathbringer. More shapes emerged from the woods. Carlton saw people he'd known in his day-to-day life. Many of them had grisly wounds of varying sorts. He knew that they were all dead. And that he was one of them now, the Deathbringer's newest foot soldier in an army of walking dead.

The Deathbringer moved away from the campsite and started down a trail that would lead out of the woods and back toward town. His army of dead followed, and Carlton fell in line with them. The girl he'd killed was just ahead of him. He looked at her and felt a weird kind of love for her. He saw her murder of him in an entirely different light now, saw it as an act of mercy—she'd removed him from a hate-consumed life of misery and loneliness.

Carlton looked at more of his new companions and smiled, knowing he would never be alone again.

Soon, he knew, the whole world, every man, woman, and child, would know this same joy.

CHAPTER SEVENTEEN

The truck's headlights picked out the words on the green road sign for an instant before the sign flashed by and receded into the darkness. But it was long enough for Hawthorne to see that his destination remained too far away for his liking.

He looked at the driver, who'd been staring stiffly ahead since picking him up a half hour earlier. "Can't you go any faster? At this rate, we'll be too late to do anything other than pull up a ringside seat for the apocalypse."

The truck driver, his mind and body hijacked to serve the Guardians' purposes, was little more than a flesh and blood autopilot. Talking to him did little good, other than to assuage some of Hawthorne's anxiousness. He wasn't much of a conversationalist, but talking at him was still somewhat better than talking to thin air.

So Hawthorne was startled enough to reach for the

door handle a moment later when the big man's mouth moved and a deep baritone filled the truck's cab: "This vessel is programmed to perform a single task, Hawthorne. To get you safely to Dandridge as speedily as possible. However, manipulation of the vessel is a delicate matter, one with little margin between success and failure. Should we attempt to deviate from its programming, to, for instance, coax it to greatly exceed posted speed limits, we run a risk of losing control of the vessel."

Hawthorne's hand came away from the door handle. "Is this you, Eldritch?"

"Indeed."

Hawthorne sighed. "Things are happening in that town. The Rogue is amassing an army. I feel it. And it grows with each blasted mile this shambling contraption slogs through. I fear that by the time I get there there'll be nothing I can do."

The driver's head turned in his direction. There was a sparkle in the man's formerly dull eyes, a glint so much like Eldritch's defiant glare that it was almost as if the man was physically in the truck with him. "Nonsense. You may well arrive too late to save anyone in that tiny village, but you will still be able to defeat him. You are still in possession of the artifact provided by our shaman, I take it?"

Hawthorne dipped a hand into a jacket pocket and stroked the object in question. As always, he derived a fresh sense of reassurance and confidence at its touch, but not enough to quell his growing unease. "I am."

The driver's jowly face formed a greasy grin. "Then all is well."

Hawthorne's face twisted in an expression of fury. "How can you say that? Maybe this thing will perform as promised. I've no reason to doubt that. What I do doubt is my ability to even get to the Rogue when he's surrounded by an army of followers he can manipulate at will. I'll be dead before I get within a hundred yards of him."

"You cannot fail."

Hawthorne laughed bitterly. "Nonsense. Of course I can fail. I'm only human. A human with a great deal of arcane magical knowledge, granted, but only human nonetheless. It's insane that the fate of the world rests on my narrow shoulders. I still don't understand how such a thing could happen."

The driver's booming laughter filled the cab. "Such things happen more frequently than you realize. This is why our organization exists. We analyze rapidly changing and volatile situations, potentially world-changing crises governments are incapable of handling. We've had centuries of practice. And we always know what we are doing, even when it appears otherwise. You were the right agent to send this time. You may not survive to tell the tale, Hawthorne, but we are confident you will succeed when you confront the Rogue."

Hawthorne settled back in his seat, letting his head fall back against the headrest as he closed his eyes and listened to the hum of the tires rumbling over the road. "I wish I could say I shared your confidence in me, but I do not."

"It is not necessary that you see things as we do. We only require that you perform as instructed."

Hawthorne's eyes fluttered open. He looked at the big man in the driver's seat. "You know I'll do that."

Eldritch-by-proxy chuckled. "Yes. We know that."

Hawthorne frowned and looked out the window at

the passing dark countryside. "I'll do what I'm supposed to do. Or die trying. That's not in question. I only wish I could discern some way to gain an advantage prior to engaging the Rogue. Some way to drive a wedge through the heart of his army."

"There may be a way."

Hawthorne looked at the driver. Hope flared within him, an emotion he knew from deep experience could be dangerous. He strove to keep his voice uninflected when he said, "Yes? And how do you propose to do this?"

"The Rogue, as you know, left a copy of *Invocations of the Reaper* with the grieving lover of the Prime. He was, of course, drawn to the book and was compelled to recite the resurrection spell, setting in motion the most crucial component of the Rogue's scheme to force a confrontation with the ruling power."

"You mean with God?"

Eldritch-by-proxy hesitated, then said, "As you wish."

"But—"

"What you choose to call the ruling power is irrelevant. Call it 'God' if you like." There was a previously absent curtness in the man's tone now. "That's not important now. What you need to know is that the Prime's lover has proven resourceful and may be an effective ally in your coming struggle."

"How so?"

"That is for you to figure out. But consider this. He has already contacted us."

Hawthorne's frown deepened. "How is that possible?"

More baritone laughter resonated in the truck's cab. "Via the miracle of modern technology. He found us through a Web search and sent his contact information via e-mail. You'll need to get in touch with him when you arrive at your destination."

A period of silence ensued. After a time Hawthorne's gaze drifted back to the silent driver, who was staring rigidly ahead again. He didn't need verbal confirmation to know Eldritch had withdrawn from the "vessel" for now.

So be it.

Talking to Eldritch had in some ways been as maddening as talking to himself. He could use the remaining quiet time he had left to do some serious thinking. Because he had a feeling that when he arrived in Dandridge things would move quickly and there'd be scant time for reflection.

His gaze went back to the passing darkness beyond the side of the road—a blackness so absolute he could imagine being swallowed by it, permanently devoured, like a fly snapped out of muggy swamp air by a fat toad. He shuddered at the image. It was too easy to imagine the Deathbringer plucking his heart out in much the same manner before the battle royale could even commence.

He pulled the shaman's gift from his pocket and looked at it.

Not for the first time, he felt astonishment at the notion that something so small could defeat such immense evil.

But, as always, he could feel its power flowing into him, and suffusing him with a degree of confidence that made him feel shame for his doubts. And he knew that so long as he retained possession of this remarkable artifact one thin ray of hope would remain unextinguished.

Chapter Eighteen

"What are you doing, asshole? Get the fuck out of here!"

Avery flinched. "Do you need to be so loud, girl?"

"My name's Melinda, fuckface. You can stop calling me 'girl.' And I'll be as loud as I need to be until you turn around and take us out of here."

Avery smirked. "Pleased to make your acquaintance, Melinda. Sort of. And you can stop calling me 'fuckface.' My name's Avery Starke, and I've been told I'm a pretty good lookin' guy."

"You've been lied to a lot. Fuckface. Now get us out of here, or I swear I'll be loud enough to raise the dead."

Avery laughed. "Interesting choice of cliches there . . . girl. Considering our current zombie epidemic."

Melinda's expression became so severe that in the darkness she looked like a constipated old lady. Avery assumed the cause of her concern was the patrol car parked outside Mike's house. Which was understandable, given their recent narrow escape from a cop infected with whatever inexplicable force was killing and resurrecting people in Dandridge. But he needed to get her calmed down long enough to make her understand why the presence of a police vehicle outside this particular house was no reason to panic.

"Look. Melinda." Avery found it hard to maintain an even tone while staring into the face of such quivering fury, but he pushed ahead anyway. "You can relax. Mike, the guy I told you was a friend, the guy who lives here, is actually the man who was supposed to marry my sister."

Her expression remained fierce, but she abruptly no longer seemed on the brink of explosion—he even detected a note of real curiosity in the set of her eyes. "Yeah?"

Avery nodded. "Yeah."

He had to pause a moment to allow a fresh welling of emotional pain to ripple through him. Then he sighed and steeled himself to continue. "A week ago some rotten sick fuck murdered my sister. The man she was to marry is a cop. Mike is a good guy. He's going through a shitty time right now, but he'll help us. I know he will."

Melinda frowned and appeared to think about it. Then a smile slowly spread across her pale face. "Okay. I trust you . . . Avery. You wouldn't let anything bad happen to me—would you?"

"Um . . . I . . . don't see why I would, so long as it's within my ability to do so, that is."

Melinda's prim response was like a mockery of real gratitude: "Thank you, Avery." She sounded like a

Texas debutante thanking her date for holding the limo door open. "Thank you *ever* so much."

Then Avery gasped as she shot across the gap between the seats, locked a slim hand behind his neck, and pushed her tongue into his mouth. He made a sound of protest and struggled for a moment—until he felt her other hand on his crotch. She kept up the assault, driving his head back against the headrest as her bare breasts pushed against the thin cotton fabric of his shirt. He felt her erect nipples sliding against him and became aware that the girl's ministrations had caused the crotch of jeans to become uncomfortably taut.

It felt good. Sinfully good. And for a brief time he considered ignoring the disintegration of the world around him in favor of having a go at the girl. But he managed to come to his senses and push the girl away.

She grinned and made a sound like the snarl of a jungle cat and came at him again. But this time he managed to ward her off before she could get her hands and mouth attached to him in ways he wasn't sure he'd be able to resist again, regardless of how wildly inappropriate such a surrender would be.

He laid the base of a hand against her flat belly and gave her a hard shove. She fell back against the passenger-side door and remained there. Her smile shifted, became a seductive pout. She cupped one of her breasts and rubbed the nipple slowly with the ball of her thumb.

Conflicting feelings warred within Avery as he watched this brazen display. The girl's behavior was repellent in the current context. It was clear to him that she was mentally unwell. Normal people just did not engage in this extreme form of acting out when faced with circumstances as dire as the ones in which they were embroiled. But he also wanted to fuck her. No need to pretty the feeling up—it was just as simple and vulgar as that. But he could not allow himself to give in to that base desire, not if he expected to ever again retain any measure of self-respect.

Still, it was touch and go there for a handful of moments. Melinda even seemed to sense he was still vulnerable and appeared poised to renew the attack. She came away from the door and slithered toward him. Avery sat stiff as a statue in the driver's seat, knowing he might well crumble when he felt her hands on him again. Then an image so powerful it pierced the sexual tension like a balloon filled his head, making him wince involuntarily. He saw Hannah's lifeless body laid out on plush purple velvet at her open-casket service. Saw the filled-in round dimple marking the entry wound caused by the bullet that killed her. This time anger commingled with grief and he gave the girl a harder shove than before, causing her back to thud against the door behind her as she pitched backward.

Anger flared in her eyes. "You're gonna pay for that, cocksucker."

Avery opened his mouth to reply but the words died at the tip of his tongue as a hand appeared through the open window behind Melinda and clamped hard around her throat, eliciting a strangled gasp and causing her eyes to bug out like those of a cartoon villain. The assault startled Avery and rendered him incapable of action for a moment. He stared wide-eyed at the spectacle of a snarling and feral-looking Marisol Roth. The nineteen-year-old girl was the daughter of Stan and Margaret Roth, Mike O'Bannon's next door neighbors.

She was dead.

Melinda flailed at her attacker, raking hands and arms with nails sharp enough to draw streams of blood. Avery puzzled for a moment over the idea of blood flowing freely from an animated corpse. He supposed whatever power initiated resurrection would also restart the dead heart, because a pumping heart was the only explanation for the free flow of blood. He further supposed this meant these reanimated things were not actually zombies in the sense he was used to from movies and tales of voodoo. They were actually alive again, just—altered.

Melinda's hands came away from the hands encircling her neck and reached out for him. Her mouth opened and issued a strangled plea: *"Heeeelllppp . . ."*

Avery, recalling the way Melinda had come to his rescue earlier in the evening, snapped out of the state of shock. He threw open the driver's side door, got out of the car, and hurried around to the other side. He'd managed to pry one of Marisol's hands away from Melinda's throat when he looked over the Mustang's hood and saw Stan and Margaret Roth emerging from the darkness. One side of Stan Roth's head was sharply caved in, as if someone had bludgeoned it with an anvil. And the center of Margaret's face was . . . gone. There was a big, ragged, blood-encrusted hole where her mouth and nose had been. Someone had shot her point-blank in the face with a big-caliber gun.

For a moment despair weighed Avery down. Wherever they went, dead people (as he continued to think of them, if only to put aside the troubling existential implications of living zombies) were popping up to attack them. It was as if a plague, some strain

148

of malign and rampaging virus, was making short work of the citizenry of his hometown. With the exception of Melinda, he hadn't been in the presence of an uninfected human being since those moments just before Tom succumbed to the contagion, or whatever it was. Hell, for all he knew, Mike O'Bannon had succumbed as well—and at this point he'd be pretty fucking surprised to learn otherwise.

The spell of melancholy passed in an instant, though, because Marisol Roth chose to abandon her assault on Melinda in favor of dealing with his interference. She whirled to face him and seized him with hands as powerful as those of a hardcore weight-lifter. She squeezed and Avery felt his throat constrict to an alarming degree. Unable to breathe, he flailed at her arms and kicked at her, but her limbs remained as stolid and unshakeable as the branches of a towering redwood tree. He heard Melinda scream and managed to focus enough to see that Stan and Margaret had arrived at the Mustang and were utilizing a pincer strategy to trap the girl in the car. Stan leaned through the driver's side window and Margaret ducked her head through the passenger-side window and groped for Melinda's flashing pale torso.

That's it, then, Avery thought dimly. *We'll be dead soon. Probably better this way. . . .*

Except that the festivities weren't quite over yet. Others were hurrying to join the party. He heard footsteps pounding across the lawn behind him, as well as a grunt of frenzied exertion.

Then, suddenly, the pressure around his throat decreased by half and he was able to draw in wheezing breaths again. He blinked. Frowned. And the first thing that came to mind was a Monty Python line, which emerged from his raw throat in a croak: "Your arm's off."

And so it was. There'd been a blur of something flashing through the air, then Marisol's arm was lying on the ground. Blood jetted from the twitching stump, staining the few bits of Avery's clothing that had thus far managed to avoid a blood bath over the course of this strange night.

Marisol's other hand relinquished its hold on him and she staggered backward in a futile attempt to avoid the oncoming wedge of blade. An axe, that's what it was. The sharp edge of it whistled through the night and chopped through Marisol's slender neck, sending her head spinning through the air like a blond bowling ball.

Avery saw his benefactor sprint forward and raise the axe again. And a sense of elation shot through him when he realized it was Mike O'Bannon wielding the axe like some sort of champion . . . axe-fighter, or something.

The blade came down yet again and relieved headless Marisol of her remaining arm. Mike delivered a kick to the still upright dead girl's midsection and sent her stumbling away. Somehow, the body remained upright, but its frantic, directionless movements made Avery think of what he'd always heard about decapitated chickens.

Margaret Roth abandoned her attempts to get at Melinda to face Mike O'Bannon and his axe. This turned out to be a predictably bad move on her part, because the next blow of the axe punched through the hole in her face and cleanly removed the top of her head, which landed with a splat on the roof of

Avery's Mustang. Avery saw the eyes still darting in their sockets and decided then and there that if he could get his hands on some very strong psychedelic drugs, he would unhesitatingly ingest a large quantity of them. Because, hell, there was no way mushroom or acid hallucinations could be any worse than the bizarre and grotesque things his damnable eyes had been forcing him to look at all night. Drug hallucinations would be a goddamned *improvement* at this point.

Mike laid waste to Margaret's body with the axe, disassembling her with what appeared to have become a series of practiced and brutally accurate blows. Melinda scrambled through the passenger-side window and moved to a point behind Avery while Mike moved to deal with the sole remaining member of the Roth family (the last one still a threat, anyway).

Melinda seized Avery's right elbow and leaned into him, clinging to him like a teenage girl glued to her boyfriend during a scary movie. Avery made no move to disengage himself from her. At this point all his previous inhibitions had fallen to dust. If the girl was determined to attach herself to him for the duration of this descent into madness, so be it, it was better than being alone.

Mike finished off Stan Roth and turned to face them. "Avery . . ." His gaze went to the girl at his side and his grim and determined expression flickered a moment, threatened to become a frown before asserting itself again. "You and your friend better get inside." He was already moving past them and toward the house. His next words came at them over his shoulder. "Right now."

Avery sensed Melinda staring up at him and glanced down at her. He held her gaze a moment and her grip on him tightened.

"What do we do, Avery?"

Her voice sounded smaller, less sure of itself than at any other point that night. Looking into those wide, imploring eyes and listening to her frightened tone, Avery felt a new sense of purpose.

He would make a stand here with Mike O'Bannon, help the man do whatever they could to fight this nightmare.

And he would protect young Melinda to his dying breath.

He managed a weak smile and touched her hair. "We do what the man says."

This elicited a smile from Melinda in return. "Okay."

And together they turned and crossed the lawn toward Mike O'Bannon's home.

CHAPTER NINETEEN

The head on the dashboard was trying to talk. Its mouth worked and Hannah could see the gore-flecked sliver of tongue struggling to form words, a task rendered futile by the glaring lack of a larynx. It was a fascinating thing to observe. Apparently some level of brain function and sentience remained, but it was clear this was greatly diminished. The head's features hung slack, making its face look like that of a drooling, lobotomized idiot. Its eyes were dull and glassy and looked like two bloated grapes wedged into a pair of smallish holes cut into a rotting melon.

Hannah was in an experimental mood, so she extended a forefinger and pushed the edge of a sharp fingernail into one of the eyes. The orb was made of tougher stuff than she expected and so she redoubled her effort. At last, the tissue parted and her finger dug deep inside the orb. The invasion restored a higher level of animation to the head and its mouth worked frantically, evidently endeavoring to produce a scream. Hannah looked at the wide open mouth and its silent exhalation of agony—and laughed. She retracted a finger and plopped it into her mouth, then tongued off the viscous fluid with great relish. A shudder of pleasure went through her and she dipped her finger into the socket another time. Then she decided to go whole hog and reached into the socket, probed around the slitted eye until she got a grip on the eye stalk, and yanked the drooping orb out. She tipped her head up and held her mouth open and dropped the eye down her throat. An orgasmic sound of pleasure slithered out of her as the damaged organ slid down her gullet.

She laughed.

"Why, I do believe I've found a new favorite snack." She looked at the head, smirking at its distraught expression and addressing it as she would any intact and fully functional human being. "Even better than fresh shrimp. I bet that would be awesome with cocktail sauce"

She was reaching for the head's remaining eye when she caught a flicker of something just beyond the cone of light projected by the Corvette's headlights.

Her foot pushed the accelerator closer to the floor and in a moment she saw a man walking along the shoulder of the road, heading in the direction of the cemetery. He was a portly guy, looked to be in his late thirties, and he had long, stringy dark hair tinged with gray. He wore a dirty and tattered Bud Light T-shirt that was a minimum of two sizes too small for him, as it failed to entirely cover the enormous beer belly that hung over the edge of his jeans.

She glanced at the head and winked. "You're off the hook for now. I just thought of another way to have some fun."

Not wishing to unduly startle her intended target, Hannah kept the Corvette between the yellow lines until the last possible moment. Then she wrenched the steering wheel hard to the right. The head tumbled off the dashboard and thunked against the passenger-side window. It fell to the floorboard and left a smear of blood on the window. The front of the Corvette slammed into the long-haired redneck and folded him like a lawn chair.

Hannah stomped on the brake, put the car in reverse, and backed speedily away. She looked at the man lying on his side at the edge of the road. He looked like a broken doll. Blood trickled from his mouth and one hand clawed feebly at the asphalt. Hannah chuckled and revved the Corvette's finely tuned engine. Then she slammed the car into gear and it shot forward again. She cackled gleefully as the front and back wheels bounced over the bulbous body, rocking her in her seat like a child on a roller-coaster. She stomped on the brake again and glanced in the rearview mirror.

The man wasn't moving, and was almost certainly dead.

But Hannah wasn't through with him. She maneuvered the Corvette with greater care and precision this time, angling one of the rear tires so that it rested against the dead redneck's head. She wished she could figure a way to get a better view of what was about to happen, but she knew time was of the essence. If she waited more than another moment or so, the big corpse would reanimate and come after her.

She sighed and rolled down both windows so she could at least hear the sound effects. Then she pushed the gas pedal down and the right rear wheel of the car rolled over the redneck's head. When she heard it pop like a ripe grapefruit dropped from a great height, she clapped her hands in delight.

She felt giddy, like a schoolgirl giggling over cute boys with her girlfriends. Except that this was even better, was more fun by far. But the euphoria was undercut a moment later by a sudden intrusion of darker thoughts. There was something incongruous about them, as if they weren't internal in origin. Given the inexplicable nature of everything else connected with her unnatural return to the world, this didn't surprise her. This voice in her head, which was like an insidious and chilly whisper at the back of her neck, was telling her the time for fun and games was just about over.

She had important things to do.

The thought made her frown.

I do? Like what?

But the voice had fallen silent.

After a contemplative moment or two, Hannah shrugged and dismissed the notion as a figment of her suddenly quite warped imagination. She seized a handful of the businessman's hair and plucked his head off the floorboard. Then she extracted the remaining eyeball, popped it in her mouth, and chucked the now useless head out the window.

She was chewing the tasty morsel when she saw something else emerging from the darkness ahead of her. At first she smiled at the prospect of playing with another pedestrian out for a leisurely stroll and a taste of crisp night air.

But the smile faded as the figure's outline grew clearer.

For reasons she was unable to comprehend, she got out of the car and approached the stranger.

He was tall, thin, and clad all in black.

She liked the long dark coat he wore. And she smiled when she saw the leering wedge of white face beneath the tilted brim of the stranger's hat. The stranger, whoever he was, had come out of the woods bordering the road. Her gaze went to the line of trees and she saw shadowy forms lingering there. More re-animated dead people, she was certain.

This man's . . . this *thing's* . . . followers.

It was then that Hannah knew she'd been brought back to join this dark stranger and his growing legion of followers. This bit of knowledge arrived fully formed in her head, almost as if it had been there all along, locked away, just waiting for the dark man to come along and release it.

And now a sense of peace invaded her. It didn't diminish the blood lust that continued to sear through her. In fact, it fueled it, fanned it higher and higher. But she had a sense of purpose now.

She knew what she needed to do.

The tall, dark stranger turned away from her and rejoined his army of followers in the woods.

Hannah returned to the Corvette, performed a sloppy U-turn, and headed away from the road leading into Dandridge.

Home, she thought.

I'm going home. Going home to see my baby.

She laughed and pushed the accelerator to the floor. She threw her head back and savored the wonderful feeling of the cool air whipping through her long hair. It was amazing—even when she'd been alive she'd never felt this . . . *alive.*

She couldn't wait to acquaint dear, sweet Mike with this exquisite feeling.

CHAPTER TWENTY

Melinda struggled not to smirk or outright laugh as she followed the adults into the kitchen. Just over a week had elapsed since she'd last been in this very room. This was just too trippy. Of all the places Avery, her clueless benefactor (who, holy shit, had turned out to be Hannah's fucking brother), could have taken her to, it was this place. An image of a frightened and trembling Hannah on her knees snapped into her brain and made her feel all tingly in her nether regions. Mike, en route to the refrigerator, passed over the spot where Melinda had stood on that wonderful day as she aimed the gun at his intended's prone form and pumped bullet after bullet into her.

It was a bit troubling, though. It was the kind of thing that could almost make a girl believe in things like predestination and grand schemes devised by divine beings. And if God, or whoever, had steered her

159

back to this place she should probably be concerned about that. There could be some kind of cosmic retribution for her sins coming. On the other hand, it was out of her hands, so fuck it—it wasn't like she could go back out into the disintegrating world beyond the walls of this house. Unless, of course, some set of desperate circumstances drove her to do so.

She heard the refrigerator door swing open and her gaze moved from that sweet spot on the floor—from which every visible trace of the blood spilled there had been scoured—to Mike's broad, muscular back. And she had to bite her lower lip hard to keep from smiling. She knew it was well beyond the realm of possibility, especially considering the irritating presence of this bitch Erin, but it would be so wicked fucking cool if she could seduce Mike and fuck him right there on the floor where Hannah's life and brains had seeped out.

But she was smart enough not to attempt anything so brazen. At least not in this mixed company. Maybe if she could somehow get rid of Avery and Erin, but that clearly wasn't going to happen. The situation was complicated by the fact that these people were Mensa material compared to Beau and Doug. They would not be so easily manipulated as those redneck buffoons.

Mike removed a six pack of beer from the fridge, pried three cans from the plastic binder and passed two of them to Avery and Erin. He popped the tab on the third and downed half of it in one long swallow.

Melinda pouted. "What about me?"

Mike looked at her. "You're too young."

Melinda narrowed her eyes and curled her lips in a sneer. She was in the midst of trying to compose an appropriately snide response when Avery beat her to the punch: "Oh, Christ's sake, Mike, we're facing what looks to be the end of the world as we know it. Let the girl have a fucking beer."

Melinda's sneer became a smile. "Yeah, Mike. Let the girl have a fucking beer. We might all be dead by sunrise." A mock sincerity infused her voice now. "And I've never had a beer. Never, ever. You wouldn't deny me that basic life experience—would you?"

Mike rolled his eyes. "I'm not wasting time arguing trivial shit with either of you."

He pried a fourth beer from the binder and tossed it to Melinda, who uttered a startled gasp and reached to snag the beer out of the air. She nearly dropped it but managed to hang on. Then she popped the tab and chugged from the can. She belched like a sailor on leave and smirked at the sour expressions on the faces of Mike and Erin.

"I lied. It's not my first beer."

Erin sighed. "Surprise, surprise."

Melinda blew the woman a kiss and tried not to giggle at the grimace that crossed her face. Then she looked at Avery. His expression was a mixture of embarrassment and the clumsily concealed lust she'd had such fun exploiting when they'd been alone in the car. She realized she'd be better off continuing to sink her claws deeper into him rather than continuing to entertain notions of making a play for Mike. And she should damn well rein in this impulse to shock the adults, lest she risk alienating Avery.

She sighed and made her face twist into an expression of exaggerated fear. "I'm sorry." She faked a sniffle. "I'm just nervous. I can't believe what's happening out there. I'm so s-scared. . . ."

Erin's expression softened. "We all are."

The older woman held Avery's wounded forearm and daubed at the ragged bite marks with cotton balls soaked in hydrogen peroxide. She put a pad over the damaged area and carefully wrapped it with gauze tape.

Avery grimaced during the application of antiseptic, but smiled when she was finished patching him up. "Thanks, Erin."

Erin acknowledged his gratitude with a tired smile of her own. She drank a bit of her beer, then put the can down and glanced at Melinda. "She needs to cover up. Is it okay if she . . ."

Mike closed his eyes and didn't say anything for a moment. Then he nodded. "Yeah." He sighed. "You know where the room is."

Erin put an arm around Melinda and began to steer her out of the kitchen. "We'll be back in a few minutes, boys."

Melinda's breath quickened at the feel of the woman's arm draped over her bare shoulders. Instantly thoughts of the comparative merits of Mike and Avery fell away, and were replaced by a profound awareness of Erin's attractiveness. The woman wasn't in Hannah's league in the beauty department—a fact she shared in common with most women—but she was definitely pretty, with a slim, compact body, largish breasts, and a face with delicate, soft features. And full lips that looked soft and kissable.

Erin's hand was splayed against the small of her back as she directed Melinda through an archway and toward a staircase. Melinda wanted to feel that hand moving over the rest of her body. But now she felt awash in self-doubt and all those old conflicting feelings. She couldn't understand it. Other girls dealt with feelings like this and didn't get all fucked up in the head about it. She knew it, because she saw them on TV and read about them in magazines.

They arrived at the foot of the staircase.

Erin's voice was a soft rush of air against the back of her neck. Her hand moved away from Melinda's back. "Go on. It's up there."

Melinda turned to look at her. "What is?"

Erin wouldn't meet her gaze, choosing to look instead at the photograph-lined staircase wall. "The master bedroom. It's down the hall, last door on the right. There's a big walk-in closet next to the bathroom. Hannah's clothes should be in there."

Melinda frowned. "How do you know that? Were you a friend of Hannah's?"

Erin shook her head. "No. I used to live here with Mike."

Melinda's frown deepened. "What?"

Erin sighed. "It's too complicated to explain right now. Just go up there and get something on. We need to get back with the guys and figure out what to do."

Recalling how effective her frightened act had been moments earlier, Melinda pouted and invested her voice with a quality of faux-earnest fear that was just short of a truly pitiable whine. "Please, Erin. Come with me. I'm scared shitless. I don't want to be alone."

Erin met her gaze now and seemed to study her, narrowing her eyes in a weird way that made Melinda fear the woman suspected insincerity. But then she sighed and some of the tenseness seemed to go out of her. "Okay, Melinda. Let's go. But let's be quick about it, okay?"

Melinda was unable to suppress a small smile. "I'll

try. Thank you." Then she impulsively gave Erin a quick peck on the cheek. "You're an angel."

Then she turned and moved slowly up the steps, displaying her vinyl-encased, shapely ass and making her hips sway ever so slightly. She tried not to overplay it. Subtlety would be the key to getting somewhere with Erin. She could feel the woman's gaze on her and the thought of it made her heart flutter with excitement. If there was even the slightest chance the older woman had any latent girl-lusting tendencies, she couldn't help but be affected by what she was getting an eyeful of now.

She reached the hallway at the top of the staircase and moved toward the bedroom. The door stood open and she moved through it into the darkened room. She found a light switch and flipped it. The room was nice and was dominated by a plush bed with a wrought-iron frame. The walls were painted a muted shade of yellow and a large television sat on a shelf in an ornate wooden cabinet. Stacks of books on both sides of the bed were the only evidence of sloppiness in an otherwise pristine environment. Melinda heard Erin enter the room behind her and moved on to the walk-in closet, which was where Erin had said it would be. She opened the closet door, flipped on the light switch there, and rummaged through Hannah's belongings for a while. Pawing through the dead woman's things sent another wicked, delicious shiver through her. She selected a few things and returned to the bedroom, where she dumped the clothes on the bed and looked at Erin.

The older woman was clearly uncomfortable being in this room. She kept her head down, but her eyes were darting everywhere. Melinda thought she had some of the mystery figured out. Clearly Erin was a former girlfriend of Mike's. And the relationship had been serious enough that at some point they'd lived together in this house. But then something happened to split them up and Mike had wound up with his Miss America candidate. Now Hannah was dead and Erin was back. Which, even for a person like Melinda, who reveled in having no morals whatsoever, seemed awfully quick.

Which maybe boded well for Melinda's wicked intentions.

"What do you think, Erin?"

Erin blinked. "What?"

Melinda smiled. "You seem really nervous. Why is that?"

Erin shook her head. "Never mind that. What were you asking me?"

Melinda waved a hand at the jumble of clothes. "I mean, should I just put on a T-shirt so the boys won't be so embarrassed about staring at my tits, or should I pick out a whole new outfit?"

Erin frowned and looked the younger girl up and down. "Well . . . don't be offended, okay? But that getup may be a tad too slutty considering the circumstances."

Melinda tried not to smirk.

She'd been hoping Erin would say something like that.

With no further prompting she began to wriggle out of her vinyl short-shorts. Then she sat on the edge of the bed and kicked off the black heels, one of which landed inches in front of Erin. Then, taking her time, she rolled the fishnets off and tossed them aside. She glanced up and saw Erin watching her expressionlessly. She laid back on the bed, crossed her legs, and smiled.

Erin frowned. "Why aren't you getting dressed?"

"I don't want to."

Awareness dawned in Erin's eyes now. She breathed a weary sigh. "Look, I don't have time for this. Play games with the guys if you have to, not me."

She turned and started moving toward the bedroom door.

Melinda was off the bed in a flash. She raced ahead of Erin and threw the door shut. Then she leaned against it with her arms and legs splayed. She smiled. "Don't play hard to get. I only want a little loving. Is that so bad?"

Erin's mouth was a tight line of rage. "Get away from the door."

"No."

"Get away from the door, or I'll move you myself."

Melinda smirked. "Go ahead. I can't wait."

Erin looked exasperated. "Jesus Christ, girl, what the hell's wrong with you?"

Much of the playfulness leeched out of Melinda at that comment. The smirk gave way to a hard glare. "Nothing's wrong with *me*, cunt." She moved away from the door, brushing past Erin and giving her an elbow to the side like a bully bludgeoning through a crowded school corridor. "Go on. Leave."

Erin touched her side and gaped at the girl in astonishment. "Are you crazy?"

Melinda didn't say anything—she was looking at the stack of books on the left side of the bed. She heard Erin sigh and start to turn the doorknob. A mad impulse flashed through Melinda. It was crazy. It was the absolute wrong thing to do in the current circumstances. But she felt helpless to do anything but obey it. She snatched up the heaviest book she could find, a big hardback dictionary, and hurried to catch up to Erin.

She swung the book and landed a heavy blow to the back of the older woman's head. Erin fell against the door, pushing it shut again. She moaned and Melinda swung at her head again. The second blow knocked the woman to the floor. Murderous rage sang in Melinda's veins as she straddled Erin and raised the book high over her head. She felt the same primal, electrifying thrill that had so galvanized her in the moments prior to killing her other victims.

But she didn't want to kill Erin. Not yet.

She had other things planned for her. So she brought the book down one more time, but adjusted the force of the blow so that it would send the woman into unconsciousness rather than killing her.

The blow delivered, Melinda tossed the book away and studied the woman's motionless form.

Not dead, but out like a light.

Good.

She went back to the bed to pick out some clothes. When she was finished dressing, she started looking for something she could use to tie up her first hostage.

CHAPTER TWENTY-ONE

Melinda heard voices raised in heated conversation as she hurried down the stairs. She paused in the foyer as the words became intelligible and she realized the topic of discussion was none other than herself. She moved quietly across the foyer floor and stopped short of the archway leading into the kitchen. She tilted her head a few degrees to the left and saw Mike O'Bannon gesturing angrily. He started to turn her way and she shuffled backward until her back met the wall, where she stood rigid and strove to keep her breathing inaudible.

"Okay, whatever. She saved your life. I'll take your word for it. But I don't trust her. There's something . . . not right about her." The fierceness of Mike O'Bannon's tone made Melinda flinch. The loathing he felt for her was obvious. It pissed her off. What had she ever done to him (that he knew about, that is)? Nothing, that's what. Other than maybe act a bit immature, but she failed to see how a little rude behavior warranted this degree of hate. It was so odd she could almost believe some subconscious part of him sensed the truth about her, knew what she had done to Hannah.

Avery grunted. "Oh, great, you'll 'take my word for it.' Thanks for the fucking favor, Mike. I'm glad you've got such faith in me. You may not like Melinda, fine, whatever. I admit she's a bit rough around the edges."

Melinda frowned.

What the fuck does he mean by that?

"But it's a fact that I'd be dead now if not for her. That fucking cop was gonna rip my throat out. She stopped him. She could've driven away from there and not worried about me. But she didn't do that, and I think I owe her something for that."

Melinda's frown became a smile.

Sweet Avery, she thought, *I think I love you. Like a hunter loves his faithful hound dog, anyway.*

Before the argument could continue Melinda pushed away from the wall and strode nonchalantly through the archway into the kitchen. She smiled as the men turned to look at her, knowing what they were thinking as they appraised her new appearance. A loose purple V-neck shirt and a pair of ragged denim cut-offs had replaced the goth-punk attire. Mike looked relieved, but she was sure she detected a glint of disappointment in Avery's glancing gaze.

Mike glanced behind her as she moved farther into the kitchen. Then he looked at her and said, "Where's Erin?"

She shrugged. "Oh, she said she'd be a while in the bathroom." She smiled. "Feminine issues, you know how it is."

Distrust flickered in the shift of his brow and the set of his jaw, then was gone in an instant as he again addressed Avery. "I think it's clear what we need to do."

Avery groaned. "Not this again."

The exchange piqued Melinda's curiosity. So they hadn't spent the whole time she was away discussing her, after all. The notion was slightly ego-deflating, but the sting of it was overridden by the need to know what the nature of this current rift was.

"What are you boys talking about?"

Mike looked at her. "I've been trying to make Avery see that the only viable course of action now is obvious—we have to get out of Dandridge. Just get in our cars and drive away. What's happening here is beyond our ability to either comprehend or solve."

Melinda nodded. "I see."

Avery sighed. "And I say the only thing that'll accomplish is to expose ourselves. The biggest flaw in Mike's plan is that we have no way of knowing whether this is a localized event. For all we know this could be a global problem."

Melinda tried not to smirk—the expression that twitched at the edges of her mouth just managed to look like a nervous smile. "Have either of you thought of checking CNN? Or the Internet?"

The expressions on the men's faces changed so dramatically Melinda was unable to suppress a giggle. Looks of intense concentration and barely concealed anxiety gave way to slack-jawed expressions of disbelief and embarrassment. Avery smacked his forehead with the palm of a hand.

Mike recovered first. He strode past them and out of the kitchen. Avery moved to follow him, but Melinda put herself in his path and he came to a halt.

He frowned. "What's up, Melinda?"

She gripped his crotch and gave it a hard squeeze. Then she pushed herself against him and whispered into his ear, *"This."*

She smiled as she felt him swell against her hand.

Avery swallowed hard. His voice emerged as a croak: "Melinda . . ."

She made a shushing noise and put a finger to his lips. "Not now."

Then she disengaged herself from him and spun away, sashaying out of the kitchen like a model strutting down a runway. She felt his gaze on her like a physical thing, like something warm and arousing on her skin. She could feel his need rolling off him in waves. Such a pathetic creature he'd turned out to be. He was like putty in her hands, as much a slave to hormones as boys half his age. Sure, he had a lot more going on in the brains department than dear, dead Beauregard (but then, so did your average cockroach), but in many ways he was a weaker thing than her deceased lover had been.

She entered the living room and saw Mike standing in front of the TV aiming a remote at the screen. He clicked through the various news channels several times, occasionally lingering at one longer than another when it seemed there was about to be a transition between stories. But each new story reported failed to include any mention of either mass resurrection of dead people or supernatural forces of any type wreaking havoc. Satisfied that the events in Dandridge remained unknown to the outside world, Mike clicked the TV off and tossed the remote onto the bloodstained coffee table.

His eyes gleamed with renewed determination.

There was also an unmistakable hint of smugness. Mike was a guy who liked to be proven right. Melinda realized then how perfectly matched this hunk and Hannah had been. They both believed they were smarter and better than everybody else. The revelation had the effect of simultaneously stirring her anger and amplifying the lust she felt for dead Hannah's lover-boy. She wanted to break him the way she knew she'd already broken Avery, but this desire was accompanied by the knowledge that he was likely unbreakable. A man like this one wouldn't be susceptible to her manipulations.

He was too . . . sophisticated.

Fine, then.

She would do to him what she'd done to Hannah—and in that last moment before snuffing out his life she'd let him know he was about to die at the hands of his lover's killer. She'd let him have one little moment to think about that, and to know how helpless he was to do anything about it. It made her wet just thinking about it.

But Mike wasn't even thinking about her just now. He was looking at Avery. "Okay, there's your proof. It's a localized event. At least for now. But I don't think it'll remain one for long. I think it'll spread like a plague. It's imperative that we get beyond the center of this storm as soon as possible. If we wait too long, it will consume us."

Avery heaved another weary sigh, but now there was a clear note of defeat in his posture. "Fine. I guess you're right. I just dread the idea of heading out into . . ." His gaze went to the living room window as his voice briefly trailed off. Then he met Mike's steady gaze again. "Into that madness."

Mike nodded. His expression softened. To Melinda it was as if he felt he could be magnanimous now that he'd won. The smug fucker. "I know, Ave. I understand. I'm scared, too. But we really don't have a choice."

Mike's words had a rejuvenating effect on Avery. He straightened up and cleared his throat. "Then let's stop fucking around. Let's get out of here."

Mike's expression became grim again. "We will, but slow down a bit. We need to go about this the proper way instead of just rushing out the door. There are preparations to make. We need to first gather the means to defend ourselves. We have two guns, mine and Gowran's."

"Three."

Mike at last looked Melinda's way. "Oh?"

Despite the loathing she felt for the kind of person he was, her heart raced at the undivided attention. "Yeah. The gun I took from the cop who tried to kill Avery. It's still in the Mustang."

Mike smiled—and sent her heart rate even higher. "Good. We'll fetch it soon. I've got plenty of ammunition for all three guns." Then his attention shifted back to Avery. "But we'll need more than just guns. Bullets are like bee stings to these resurrected people. You can deter them momentarily by shooting them, but you will not stop them."

Avery grunted. "So we're fucked, then?"

Mike's expression sharpened. "No." He nodded at the blood-soaked axe propped against a side of the sofa. "You saw how I dealt with them when you arrived. Dismemberment is the only way to stop them. I have a machete and another axe in the shed out back. We'll take those and whatever else might be useful. And then we'll need to agree on a path out of town. We'll take two cars. Your Mustang, Avery. And the cruiser parked out front. There'll be other weapons and things we can use in there. But I want us to be a well-oiled machine before we enact our exit strategy. That means all four of us discussing everything to the last detail before heading out that door."

Mike looked at Melinda again. Some of his earlier distrust was evident again. "Speaking of that, where is Erin? She's taking a long time."

Melinda managed not to seem nervous as she began moving back toward the foyer and the staircase. "I'll go check on her."

Mike held her gaze for one long, pendulous moment during which she was certain he would rush past her and run up the stairs to check on the bitch himself. Which would ruin everything. Only a great effort of will kept her knees from shaking. Then he just nodded and picked up the bloody axe. "Okay. But be quick about it."

And then he was addressing Avery again. "Take this." He proffered the axe. "Go out to the Mustang and get that gun. If you see any walking dead, don't hesitate. Be merciless."

Melinda couldn't help smiling. "Chop the fuck out of 'em."

Mike grunted. "Basically, yes."

Avery took the axe without enthusiasm. "Sure, whatever. What're you gonna do?"

"I'll be out back fetching things from the shed." He clapped his hands in a brisk manner that made Melinda think of a football coach or general sending his troops into battle at the end of a strategy session. "Let's get to it."

He strode purposefully out of the living room, passed through the archway leading into the kitchen, and within moments they heard the trod of his booted feet over the broken glass around the rear door.

Avery remained where he was. He stared at the axe in his hands and shook his head. Then he looked at Melinda. "Fucking bullshit. That guy's not scared. Not really. He's got ice in his veins."

Melinda faked a smile of encouragement. "You can do it, Avery. You're as strong as he is, deep down. I know you are."

Avery returned the smile. "You really think so?"

Melinda came at him so fast it made him gasp. She threw herself on him and pushed her tongue into his mouth. She heard the axe clatter to the floor. Good. She felt Avery's immediate physical response, the hardness at the center of his body pushing against her. She disengaged herself and gripped his hands, tugging him through the foyer and past the staircase. He stumbled along with her, helpless to do anything but be steered by her. They passed through another archway into a sitting room, then through that into Hannah's office. She closed the office door and pulled Avery down onto the plush rug in front of Hannah's desk.

Her voice was husky and insistent. "Do it now. While he's gone." She wriggled out of the cut-offs. "Please, Avery. *Please.*"

Avery looked at her with eyes full of lust, but still he hesitated. "He'll be back soon."

She snarled at him. "So do it *fast,* fucker. Do it *now.*"

And he needed no further prompting. He got his jeans off and slammed into her. They grunted and thrashed for maybe a minute and then it was done. It was raw, sweaty, and animalistic. And Melinda loved it for that minute. But then she pushed Avery away and snatched up her cutoffs, stepping into them quickly while Avery remained prone where he was, still panting face down on the floor.

Melinda scanned the office, looking for the right tool.

Her gaze swept over Hannah's desk and she saw what she needed. It was in her hands when Avery at last began to push himself off the floor. Melinda planted a foot in the small of his back and drove him back to the floor. Avery let out a cry of surprise and tried to turn over.

But Melinda was too fast.

She pinned him down with a knee and crashed the flower pot over his head. Avery didn't quite lose consciousness, but he was close enough that Melinda had time to do what she needed to do. Once she'd secured him by hog-tying him with coaxial cables, she stuffed a pair of Hannah's panties into his mouth as a gag.

Then she left the office, searched around a bit until she found the next thing she needed, and went into the kitchen to await Mike's return.

CHAPTER TWENTY-TWO

As if from some subliminal signal, Hawthorne emerged from his light doze in time to blink his eyes clear of moisture and read the green road sign that flicked by to his right.

DANDRIDGE
29 MILES

He sighed.

In another half hour, maybe less, he would arrive at ground zero of a potential apocalypse. The enormity of what he was facing (as well as the depth of his personal responsibility) hit him again and he experienced another fleeting moment of hopelessness. He was tempted to reach into his jacket pocket and again tap the shaman's gift for a renewed surge of confidence, but he resisted the impulse. Now, as the moment of his rendezvous with destiny was becoming imminent, he needed to look within himself for the strength to do what must be done.

So he looked within and found what he expected. Fear. Terror. The coward's impulse to turn tail and flee the site of danger. But that was fleeting, just a surface skein of protectiveness woven by the survival instinct present in every human being. Beneath the fear was a stronger mass of steel, a hard, unyielding part of him that would never waver in the face of death. This part of him, he knew, would banish his baser instincts when the moment of truth arrived.

He thought of men at war, preparing to go into battle. He thought of landing boats full of soldiers approaching the beaches of Normandy, young men in the last moments of their lives who *knew* they were about to die. And yet they had done what needed doing. They had emerged from those boats and stormed straight into the teeth of the slavering German war machine. So many other men had done the same in countless other conflicts throughout history.

There was one glaring difference, however—those men had been surrounded by comrades. For now, at least, Hawthorne was all alone. He was a real army of one. The thought produced a helpless, nervous giggle.

He sobered himself with thoughts of what might happen should he fail to win the coming battle. He knew only what he'd been told, but that was enough. The survival of the human race was at stake. The Deathbringer meant to kill and then resurrect every single human being on the planet. He was gathering his forces in an effort to force a confrontation with the ruling power of existence. Not for the first time, Hawthorne wondered what the Rogue hoped to accomplish by bringing such a thing about? Did he really imagine he could grow so powerful as to be able to kill God? The idea seemed grandiose and delusional, and yet Eldritch implied this was precisely what the Deathbringer intended.

It was beyond insane. And therefore, Hawthorne concluded, beyond comprehension. There was no way to truly understand a mind as diseased as the Rogue's. His continued existence constituted a dire threat to the world. And Hawthorne was rather fond of this world, despite its many faults and the petty differences of its constantly warring peoples.

He watched mile marker after mile marker tick away. Tick by tick, Dandridge and the ultimate battle drew closer. So Hawthorne closed his eyes and bowed his head. And he mouthed a solemn prayer to God, or the "ruling power," or whatever force he really served.

Please, he prayed, *give me strength. . . .*

CHAPTER TWENTY-THREE

Erin groaned as consciousness at last returned. Her head throbbed and she felt woozy. She wondered for a moment why she was feeling this way, thinking she'd maybe gone out for a night of drinking and had indulged a little too much. But no, this headache didn't feel like a hangover. She could feel welts at the back of her head and just above the hairline over her forehead. She'd been attacked. Her first thought was that a predator of some sort, a rapist maybe, had waylaid her outside a bar. The thought sent a burst of panic through her, a feeling that surged even higher when she realized she was bound and gagged and confined in some tight space.

But then the memories came crashing back. She was somewhere in Mike's house. She moved her head and felt the soft brush of clothes against her hair. She knew then where she was—the closet in the master bedroom. Melinda, that strange girl who'd shown up with Avery, had clumsily attempted to seduce her. Then, stung by Erin's rejection, the girl had attacked her, striking her with something heavy. Erin had a dim impression of something thick and rectangular. A big book, maybe.

Then . . . nothing.

Her memories ended at that point. But she knew it was a good sign that she remembered these things. It meant there was no brain injury, that she hadn't suffered a concussion. Which was a kind of miracle. She wondered what had stopped the girl from just beating her to death. How long did the little bitch imagine she could conceal what had happened? At some point, surely, Mike and Avery would come looking for her, regardless of whatever cover story Melinda invented.

A point Erin fervently hoped would be soon. The crushing terror of claustrophobia loomed like an approaching storm. She struggled against her bonds and they gave a little but not much. The texture of them was familiar. In a moment she realized they were coaxial cables removed from the television and VCR. This was good. She would've been fucked if Melinda had secured her with rope. Rope was supple, more conducive to thoroughly binding a person. Coaxial cable could be manipulated and shed, given enough time. With that goal in mind, she started working her wrists back and forth. The tightly drawn cable abraded her skin and initially failed to yield, but she increased the flexing motion and the coils began to loosen slightly. But not enough. Not yet. She went to work on the cable around her ankles, too, moving her legs in a scissoring motion. Her feet skidded against the closet door and a new strategy came to mind.

She wriggled into a position affording maximum leverage and kicked her feet against the locked door. The kick resulted in a satisfyingly loud noise as the door rattled in its frame. Emboldened by this small success, she kicked the door again, managing a bit more force this time and a louder thump and rattle. Then an alarming thought went through her like a knife. She hoped Melinda wasn't still in the bedroom. That would mean a premature end to any attempt to extricate herself from this situation. Hell, the girl probably really would kill her then.

She held her breath and waited a moment, half-expecting to hear footsteps padding across the carpeted floor. She waited for the closet door to be yanked angrily open and to see a spill of light framing Melinda's furious, leering visage.

She waited. And nothing happened.

So she wasn't in the room anymore. Good. Or was it? She thought again of the likelihood of Mike and Avery coming to investigate if she didn't return soon. Melinda would know that was inevitable, of course. And she wouldn't stop at what she'd done to Erin. She could even now be doing something awful to Mike or Avery, or both of them. They might even be dead already.

Tears welled in her eyes at the thought of losing Mike. And of being left to face that crazy girl and the horrors lurking outside alone. So she refocused her efforts on the gag in her mouth. She had to call out a warning before it was too late. The texture of the gag was familiar. It was some flimsy bit of silk. Then she detected a lacy bit of frill and knew Melinda had gagged her with a pair of Hannah's panties. The thought made her vaguely ill, but she realized she was just lucky the girl hadn't slapped a strip of tape over her mouth, too. She worked her jaw and pushed the bit of fabric forward, managing to expel it after barely more than a minute.

She drew in several ragged breaths and paused to gather strength. When she was at last breathing more easily, she maneuvered herself into a sitting position, sucked in a deep lungful of air, and opened her mouth wide—

CHAPTER TWENTY-FOUR

Mike knew an instant too late that he'd been a fool to let his guard down. He'd ventured into the night unarmed, emboldened by a primal instinct that said a man was safe on his own property. He felt a tingling along his spine as he pulled the cord to illuminate the shed's interior, a vague sense that something wasn't as it should be. Then the light flickered on and he saw the grinning face of a wild-eyed child. A kid in X-Men pajamas with shaggy sandy blond hair and a smear of blood across his mouth. In the kid's hand was a disemboweled squirrel. Mike felt something twist in his stomach at the realization that the kid, who he recognized as the youngest boy of a family two streets over, had eviscerated the dead animal with his teeth.

His sickened reaction paralyzed him a heartbeat too long, because the kid was on him in a flash, dropping the mutilated animal and propelling himself at the adult intruder, moving with the astonishing quickness of a racing dog bolting off the starting line. The kid latched onto Mike's left leg and tried to push teeth through denim. The kid's head thrashed like that of a lion tearing at its prey and the fabric actually began to give way. Mike tried to kick the boy away, but he held fast, clinging to the older man and continuing to assail him with an animal tenacity. Mike seized handfuls of the boy's hair and tried to pry his head away from the newly opened rip in his jeans, but the kid changed tactics and sank his teeth into the meaty part of a palm.

Mike howled with pain and fury. He was hesitant to use brute force on a kid, but the reality was this thing was no longer a kid in the true sense. It was a deadly *thing*. A rabid beast. So he brought a knee up and slammed it into the kid's jaw, which had the effect of driving the boy's teeth deeper into his palm. He felt warm blood flow out of the gash in his flesh. But a follow-up blow shook the boy loose and Mike pushed past him into the shed. His eyes scanned the row of pegs along the wall to his left. The machete he used for hacking away at overgrown shrubbery was missing. He whirled about in time to ward off another lunge by the boy, hammering a closed fist into the center of his face that crushed his nose and sent him toppling backward.

A long shadow fell over the boy and Mike looked up to see the thin figure of a lovely young woman framed in the open doorway. She stepped into the shed and leered at Mike. The machete, caked with blood along its edge, was in her hand. Mike recognized her. She was Michelle Flynn, the little boy's mother. He'd given her a speeding ticket a month ago, which she'd tried to flirt her way out of, which just wasn't possible given that she'd been hurtling along at twice the posted speed limit.

The boy looked up at her. "Mommy. The bad man hurt me."

Michelle Flynn smiled down at him. "Aw, poor little baby." She flashed a grin at Mike. "Don't you worry 'bout a thing, sweetie. Mommy will make the bad man sorry."

She raised the machete and took a step in Mike's direction. As she stepped beneath the flickering bulb Mike saw a lumpy red blotch across the front of her blue sundress. A pink length of intestine poked through the hole in her belly. It looked like a plump sausage link. Mike's stomach knotted up again and he moved backward. His butt bumped the edge of a rickety work table and he slid sideways and stepped behind it, happy to have even this flimsy barrier between himself and the blood-hungry mother-son duo. His glance flicked downward and did a rapid inventory of the work table's surface. His gaze snapped back to Michelle and in that moment of eye contact he knew he had no time to think things through any further.

He snatched a hammer off the table in the same instant Michelle snarled and leaped forward. He whipped his hand back and snapped it forward. The hammer streaked through the air and hit the woman between the eyes. She staggered backward and the machete slipped through her fingers. Mike saw her boy's eyes go to it and knew he had no time to consider another course of action. He scrambled over the table, sending up a puff of dust and causing an array of tools to clatter to the floor. He swung his legs off the table and landed on the floor in a crouch. He was face to face with the boy for a nanosecond. They reached for the machete in the same moment, but Mike was quicker. He had it in his hands and was standing upright just in time to face a renewed assault from Michelle Flynn.

He swung the machete and the tip of the blade cut a line through her throat. Blood seeped through the rip in her flesh like water leaking through a tear in a plastic bag. But she was only momentarily deterred by the wound. It caused her no pain, or at least it seemed that way. She hissed at him and threw herself at him like a woman leaping off a cliff into a lake. Mike held the machete straight out and she impaled herself on it. The blade punched through her, exiting out her back. Mike yanked the blade out, shoved her back, and swung the blade again. This time it punched into her throat. Blood erupted from the wound and her head tipped to the left and fell against her bosom, still attached to her body by a bit of tissue. One more frenzied blow disconnected it.

The boy made a sound remarkably similar to that made by an air raid siren and came at Mike like something shot out of a cannon. Mike acted without thinking now, surrendering fully to pure, brutal instinct. The boy's head came off with greater ease than Michelle's had. The two headless bodies staggered about the shed's interior, reaching for him with groping hands. Again shutting off the part of himself that was a thinking and feeling human being (a thing that was becoming disturbingly easy), he went to work with the machete, reducing the bodies to a pile of quivering but harmless limbs.

Mike allowed himself a brief moment to recover.

He leaned panting against the work table and stared at the mass of flesh that had until just recently (perhaps even within just the last half hour or so) been the bodies of two decent human beings. A mother of four and a handsome young boy with a winning smile and the whole world ahead of him. They had been real people. Not *things*. Other people had loved and cherished them, and would grieve for them, just as he'd grieved for Hannah. He grunted at his use of the past tense. The grief was still there, but suppressed for now. If he survived this insane night, then he might have time to miss her again.

But now he had business to take care of—and people to protect.

He looked at the row of pegs along the wall and found the other axe. It was an old one, rustier and duller than the one he'd given to Avery, but it should still be able to the job. He did a quick check for anything else that might be of use. There was the chain saw, but there was no gas for it, so lugging it along would only bog them down. There was nothing else useful that he could see.

Mike heaved a big sigh. Then he moved around the pile of body parts and left the shed. He crossed the lawn quickly, anxious to be back inside and coordinating the logistics of their escape with the others. He'd arrived at the shattered rear door and was stepping into the dark kitchen before he realized that he'd yet again let his guard down.

The kitchen lights had been on when he'd left the house. He frowned, but before he could assess how to deal with this disquieting development a scream emerged from somewhere inside the house.

He recognized immediately who'd made the sound.

Erin.

Instinct propelled him through the shattered door.

Then something was coming at him out of the dark.

Moving in a vicious arc straight at his face.

He tried to dart out of the way.

Too late.

Something slammed against his head and the world spiraled down into darkness.

CHAPTER TWENTY-FIVE

Being a homeless man in a small town like Dandridge wasn't quite the same as being a big city bum. Jim Walker knew this because he'd spent time living on the streets of some of the country's biggest cities, from New York City to Los Angeles to Miami. He'd roamed the length and width of the land. Partly because of the wanderlust that had been so much a part of his youth, but also because he was driven forward by a need to find a place where he would feel at home, a place where, at long last, he could come to feel a sense of belonging.

But, no matter where he'd gone, Jim never found what he was looking for. The big cities were inhospitable and sprawling. The homeless populations were too high, thus creating too fierce a competition for already slim pieces of the panhandling pie. Most city folk kept their heads down and bustled right on by you, pretending not to see you. And a high percentage of the ones who would look at you were people looking to heap abuse on beggars.

So Jim gave up on the big cities of America. He would've gone overseas to check out places like London and Paris, but transatlantic transport was beyond the meager financial means of a career hobo. So, weary of the cutthroat world of New York City street life, he'd finally drifted back to Dandridge, the town of his birth. He'd vowed to never return when he left twenty years ago. But that had been when he was young, all defiant and full of vim and vigor. Now he was old and defeated. It stung a little to slink back into town after all these years, but not as much as he would've thought.

Twenty years was a lifetime. A generation of babies had grown to adulthood. Dandridge had changed. It was still small, but it had grown in significant ways. There was more business, including a big industrial park where there'd just been a big, dusty field when Jim was a kid. There were more stores and fast food franchises. Some of the fixtures of his youth were gone. Places like Kotzwinkle's Five & Dime and Walker Feed and others had been replaced by pawn shops and tanning salons.

And yet some things hadn't changed. Life in Dandridge was slower paced and less severe than what he'd become used to over the last two decades. The people were kinder. A few citizens even remembered him from all those years ago. He was able to find enough odd jobs to have booze money, especially now that summer was drawing near. He supposed he'd mellowed quite a bit, because the truth was life was easier here. And better. The special home he'd been looking for all these years had turned out to be the one he'd fled so long ago. Life was a funny old bitch that way sometimes.

Jim pondered all this as he wandered the length of Main Street with a forty ounce bottle of beer in his hand. The bottle was wrapped in a crumpled paper bag meant to disguise the fact that it was a booze container, although any mildly perceptive Dandridge cop would likely see right away what it was. Fortunately for Jim those boys didn't hassle him too much. He didn't drink during the day and he only wandered the streets like this at night, long after most of the shops had closed down. He wasn't out to cause any harm. He just liked to walk. And so long as he didn't bother anyone, the police let him be.

His destination tonight was the park in the town square. He wanted to sit on a bench and stare up at the cloudless sky while he drank the rest of his beer. Then maybe he'd head down to Stu Smith's bar and have another beer or two. More and more these days Jim craved human company. He'd been a loner for so long, even during his days in New York and L.A., that he'd forgotten the simple pleasures of sitting with other people and just shooting the shit.

Yeah, that would be fine.

But for now he needed that quiet time in the park. He crossed Main Street and moved down the opposite side of the street toward the town square. When he entered the park, he was struck by how quiet it was. It wasn't that late in the evening. Usually there were a handful of people wandering around, kids in groups or couples holding hands.

Tonight there was nary a sign of life.

It was a tad puzzling, but Jim dismissed it and headed for his favorite bench, which he was pleased to see was unoccupied. He sat down, set his bottle of beer next to him, spread his arms over the back of the bench, and tilted his head back to stare at the moon.

He saw something else instead.

In that moment Jim Walker became the first person in Dandridge to get an unobscured look at the Death-bringer's face. He might have screamed, but his heart stopped beating in that instant. He'd never seen, or even imagined, something so obscene. So when the world winked out, the last feeling he had was a sense of relief; he didn't want to go on living in a world in which something so awful could exist.

But the darkness lasted only a moment.

He opened his eyes and again saw the Death-bringer's face. But now he was mystified by his initial reaction to this visage. The Deathbringer's pale flesh exuded a ghostly beauty. This was the face of an an-gel, come to deliver the suffering from a place of pain to an exalted, transcendent place. This thing, this glo-rious creature, was the true savior of the world.

The savior grinned. Then spoke, his voice emerg-ing in a dusty hiss: "Go forth and kill, my son." The thing laughed, a sound like rusty nails rattling in a jar.

Jim laughed, too. Because the sense of liberation flowing through him was a wondrous thing. He was now free of society's constraints. No more would he have to humiliate himself and beg for what he needed.

Now he would take. And, yes, *kill.*

He stood and walked out of the park, leaving the beer bottle behind. He didn't need it anymore. There was something else waiting for him out there, some-thing he needed more than he'd ever craved alcohol.

Warm, human blood.

* * *

The Deathbringer watched his newest acolyte disappear into the night and felt a sense of accomplishment. Things were happening fast now. What he'd set in motion had acquired a relentless energy of its own and could not be stopped. Soon every living human in this miserable little burg would be dead, transformed into the first brigade of his army of darkness. Then, this one small corner of the world converted, he would send his soldiers out into the wider world. And his plague of death would spread with greater lethality and virulence than any virus the world had seen. There would be no way to contain it, and within days every human would be dead. Envisioning a world devoid of life instilled within him a pleasant feeling that was as close to happiness as he'd known during his time as a Reaper.

There was no real need to personally snuff out any more lives, and he hadn't intended to kill the bum. That had just been a happy accident. All he needed to do now was gather his army about him and wait for the confrontation he knew would come. There was an opposing force out there, and it was sending a representative.

But he could not be stopped.

And he relished the prospect of confrontation.

An object in his clenched fist dripped blood onto the grass. He raised his fist and opened the fingers. A human heart, formerly housed within the torso of this town's mayor, throbbed against his cold flesh. He squeezed the organ and heard a squeal from the ground behind him. He turned and regarded the wretched creature who, until tonight, had been the most powerful man in town. Now he was a pitiful, sniveling worm, a puppet kept alive for the Deathbringer's amusement. He squeezed the heart again and elicited another wail of agony.

"Come to me."

The mayor of Dandridge, Jerry Hogan, had suffered what should have been a mortal wound. By all rights he shouldn't still be alive without a heart to pump blood through his veins. But the Deathbringer had the ability to keep the man's live body functioning for a brief time. This skill wasn't derived from the standard body of knowledge taught to Reapers. *Invocations of the Reaper* was rich with lessons kept from his kind, the theory being that some ideas were too dangerous to expose to beings already nearly as powerful as gods. Doing this thing to the mayor served no practical purpose—other than, perhaps, as an additional way to show the depth of his spite for humankind.

He wondered what the man he'd been centuries ago would think of the cruel and sadistic thing he would eventually become. It was difficult at times to reconnect with those old feelings, but he was sure that man would have felt revulsion. But that man no longer existed. He'd been human. And therefore weak.

Like poor Mr. Hogan.

His grin widened as he gripped the twitching heart tighter. The mayor moaned and writhed in the grass, his fingers groping weakly at the ground as he tried to pull himself toward the Deathbringer.

His tormentor increased the pressure.

"Come!"

The mayor managed to push himself another inch or so forward, then could move no more. The Deathbringer knelt next to him and flipped the man onto his back. Then, cackling, he pushed the still-beating heart into the man's open mouth and forced him to chew. The man's body spasmed like a live electrical wire exposed to water, then went still as lumps of tough heart muscle passed through his esophagus and dropped into his stomach.

The Deathbringer stood erect and waited.

The mayor's eyes snapped open. He looked into the black eyes of his killer—and smiled. He got slowly to his feet, then looked down at the gaping hole in his chest. He probed it with a tentative finger, the tip of which he then popped into his mouth.

The Deathbringer spoke: "Look at me."

The mayor looked at him, his wide eyes full of awe, love, and reverence. The Deathbringer smiled. "Go. Kill. Help me bring the world to its knees." Mayor Hogan, or the thing that had once been that man, turned without a word and walked out of the park. The Deathbringer watched him start to cross Main Street, then come to a halt in the middle of the street as a squealing car came around the corner and bore down on him. The car's driver stomped on the brake pedal and the car shrieked to a halt, leaving a path of smoking rubber on the asphalt behind it. The driver's side door flew open and a middle-aged, pudgy white man emerged from its interior.

The man appeared to recognize the mayor. "Jerry? Is that you? What the hell are you—"

The man never had a chance to finish his flustered query. Mayor Hogan launched himself at the man, tackling him about the midsection and driving him to the street. Screams resounded along the otherwise empty Main Street, commingling with the lower-pitched snuffling sound of something manic devouring raw meat.

The Deathbringer closed his eyes and listened.

Enjoying, for a moment, this latest movement in his symphony of fear and pain.

CHAPTER TWENTY-SIX

Anger, coupled with the natural thrill of violence, sent adrenaline pulsing through Melinda's veins. Satisfied that Mike O'Bannon was down for the count, she dropped the baseball bat and raced out of the kitchen and through the foyer. She took the stairs two at a time, flew down the second floor hallway, and entered the bedroom in time to see the splintered closet door burst open. Erin's bound feet poked through the ragged hole in the door.

At least the bitch was still tied up. She went to the closet and yanked the door open, and sneered down at Erin's sweat-drenched face. "Hey, bitch. Just wanted you to know your screaming didn't do any damn good."

She knelt and seized the front of Erin's shirt. "You almost fucked everything up. I ought to kill you now."

Erin's jaw quavered as she tried to speak. "N-no . . ."

Melinda punched her in the throat. "Shut up."

Erin coughed and made a strangled sound of pain. Then Melinda punched her in the throat again, making her yelp. She let go of Erin's shirt and gripped handfuls of her hair, then stood semierect and began to pull her out of the closet. Erin's mouth opened wide, emitting a high-pitched squeal of agony. Melinda was fascinated by the sight of the woman's taut hair and stretched-out scalp. She coiled loops of hair around her fists and pulled harder. The sound coming from Erin's throat was now a relentless, ululating peal of pure agony. Hearing it made Melinda laugh. She wondered whether she could pull hard enough to actually tear Erin's scalp off her head. It was a fun thing to consider, but dragging the bitch this way was too much work.

So she let go of the hair and started working at the knotted cable around Erin's feet. When the cable was removed, she warded off a weak kick by Erin and moved at a speed too fast for her first (and favorite) hostage to match. She looped the cable around Erin's neck, fashioning a kind of choke leash out of it and pulled it taut.

She stood and hauled a limp Erin to her feet. She slapped the older woman and clamped a hand hard around her jaw. "You and I are going downstairs. You're gonna walk ahead of me and not try anything funny. If I even feel like you're gonna try something funny, you're gonna stop being able to breathe."

Melinda pulled on the length of cable, making Erin gasp. "Do you understand?"

Erin just looked at her with eyes wet with tears. They were hurt puppy dog eyes. Uncomprehending, bloodshot eyes.

Melinda jerked the cable harder. *"Do you understand?"*

Air wheezed through Erin's constricted throat. She sniffled. Melinda decreased the pressure enough to allow her to say, "Yes. I understand."

Melinda stroked her cheek with the back of a hand. "Good. Good girl. Now turn and walk."

Erin's shoulders sagged as she turned and began to shuffle out of the room. She had a dejected air about her. Seeing it made Melinda smirk. The bitch wasn't so smug now, was she? Where was that haughtiness, that casual sense of ethical and intellectual superiority? It was gone, excised from the broken slug of a woman like a sickness.

She followed Erin out of the room and down the stairs, then through the foyer and into the kitchen. She was pleased to see Mike still sprawled unconscious on the floor amidst the spray of shattered glass. Erin whimpered at the sight of him.

Melinda summoned her cruelest laugh. "He's not dead. But I don't know if his brain's still working. He just took a baseball bat to the head."

Erin started to say something, but Melinda jerked the cable tight again, silencing her. "I didn't say you could talk. There, sit in that chair."

She steered Erin over to the kitchen table. Still too weak to mount even the most feeble attempt at fighting back, the woman did as instructed. She sat in a chair and Melinda removed the makeshift leash, using the length of cable to bind Erin to the chair.

"Now, then." Melinda straightened up and stood before Erin with her arms folded beneath her breasts. "I'm gonna get the boys situated. I want you to be quiet while I'm doing this. If I hear one word from you, I'll cut your tongue out." Now she leaned forward and laid her hands on Erin's trembling shoulders. "Do you believe me?"

Erin's head tilted upward. Her mouth opened, then snapped shut. She nodded.

Melinda smiled. "Good."

She planted a light kiss on Erin's mouth and stood erect again. A jolt of terror snapped her body rigid as she heard Mike groan. She couldn't afford to let him come to, not yet. She retrieved the discarded baseball bat and delivered a solid tap to the back of his head. Mike didn't move, nor did he groan again. Concerned that the relatively light blow might have finished him off, Melinda listened for the sound of his breathing. When she heard it—low, barely audible—she started looking for something she could use to bind him. The coaxial cables didn't seem to be as effective as she'd imagined they'd be, so she needed something else.

A trip through the living room produced results. On the coffee table, next to that weird black book, was the belt formerly worn by the police officer Mike had chopped into little pieces. She removed a set of handcuffs from the belt and returned to the kitchen, where she knelt next to Mike's prone form and pulled his hands behind his back. She snapped the cuffs around his wrists, then rolled him onto his back. She hooked her hands under his armpits and dragged him to the table. Getting him up into a chair turned out to be a miserable chore. He was big and muscled, and weighed maybe seventy-five pounds more than she did. By the time she managed to get it done, she was drenched in sweat.

And Mike was groaning again. Rather than belting him into unconsciousness again, she returned to the living room and pulled the television, stereo, and VCR out of the entertainment center. The electronic components crashed to the floor. The TV's screen shattered and emitted sparks.

Melinda returned to the kitchen with a fresh set of cables and cords, with which she went to work binding Mike to his chair. There was just one more thing to take care of, then the party could really begin.

She left the kitchen and went to Hannah's study to fetch Avery.

CHAPTER TWENTY-SEVEN

The Corvette came roaring around a sharp curve in
the road. Its driver saw the obstruction ahead and
jammed the brake pedal to the floor. The car went
into a spin and slid off the road into a ditch, coming
to rest on its side amid a cloud of smoke and dust.

Hannah, who had not been wearing a seat belt,
cried out as she fell against the crumpled driver's side
door. She'd finally discovered a drawback to being a
resurrected person—even in death, or rather this per-
version of death, there was still pain. The slide and
crash had whipped her about the car's interior like a
rag doll in a dryer. After taking a moment to get her
bearings and verify that all her parts remained unbro-
ken, she stood and hauled herself out through the
passenger-side window. She sat on the side of the car
and regarded the road blockage with a mixture
of rage and contempt. Someone had positioned a
garbage truck so that it was blocking both lanes of

BRYAN SMITH

traffic on the narrow road. But the truck was empty and there was no sign of whomever had done this thing. Which was a shame, because she was in a mood to tear someone apart.

With a sigh, she pushed herself off the Corvette and landed on the road's shoulder. She stood there a moment, listening for any indication of human activity. Her other senses were alert as well, working to detect the faintest pulse of warm blood. But she only heard the scritching of cicadas and various clicking, ratcheting sounds from the Corvette's engine. The strongest smell was that of sizzling rubber on asphalt.

She was alone. And yet *something* didn't feel right. She had a sense of being watched, but from which direction she couldn't discern. Remaining where she was, she turned in a slow circle, straining to make out any lurking shape in the dense and dark stands of trees lining both sides of the road. She saw nothing. But the feeling of being watched failed to diminish. For the first time since clawing her way out of her grave, she felt something close to fear. It was disconcerting. Up until now, and even during her encounter with the strange dark man and his army of dead, she'd had a sense of invulnerability. She was dead, after all, and there was no longer any reason to be afraid. So how to account for this slowly dawning feeling of dread or for this ripple of fear shimmering through her body?

She sighed. "Just move, girl. Take your dead ass on down the road." She spoke in a whisper, as if concerned some unseen entity would hear her. "You have places to go and people to kill, so get it in gear."

So she began to move forward, progressing slowly at first, with great caution. She was close enough to the truck now to confirm that it was empty. She gave the front of the truck a wide berth, placing herself in a spot midway between the truck and the line of trees to her left. Her gaze tracked smoothly left to right the whole time as she strove to remain on guard for any potential assault. And then she was on the other side of the truck and could see that there was no one lying in wait for her there, either.

Hannah released a big breath she hadn't been cognizant of holding. Whoever was responsible for this act of irritating fuckery, he or she was gone. The realization triggered conflicting feelings. On the one hand, it was nice to shake that odd feeling of being watched and preyed upon. On the other, it sucked that there was no one around she could punish for causing a wreck that would've killed her had she not already been dead.

The neighborhood where she'd shared a home with Mike wasn't terribly far away. Or at least it wasn't by car—it would, however, be a hike of some significance on foot. She turned and appraised the empty truck again. Indecision held her in place another moment; then she went to the truck and peered through a window. The vehicle's key, a thin sliver of silver that glinted in the light of the full moon, was in the ignition.

Hannah frowned. She again turned her head to the left and right and searched for the presence of others. The result was the same as before—she was alone. She remained where she was another moment and thought things over.

This was such an odd and inexplicable thing. The way the truck was positioned, it was clear it had been placed here to block access in and out of town. But what didn't make sense was the presence of the key. Why deliberately block the road and yet provide anyone who happened along with the means to remove the obstruction? It troubled Hannah, because she could almost believe this had been done with some design, some specific purpose, in mind—something aimed at her.

Which was crazy and paranoid. Except that those words no longer quite possessed their former meaning. The rational world she'd known prior to her death had given way to an inverted, bizarro realm in which even the wildest conspiracy theories could have a hitherto unimagined degree of plausibility.

But, hell, she couldn't stand here all night thinking about it. She needed to get to Mike soon. She wasn't sure why (though the seemingly non sequitur word "prime" kept coming to mind), but why didn't matter. Not yet, anyway. All she knew was the dark man wanted her there—for a purpose that would be revealed later on. So her predicament boiled down to a simple dilemma: get in the truck and be there within ten minutes or proceed on foot and maybe miss the big party.

She sighed. There was no real choice.

She moved to the other side of the truck, opened the door, and slid into the driver's seat. Her hand went to the key and gave it a twist. She heard the rumble of the diesel engine coming to life and caught a whiff of something that smelled like burning powder. Then flame engulfed her and an explosion propelled her through the windshield. For a moment she was airborne and aflame. Then she dropped like a rock tossed into a well, struck the pavement, and skidded across the road's rough surface. She surged to her feet and stared in horror at her burning arms. Memories embedded in her subconscious since childhood came to the surface and sent her running into the woods, where she dropped to the ground and rolled back and forth to smother the flames. Soon she was no longer on fire, though patches of her hair and clothing continued to smolder. She touched her face to check for burn blisters and found only grime. Her hands were another matter—though still functional, the tops of them had been scorched. They were black and pebbled with blisters.

She bent forward and felt something twisting in her guts. She glanced down and saw a piece of shrapnel protruding through a hole in her abdomen. The flesh around the piece of twisted metal had a puckered, cooked texture. She gripped the hot bit of metal and pulled it free of her flesh. It slithered loose, trailing a mass of stretched-out tissue and intestine; she thought of gooey cheese dripping from a fresh piece of pizza. She twisted the foreign object free of her flesh, chucked the scorched hunk of metal over a shoulder, and stuffed the bits of her that should be inside back through the hole. It hurt and was yucky in the extreme.

But she didn't care. Her beautiful face was unmarred, that was the important thing. Thinking it almost made her laugh. Should a dead person still feel vain? Wasn't her appearance irrelevant now? She was surprised to discover that it was not. She'd always been proud of her looks and death had not changed that. Besides, she wanted to look good for Mike when they were reunited.

She stood up and walked out of the woods. She stood at the edge of the road and frowned at the still blazing interior of the truck's cab.

A bomb.

She shook her head in astonishment. Why would anyone rig a truck with a bomb, then leave it like this? She thought again of the odd and frightening notion that it had been left here specifically for her. If true, there could be only one logical conclusion— that someone, or some force, hoped to prevent her from reaching her destination. And the next logical deduction was that whoever, or whatever, was responsible was working in opposition to the goals of the dark man. And if this theoretical opposing force had managed to arrange this failed assassination attempt, it would mean that they were nearly as powerful (and seemingly omniscient) as the dark man.

Whatever the case, Hannah was certain of one thing. She would not be deterred, regardless of whatever obstacles were placed in her way. Not because she believed fervently in the dark man's cause— which was something she understood in only the vaguest way, anyway—but because the other side had just tried to kill her. She had died once already and had no desire to repeat the experience. So, then, the dark man's enemies were now her enemies. Given the chance, she would eradicate them from the face of the earth.

There were, however, some basic problems with that. One, she had no clue who or what the opposing force was. Two, she hadn't the faintest notion of where to look for them, or even who or what she would be looking for.

There was just one thing she *could* do.

So she did it—she turned away from the ruined vehicles and set off on foot down the road. She grinned. Her would-be assassins had only succeeded in slowing her down. No matter. She would get where she was going one way or another. As she continued down the road, she entertained herself with vivid fantasies of what she would do to her new enemies should she ever have the chance to physically confront them.

CHAPTER TWENTY-EIGHT

The truck was nearing the outskirts of Dandridge when Hawthorne heard the low, almost inaudible trilling sound. He frowned and glanced at the somnambulistic driver, thinking perhaps he'd begun to come out of his trance and was whistling some odd tune. But the big man's mouth was shut and his glassy eyes continued to stare at the road ahead. The noise continued, pulse after pulse, and Hawthorne at last realized he was hearing a cell phone, one of those tiny wireless contraptions that had become so ubiquitous during his time of semiseclusion with the Guardians.

He sat still a moment and held his breath, striving to make out the source of the sound. His gaze went to the glove compartment and stayed there while he waited to hear the sound again. The pulse came again and he knew he'd homed in on it. He opened the glove compartment, sifted through the stack of manuals, receipts, and paperwork until his hand closed around a small lump of plastic that fit into his palm like an egg. A small egg. He turned it over in his hand, looking for anything that resembled an instrument panel or mouthpiece, until he figured out that the thing flipped open like the communicators in an old sci-fi show he'd enjoyed as a teenager in the late 60s, way back in the last phase of what he still sometimes thought of as the end of his "normal" life.

He flipped the phone open, frowned again at the disconcertingly small miracle of modern technology, and put the flip-up part of the little phone to his ear and said, "Hello?"

Eldritch's voice intoned: "It's about time."

Hawthorne grunted. "If you'd told me earlier where to look for this Lilliputian device, I could've answered much sooner. And anyway, why call? Why not just establish a link with the vessel again?"

Eldritch sighed. "Because our magical resources are stretched thin as it is. Do you imagine that communicating that way is as simple as dropping a few coins in a pay phone? Each connection of that sort requires a vast expenditure of magical energy that places tremendous strain on both the spell caster and the vessel. Overdo it, and you risk killing one or both."

Hawthorne sighed. "Okay. Fine. I assume you know I'm arriving in Dandridge as we speak."

"Of course." Eldritch sounded a smidgeon too smug to Hawthorne's ears, considering the man had intimated that his ability to affect events in Dandridge was nearing an end. "And there are some things you should know. Our energies have been further depleted by our endeavors in another area. We set a trap for the Prime. We were able to deduce her likely route away from the scene of her resurrection, and our guess proved correct."

Hawthorne's pulse raced and he was unable to contain his excitement when he spoke: "So she's dead?"

Eldritch groaned. "Of course. She's been dead a week and a half."

Hawthorne closed his eyes. "She got away, didn't she?"

A pause. Then a reluctant, "Yes."

Hawthorne sighed. "My God, Eldritch. You were able to cause someone to set a trap. Couldn't this person, or persons, also have been made to detain the Prime once this trap failed to ensnare her?"

There was an edge to Eldritch's voice when he said, "No. I don't think you appreciate the extraordinary lengths we've gone to just to do what we've done. If you must know, one of our own, a member of the Guardians for nearly as long as I've been with the organization, volunteered for what amounted to suicide duty. His consciousness was sent through the ether and was temporarily installed in the body of a citizen of that village. He had twenty minutes to rig a crude incendiary device and plant it in the appropriate place. When that was done, he waited to see whether his efforts would succeed. The device was ignited, but it wasn't powerful enough to destroy the Prime. Our agent saw this in the last moments before he took his own life."

Hawthorne's jaw dropped. "He killed himself? But . . . why?"

"Two reasons. The spell used to send him to Dandridge amounted to a one-way ticket. He could not return through the ether to his own body." Eldritch's flat tone made Hawthorne think of a newscaster matter-of-factly relating the details of a tragedy. "So he was doomed regardless. Moments before his consciousness would simply cease to exist, at least in a form valuable to us, he killed the body he was inhabiting."

A grunt of disgust came from Hawthorne. "My God."

"The agent had no choice. He didn't know precisely how much time he had left and he couldn't risk discovery by the Prime. So he sacrificed himself to the greater good." Eldritch paused in a pointed way before continuing. "Which, as you well know, you may also have to do before the night is through."

Hawthorne had not forgotten this grim fact, but having it verbalized in this blunt way made something twist inside him. He did not want to die. He would not be swayed from doing what needed doing, but he believed his cause would not be well served by failing to acknowledge his fear.

"I know, Eldritch. I won't fail you. And I won't fail the Guardians."

"I know you won't, old friend." There was a note of sadness in Eldritch's voice now, and hearing it made that knot of fear inside Hawthorne twist even tighter. "I would not have sent you on this mission had there been even the slightest doubt on that count."

The truck's driver downshifted, slowing the big truck as it moved toward an exit. The truck shuddered as it wound around the pale loop of road. Hawthorne saw an intersection ahead, replete with the usual attractions for highway travelers—a convenience store, a small hotel with a blinking neon sign, two fast-food restaurants, and a diner. The driver steered the truck through the intersection and continued down a narrow two-lane road. Less than a hundred yards down this road, Hawthorne got a look at the sign he'd been waiting all night to see.

WELCOME TO DANDRIDGE

He drew in a calming breath and said, "We're here."

"Good," was Eldritch's sole acknowledgement.

The driver shifted down through the gears again and brought the truck to a full stop alongside a tricked-out black 1970s Firebird parked on the road's shoulder. Hawthorne looked at the vacant face of his chauffeur. He felt an absurd need to thank the man for delivering him to his destination. The man wouldn't hear his words, nor would he remember them later when he was at the helm of his own body again. So Hawthorne just opened the door and stepped down out of the truck's cab. He threw the door shut and the truck's engine rumbled. Hawthorne moved to the shoulder of the road to stand next to the Firebird as he watched the semi roar away.

Then he put the phone to his ear again and said, "What now?"

"Now you call the man who contacted us. You will need to secure the copy of *Invocations of the Reaper* before the Prime can get to it. Tell this man his e-mail was received and that you were sent to help him. It is not necessary at this point for him to know anything else. In the glove compartment of the transportation we've arranged is a restaurant receipt with the man's address and driving directions written on the back. Emphasize how important it is that the book not leave his possession. Call him now."

"What's the number?"

Eldritch told him. Then he said, "Good luck to you. Now go do what must be done."

The line went dead.

Hawthorne stared at the phone for a moment and rehearsed what he would say to the man. None of it sounded like the utterings of a sane man. But he supposed that by this point the man he was trying to reach may well have a revised notion of where the dividing line between the sane and the crazy truly lay.

He punched in the number and put the phone to his ear.

The line rang and rang.

CHAPTER TWENTY-NINE

Avery's head hurt. He'd fallen while walking over the jagged mounds of rocks that dotted the landscape along the slight cliff that overlooked the lake. He and his sister had been out playing in the woods with their friends all afternoon on this hot summer day. Hannah had warned him not to go exploring too close to the edge of the cliff, but he'd wanted to get to a spot he'd managed to reach on his own before, a place where he could lie out flat with his head poking over the edge. He liked to watch the water lap against the rocks and try to discern the thin, wriggling outlines of fish flitting through the murky green depths.

But he'd fallen and banged his head on one of the rocks. His head throbbed in a way that reminded him of the ear infection he'd had earlier in the summer. He tried to reach up to feel for blood leaking from the gash the rock had surely opened in his head, but he couldn't make his hands move. Blind panic flashed through him for a moment during which he was sure he'd broken his spine in the fall. Tears dribbled from the corners of his eyes at the prospect of paralysis and being a cripple for the rest of his life.

Then the world—the real world—came into focus and he realized he was decades removed from that summer and his spill on the rocks. Decades older, yes, but apparently he was just as foolish as he'd been in the daredevil days of his youth. Because he'd been dumb enough to fall under the spell of a very odd girl who he now suspected was a genuine psychopath.

He was tied to a chair at the kitchen table. There was something jammed in his mouth. A gag. Mike and Erin were bound to other chairs on the opposite side of the table. Mike was unconscious. Erin was awake and looking right at him. There was no gag in her mouth. He watched her, expecting her to say something, but she remained silent. Shame coursed through Avery. Her silence was a judgment, a condemnation of his stupidity. He'd brought Melinda into their lives, when it should've been obvious from the outset that the unstable girl should've been left to fend for herself. But he'd surrendered to his basest instincts and allowed himself to be seduced by her. The thought of it made him feel filthy, like a piece of scum. Surely Erin was thinking that very thing as she watched him and said nothing.

There was likely little solace to be gleaned from anything he could say, but he nonetheless felt compelled to verbalize his regret. So he worked his jaw and pushed the gag forward with his tongue, eventually managing to expel what turned out to be a pair of green silk panties. Something from Hannah's wardrobe, no doubt. The thought of it made him ill and he made himself look Erin in the eye.

"Erin, I'm so sorry, I didn't mean for any of this to happen." He shook his head as tears blurred his vision; his words of apology sounded lame to his own ears. "I've been so stupid. Please forgive me."

Erin's gaze remained riveted on him, but she still did not speak. Her mouth opened slightly, then closed, and her eyes gleamed with a brighter intensity that made Avery think his pitiful apology had only inflamed her anger.

His face flushed and he averted his gaze for a moment. Then he forced himself to look at her and said, "I'm sorry. I have no right to ask for forgiveness. But, listen, where is Melinda? Maybe I can figure a way out of this mess before she gets back."

Erin's mouth opened again, wider this time, and her bottom lip trembled for a moment. He saw her tongue move through the open mouth and expected to hear her condemnation of him any moment. Then she closed her mouth again and shook her head. She stared down at her lap and sniffled. Her shoulders heaved as she stifled a silent sob.

Avery frowned. It dawned on him that something other than anger at him was troubling her. Well, of course. She was terrified. Her own life was in the hands of a sadistic stranger, a psycho who'd already displayed a willingness to attack and kill. And, of course, she was probably thinking about Mike, who she clearly still loved.

He bunched his fists and tried to flex his wrists against the binds. There was something strange about whatever she'd used to secure him to the chair. He flexed his wrists harder and felt something sticky peel away from a small section of his skin. Yes, something sticky overlaying something hard. A moment later he realized she'd wrapped layers of duct tape around coaxial cables. He glanced down and saw that his legs had been secured in the same manner. The method was diabolically crude but effective. No matter how furiously he tried to wriggle his way free, the binding material refused to give.

He looked at Erin again and saw she'd lifted her head to watch his attempt to get free. Her eyes were wet with tears, one of which was rolling slowly down a lightly freckled cheek. Seeing her this way broke his heart. He'd known her as an acquaintance since before her relationship with Mike and he'd always thought she was cute. Too young to make a play for (how hollow that sentiment seemed in light of the way he'd succumbed to Melinda!), he'd nonetheless always enjoyed looking at her when he'd seen her around town. Anger burned inside him as he continued to stare at her tortured countenance. It wasn't fair. She didn't deserve to be where she was, at the mercy of a crazy person. Just as Hannah hadn't deserved the cruel way her life had ended. If he could just get free, he'd snap Melinda's neck and be done with it. It'd be no different than eradicating toxic waste. It'd be a favor to society.

He gritted his teeth and flexed his wrists with all his might, yet still there was no give at all. He sagged in the chair and closed his eyes, wishing he could slip again into unconsciousness and return to that long ago summer. Then he frowned and opened his eyes. He'd heard something, a sound so low it might have been a disembodied voice whispering in his head. Then he looked at Erin and saw that her gaze had sharpened, that there was something imploring in her eyes now.

He dropped his own voice to a whisper: "What did you say, Erin? Was that you?"

Her mouth opened by the tiniest imaginable increment—but still she hesitated. Her eyes darted side to side then looked beyond him. Clearly she wanted to be certain Melinda was nowhere in the vicinity before speaking. It was odd. He understood being afraid. Hell, he was terrified. But it dawned on him that Melinda had done something to make Erin scared to death to say even a word. The realization made him want to tell her to shut up, but it was too late.

Her voice was just barely audible as she said: "She told me not to talk or . . ." She hesitated as her eyes filled with fresh tears. And her eyes scanned the kitchen again before she continued. "She said she'd cut my tongue out if I said anything." She sniffled and her jaw trembled. She was on the verge of a meltdown. Avery wanted to tell her to shut up, but was fearful now of adding to the overall noise level emanating from the kitchen. "And . . . and I believed her. I tried not to say anything. But I wanted you to know I don't blame you for this. You couldn't have known—"

She was cut off when someone came rushing into the kitchen. Avery glanced to his left and saw Melinda flash by. She'd changed back into the outfit she'd been wearing when he'd had the misfortune to encounter her outside the cemetery. She'd added a lacy black bra, probably purloined from Hannah's closet. Avery glimpsed a blur of something silver as the girl moved into position behind Erin.

A carving knife.

Avery's heart slammed. His mouth dropped open and he wanted to scream out a plea, but no words would come. Erin was wailing openly now and pleading for mercy, but Melinda wasn't listening. She twisted a handful of Erin's hair in her free hand and jerked her head back, exposing the smooth expanse of her slender neck. Then the hand holding the knife came around and laid the blade against tender flesh.

Melinda's expression was almost a parody of outrage. Her eyes bulged in their sockets. Her nostrils flared. And her lips were puckered like those of a guard dog baring its teeth at an intruder.

"I told you not to talk, you fucking cunt. Didn't I?"

Erin's only answer was the steady moan issuing from her throat.

Melinda screamed: *"Answer me!"*

But the moan just went on and on.

Avery at last found his voice: "Please, don't." It sounded pitifully meek to his ears. "Please . . ."

Melinda looked at him. And now he saw how clearly her eyes gleamed with pure madness. "Remember this, Avery," she told him. "This is what happens when people don't do what I say."

She yanked Erin's head farther back, snarled, and drew the knife across her throat. Avery's heart sank at the sight of the deep gash that opened in the white flesh. And he felt sick when he saw the stream of blood flowing out of it. This was all bad enough, but Melinda wasn't done yet. She repositioned herself and raised the knife high over her head, then slammed it into Erin's chest. The blade plunged in to the hilt and Melinda left it there, stepping back to watch Erin's body spasm a bit before going still. Avery saw the light go out of her eyes and started sobbing.

Melinda's hearty laughter provided a stark counterpoint to the sound of his grief.

CHAPTER THIRTY

Melinda went to the kitchen sink and turned on the hot water. She used the steaming water to wash the blood off her hands and arms. She dried herself with a hand towel, then leaned against the counter and watched Avery's display of emotion. It made her sick. You'd think the bitch had been his girlfriend or wife and not just some obnoxious skank who'd been too stupid to keep her slut mouth closed.

When his sobs at last started to subside, she went to the table and sat in the last unoccupied chair. She stared at Avery with a flat expression until he finally summoned the nerve to look at her; then she flashed him a falsely radiant smile.

"Hello, Avery, dear."

Avery continued to look at her, but didn't say anything. There was hate in his eyes. But that was okay, because there was fear there, too.

She laughed. "It's okay, sweetie. You can talk." She

glanced briefly at Erin's corpse and smirked. "That 'shut up or die' edict was strictly for this dead bitch. She pissed me off." She leaned forward, placing her elbows on the table. She batted her eyelashes at him in what looked like a parody of an old-time movie starlet. "But you're my boyfriend. You're not gonna do anything to piss me off? Are you?"

Avery swallowed hard and seemed about to say something, then he closed his mouth again.

The false humor leeched from Melinda's voice as she spoke again: "Do you have something to say, Avery? Are you mad at me?"

Then, in a development that simultaneously stunned and delighted her, Avery seemed to find some measure of bravery within him, because what he finally said was, "You killed Erin, you coldhearted, murdering bitch. Yes, I'm mad at you."

Melinda smiled again, but this time the expression was genuine. "Oh?"

Avery was breathing hard—she could see he was having difficulty controlling the anger raging inside him. "Yes. And I'm not your fucking boyfriend."

Melinda laughed. "Oh, yes, you are. You are because I say you are. And what I say goes. By the way, there's something you should know."

She waited, wanting him to ask. Her smile became cryptic and remained in place.

Avery just stared at her for several moments. Then he cleared his throat and said, "What?"

He sounded annoyed. But Melinda didn't mind. It just added to the exquisite pleasure of anticipation. He clearly had no clue what kind of bomb she was about to drop. She regarded him with an expression of supreme amusement for a beat longer, then unloaded on him: "This skank is the second bitch I've killed in this house."

Avery looked puzzled at first, but then his eyes went wide. "No."

Melinda laughed. She nodded. "Oh, yes."

"You're lying."

Melinda shook her head. "I shot your sister three times, right here in this kitchen." She laughed some more. "Remember how I freaked out when you brought me here?" She laughed again, this time at the light dawning in his eyes. "You thought it was because of the cop car out front. But really it was because I couldn't believe you'd brought me here, of all places. The scene of the motherfucking crime."

Avery still couldn't quite believe it, she could see that in the set of his features. The coincidence was too fantastical, so much so that he just couldn't accept it. Not yet. The firm hand of denial was closing its grip on him.

So she decided to shake him up some more.

"My old boyfriend. The one before you, sweetie. I killed him at the cemetery tonight. He dared me to do it. Stupid fucker didn't think I'd go through with it, but I showed him."

Avery slowly moved his head side to side. "No. You're lying."

Melinda ignored the comment. "I parked my car two streets over. I dressed myself up as a blonde Catholic schoolgirl. I looked like I belonged in the neighborhood. Nobody paid any attention to me, except maybe a few dirty old men peeking at me through their windows." She giggled. "When I came up to the porch here, Hannah was writing in a big yellow pad. Making wedding plans."

This detail was the one that finally got through to Avery. His mouth dropped open and there was despair etched in the lines of his face. "Oh, no . . ."

Melinda giggled again. "Oh, yes. I told her I was selling magazine subscriptions for school. She bought it, the stupid bitch. She went inside to get her checkbook and I followed her in." Her gaze fell briefly to the expanse of tiled floor on the near side of the island. "I made her get on her knees." She nodded. "Right there. Then for some fucked up reason the bitch laughed. I guess she was so scared it made her crazy." Melinda's smile broadened at the memory of it. "But it pissed me off and I hit her upside the head with the gun. She fell on her back and I started shooting. Three times. The last one went right through her forehead. Blew her brains and a bunch of blood out the back of her head. You should've seen it. It was wicked cool."

Avery lunged against his bonds and shook the chair with such force it nearly toppled over. He screamed at her: *"Goddamn you! I'll kill you!"*

Melinda threw her head back and laughed loudly. Then her head snapped forward and she grinned as she spoke. "I don't think so." Her gaze flicked up and down and the grin became a smirk. "Not unless you've got some psychic powers I don't know about."

Avery screamed again: *"Goddamn you!"*

Melinda's good humor faded. "Shut up."

Avery just screamed more.

Melinda's gaze flicked toward Erin. She wrapped a hand around the knife handle and tugged at the blade. It came loose with a wet sound. She brought the blade to her mouth and began to lick the blood off it. She knew doing this made her look like a total wacko, but that was the point. She wanted him as freaked out as possible. And it was working. He fell silent and watched her simulate fellatio with the thing that had ended Erin's life. The fury of before gave way to an expression that made her think of a frightened child lost in a big department store.

Melinda stood up and circled the table until she was standing behind him. She tugged his head back and laid the blade against his throat. She heard him swallow hard and watched the rise and fall of his chest in fascination as he drew in and rapidly expelled a series of panicked breaths. She knew he'd be thinking about how she'd positioned herself behind Erin this very way only moments ago. She let him think about that for a good while, even going so far as to press the blade hard enough against his throat that it began to open his skin. She savored the sensation of him shuddering against her. It turned her on like nothing else ever had. God, she was so glad things had gone this way. She wouldn't have been able to maintain that nervous semi-good girl facade for long. Now she was free to do what she wanted. Free to indulge in that newest and sweetest vice of all—murder.

She knelt closer to Avery and whispered in his ear. "Do you want to die?"

Avery's body shuddered some more. He was trying to keep his emotions under control now, she could tell, but a sob worked its way out of his throat. It was pathetic, a strangled, helpless, hopeless sound. She loved it.

She nibbled at his earlobe. "Answer me, Avery, or I'll give you a second mouth, like that dead bitch over there. You don't want that, I know. So tell me what I know you want to say. Tell me you want to live."

His jaw quivered and he fought for control for a few seconds, but at last he managed to say it: "I-I . . . want to live."

Then tears came pouring down his face in a steady torrent. His shoulders jerked and she made shushing noises. She kissed the top of his head and removed the blade from his throat. "There, there. That's a good boy."

The force of his sobbing increased and she knew he was experiencing a great deal of shame in addition to his fear and anger. She didn't believe she'd ever so thoroughly emasculated a man. Even Beau hadn't been broken this completely. She'd made this pitiful fuck beg for his own life even after admitting she'd killed his sister. It made her feel powerful, strong, like some kind of superwoman. She had an urge to rub his face in it some more, but she was distracted by the sound of someone stirring on the other side of the table.

She looked up, expecting to see that Mike had regained consciousness.

But Mike was still out, his head still lolling over his chest. So her gaze flicked to Erin and a jolt of terror whipped through her at the sight of the dead woman's grinning face. She gasped and stepped away from the table.

Erin's mouth opened and a ragged voice issued forth: "Hello. Did you miss me?"

Melinda stood like a statue for a moment, her heart pounding, seeming as if it might explode at any moment. Then she remembered what was going on in the larger world and realized she should've expected this. She wished she'd cut the cunt's throat deep enough to render speech impossible, as she'd done with poor, stupid Doug. The woman's damaged voice creeped her out more than any of the many strange things she'd encountered thus far.

She managed an off-kilter smile. "Like I miss a turd I've flushed down the toilet, you dead skank."

Erin laughed. The wheezy sound was even more disconcerting than the ragged voice. "Admit it, you missed me. Hell, you wanted to fuck me." More jagged laughter assailed Melinda, who cringed at the sound of it. "Still want me, girl?" She tilted her head and the gash in her throat opened wider. "Come on, honey. Untie me and let's get it on."

Melinda's face crinkled in disgust. "Oh, I don't think so. You're not so . . . appealing anymore."

Erin snarled. "Untie me anyway. I'll kill you fast. It'll be more merciful that way. Otherwise you'll only be delaying the inevitable."

Melinda shook her head. "No."

Erin's grin returned, spreading wide across her face now. And her voice was like the growl of an awakened demon: "Then I'll make you die slowly."

Melinda didn't want to admit it, but the resurrected Erin's bravado was unnerving. There was nary a hint of her former fear, nor of the submissiveness she'd instilled in the woman. She sounded certain she'd be able to get to Melinda and do what she threatened. Melinda remembered the way Hannah had clawed her way out of her grave. These resurrected things were imbued with a frightening level of unnatural strength. It wasn't much of a stretch to imagine the woman bursting free of her bonds and coming after her.

Which meant there was only one thing to do—get the axe and chop the dead whore into a gazillion itty-bitty pieces. She took a backward step, keeping her eyes on Erin as she moved in the direction of the living room, where Avery had discarded the axe. Erin started laughing, and the sound of it grew louder and throatier with each backward step Melinda took.

Then the sound of a ringing telephone made Melinda stop in her tracks and caused Erin to stop laughing. The phone rang again. And again. Melinda looked at Avery, who still looked a bit shell-shocked. Then she looked at Erin, whose smile had given way to an expression of frank curiosity. The phone kept ringing. Whoever was trying to reach the home of Mike O'Bannon wasn't giving up easily. Melinda's gaze went to the wall-mounted phone above the microwave oven. She watched it as the tone rang out a few more times, then she looked at Erin, whose smile had returned, and was now imbued with mischief.

"Don't you want to know who that is? Who'd be calling in the midst of a zombie apocalypse? I don't know about you, but I'm intrigued."

Melinda's frown deepened. She was intrigued, too. She picked up the phone and heard a dial tone. She sighed. It figured that the caller would finally give up in the same moment she finally picked up the phone. She frowned at the buzzing receiver for a moment, then thought of something. She punched in the star sign and the number sixty-nine, then put the phone to her ear again and listened to it ring.

Then the somewhat raspy voice of an older man was speaking in her ear: "Hello, is this Michael O'Bannon?"

Melinda hesitated. Her gaze went again to her trio of prisoners, one dead (sort of), one out of commission, and one who appeared to be in a state of shock.

She'd corralled them all so easily. It was amazing, really, and thinking of the scope of the accomplishment made her feel confident and strong again.

She smiled and cleared her throat. "This is the home of Michael O'Bannon." Her voice adopted the vaguely patronizing and smoothly efficient timbre of a telephone operator. "Who's calling, please?"

There was a brief silence from the other end. Then the man coughed and said, "It's critically important that I talk to Mr. O'Bannon."

Melinda just managed to stifle a giggle. "Oh, 'critically' important, eh? As opposed to mildly important, I suppose?"

The man sighed. "Who is this?"

Now Melinda did giggle; she just couldn't help it. "I'm me—who are you?"

Silence.

Then a soft click signaling a severed connection.

Melinda looked at Erin and felt none of the fear she'd felt before. She smirked. "You'll have to excuse me for a moment, but I'll be back in a jiffy to take off your head."

She turned and walked out of the kitchen.

Hawthorne snapped the cell phone shut and tossed it carelessly through the Firebird's open driver's side window. He heard it smack against the passenger's side window and tumble to the floorboard. He experienced a twinge of regret, thinking he'd probably destroyed the thing, then decided he didn't care. The phone was useless to him now. It was clear to him that something had gone horribly wrong at Michael O'Bannon's residence, which meant he had a fresh set of complications to deal with now. The situation was already problematic enough without this new bit of horseshit shoveled on top of everything else. He had to get to Michael O'Bannon and *Invocations of the Reaper* before the Prime. He wondered for a moment if the maddening girl he'd talked to had been the Prime, then dismissed the notion. She was obviously too young to be O'Bannon's murdered fiancée, which just reinforced a grim bit of reality—that there were new and unknown players in the game.

He sighed.

There was nothing to do but to go find out what was happening. "Once more into the breech," he muttered, then turned and got into the Firebird.

He retrieved the receipt with the scrawled directions, memorized them in an instant, and started the car, wincing at the muscular roar of its engine. Making a mental note to abandon the car prior to arriving at O'Bannon's place, lest it herald his arrival, he put the Firebird in gear and steered it onto the road.

Then he pushed the gas pedal to the floor and made the engine thunder as the big car rocketed into the night.

CHAPTER THIRTY-ONE

Hannah saw the VW bus weaving down the road and moved to step into its path. She remained rooted to the spot, unafraid as the lumbering old vehicle with its distinctive flat front end bore down on her. Her reflexes and quickness were such that she was confident of being able to dodge the rickety box-on-wheels at even the last nanosecond. This was the great thing about being dead, the way her physical strengths in life had been heightened and honed to an incredible degree. From what she'd seen this set her apart from the other resurrected people, who were all unnaturally strong and mobile—but not quite at the same extraordinary level.

So she stayed where she was, knowing she was in no real danger. And as it turned out, there was no need to dodge the VW. It squealed to a swerving stop several feet in front of her. The driver's side door opened and a stoner boy fell out of the vehicle onto the road. He staggered and managed to remain upright, which was miraculous, given how he was high as a goddamned blimp.

The reek of pungent marijuana smoke rolled out of the van in waves. Hannah saw the lit tips of joints rising and falling within the van's dark interior. So stoner boy wasn't alone. Good. More toys to play with.

Holding his head up in a strained way that made Hannah think of a doctor peering down a patient's throat, the boy staggered another few steps in her direction. Hannah tried not to smirk at his attire. He was wearing plaid bell-bottom pants, sandals, and a tie-dyed Grateful Dead T-shirt. A braided homemade necklace encircled his scrawny neck. His eyes were red-rimmed and heavy-lidded. A floppy green hat was tugged down tight over his head, making shaggy loops of brown hair curl outward like a collie's fur.

Dim strains of music and stifled laughter emanated from the van. The music was familiar. She closed her eyes and listened to the faint tones for a moment, trying to identify it. Then she opened her eyes and smiled. This would be fun. Her brother was a big fan of this music and she'd absorbed some of his knowledge of it. There was a role to play here, a way to amuse herself before getting on with the task assigned to her by the Deathbringer.

The boy stopped and swayed where he stood. "Hey, lady, you . . . uh . . . like . . . almost got ran over. That's not too cool. Uh . . ." His eyes went glassy for a moment and he struggled to focus. Then he blinked and squinted at her. "What, uh . . . are you doin' out here?"

Hannah's smile widened. "Like, I need, like, a

ride." There was a playful, lascivious twist to her lips now. "You're, like . . . cute."

He stared at her through those hooded eyes for another suspended moment. She could almost hear the drug-slowed gears of his mind struggling to engage. Then he made a strange sound, a low tone, a single repeating note she finally recognized as laughter. "Huh huh huh huh huh huh . . ." Then he made a snorting sound. "Yeah, like, you're hot. Wanna catch a ride with us? We'll smoke you out."

Hannah tittered like a giddy cheerleader. "Dude, a ride would be awesome. You fucking *rock!*"

The boy swayed again as he made an enthusiastic beckoning motion with his hand. "Hells yeah! Come on aboard."

He turned in a wobbling semicircle and shuffled back toward the van. Hannah followed him and stepped up into the smoke-filled vehicle. A fat stoner boy in a tentlike white poncho grinned at her from the passenger seat. A fedora sat atop his head and dark sunglasses obscured eyes that were likely every bit as bloodshot as the driver's. The rear compartment seats had been pulled out and the floorboard covered with a plush shag rug. A low-wattage red lightbulb hung from a cord near the back of this area, making it look to Hannah's eyes like a kind of mobile opium den. Two young girls sat cross-legged on the rug. They wore homemade hippie-chick clothes and were scrawny and passably pretty, but also somewhat smelly. She realized none of the van's occupants, herself obviously included, had bathed in days. And the average age—excepting herself—was somewhere around twenty.

She slithered between the front seats, intentionally sliding over the skinny driver's lap in the process, and settled into a cross-legged position near the girls, who looked at her with gaping mouths for a time before glancing at each other and giggling nervously.

One girl, the marginally prettier of the two, smiled at her. She had a cute, dimply face and blue eyes that looked big behind her John Lennon glasses. Granny glasses, the kind with the big round lenses. "Here, dude. Smoke up." She held out a joint, which Hannah accepted, taking it between the thumb and forefinger of her right hand. "It ain't gonna be the best smoke you've ever had, but it'll do the trick."

Hannah put the wet end of the joint between her lips and inhaled deeply. She hadn't partaken since her earliest college days, but there was a strong curiosity factor here—*could* a dead person get high?

The immediately apparent answer was *yes*.

Warmth suffused her and she felt lighter and more carefree than at any point since her resurrection earlier in the evening. It was a good feeling. But she didn't feel so mellow that she had forgotten her bloodlust. She looked at the girl with the granny glasses, savoring the sight of those big blue eyes. She thought of how good the eyes of the Corvette's owner had tasted and felt an urgent craving to experience that taste again.

Somehow, though, she managed to make herself hold back. She wasn't finished playing with these stupid children yet. She held out a hand and said, "I'm Whisper Starshine. What are cool people like you guys doing in this nowhere town?"

Granny glasses girl said, "Whoa, cool name. Hippie parents, huh?"

Hannah giggled. "Yeah."

Whisper took Hannah's hand and held on to it, clasping it in both of her hands. "I'm Constance Morrow." She rolled her eyes. "As you can tell, my parents weren't cool." She nodded at the other girl. "This is Lucy Diamond." She snickered. "That's a made-up name, as if you couldn't guess."

Hannah arched an eyebrow. "What's your real name, sweetie?"

The girl was a pale thing with long, straight brunette hair. She appeared to blush at Hannah's use of the endearment "sweetie." "Oh, it's a crappy name. I'd rather just be Lucy."

Hannah nodded and, using her left hand (for the right was still being held by Constance), took another toke off the joint. She held the smoke in a moment, then blew a cloud of it at the van's ceiling. She felt Constance's fingers stroking the underside of her wrist and savored the feeling a moment. It felt nice to be touched that way. She thought it was something she might have been willing to explore under other circumstances, but time was running out. She could only play with these things a few moments more before doing what she would have to do.

She met Constance's smoky gaze and smiled. "You didn't tell me why you're here in Dandridge."

Constance's eyes narrowed. "Oh . . . right . . ."

Everyone in the van, except Hannah, laughed at this.

The driver spoke up. "We're doing the, uh, cross-country thing, y'know?"

Hannah turned her head to look at him. "Oh, yeah? You following a band?"

The fat boy in the passenger seat heaved his body

around so he could look at her. "Yeah. You ever hear of the Yonder Mountain String Band?"

Hannah nodded. "Oh, yeah. Love them." The name was new to her. The driver turned up the volume on the Grateful Dead's "Ripple," and she smiled. "But nobody's better than the Dead."

She moved her head gently in time to the song and started singing the words. Avery had played this and other Dead songs endlessly in the last year before he left home, leaving the lyrics to every song forever imprinted on her memory. The kids sang along with her. They smiled and laughed and everything was cool for a few more moments. But then Constance's smile faded and she relinquished her hold on Hannah's hand. Hannah followed the girl's alarmed gaze and had to laugh at the little puff of smoke emerging from the hole in her abdomen. Apparently the shrapnel had nicked one of her lungs, too.

Constance's face twisted in a stricken expression. "My God, what's wrong with you?" She grimaced again as she glanced down at Hannah's hands. "I thought something didn't feel right. Oh, Jesus."

She scooted away from Hannah, until her back met the van's rear door. Hannah grinned and sucked in another lungful of smoke. She watched in fascination as tiny, vaporlike wisps curled out of the hole in her midsection.

"Dennis!" Constance's voice rose through several lower registers and ended in a shriek. From the direction of her gaze, Hannah deduced she was addressing the van's driver. "Stop! Stop now, goddammit!"

The van swerved in wide arcs back and forth across the road as Dennis turned in his seat to get a look at whatever had distressed Constance. Because of the dim lighting and the way Hannah had positioned herself at an oblique angle, he couldn't discern anything obviously amiss.

"Dudes, stop freaking out. You're gonna make us wreck."

Constance screamed at him. "You're gonna make us wreck, motherfucker. There's something really, really wrong with the bitch you picked up. Get her out of here!"

Lucy was staring in openmouthed stupefaction at the smoke rising from the jagged hole in Hannah's flesh. Then she lifted her gaze and stared at the older woman through squinted eyes. "Dude . . . you're, like . . . *dead.*"

Hannah cackled. "Like, *duh.*" She shook her head in an exaggerated gesture of disbelief, as if she'd never encountered anyone quite so dumb as this girl. "I can't believe it took you so long to figure it out." She sniffed at the air. "Or, no, I guess I can believe it. You guys are already half brain-dead." She laughed again. "I really ought to thank you. You've done some of the work for me already."

Lucy frowned and shook her head in a way that made Hannah think of the slow-motion replays shown during televised sporting events. "Noooo . . . ," she said, sounding to Hannah like a parody of a ghostly whisper in a spooky movie as she drew out the single syllable. "Oh, no. No fuckin' way, dude."

Hannah's mouth became a tight line. She was no longer as amused by these kids. Stupidity on so epic a scale was just annoying. So she decided to stop fucking around. She clamped a hand around Lucy's throat, turning her next stoned utterance into a strangled wheeze. Constance, screamed as Hannah pulled

Lucy close and took a big bite out of her face. Hannah wrenched her head and tore loose a big flap of cheek. The taste of bloody flesh on her tongue zapped dead the last remnants of the mellow feeling induced by the drug. She squeezed Lucy's neck until she felt tendons and cartilage give way with a crunching sound. The girl's eyes bulged and her mouth went wide as she instinctively fought to draw a breath, but Hannah's death grip could not be budged.

Hannah sank her teeth into the dying girl's other cheek and was only dimly aware of the van slowing and coming to a stop. She hungrily munched this new tasty morsel, her jaw working as relentlessly as a fat kid's at a pie-eating contest. The only thought in her mind in the moment before she felt the first stinging sensation was that face meat tasted pretty damned good. Not as good as an eyeball, or a handful of juicy viscera, but pretty damned good. It was more of a refined taste, like New York strip steak compared to a fast food burger.

Then something stung her shoulder. She knew she'd felt the same thing a moment ago, but she'd thought it was a bee. But this time the impact of it was enough to make her pitch forward a bit and finally surrender Lucy Diamond's gruesomely compacted neck. The girl fell dead on the floor and the back of her head banged the metal door and made a sound like a chintzy snare drum.

Hannah frowned and looked at her shoulder.

Blood.

Bubbling out of a small round hole. Somebody was shooting at her. And whoever was doing the shooting was a lousy shot. One bullet had already gone well astray. Blood and other fluid leaked from the space

formerly occupied by Constance Morrow's left eye.
The remaining lens of her granny glasses dangled
from her right ear as she toppled sideways and shuddered some before going still.

A big voice boomed from the forward section of
the van. *"Stop shooting!"*

"She's some kind of monster, dude," said Dennis.
His voice quavered. He sounded full of nervous energy, like a demented cross between the pot-addled
stoner dude he naturally was and a manic, tweaking
meth-head. "I gotta shoot her in the head, like they
do in the movies."

"You idiot—you'll shoot me in the head before
you're done."

Hannah turned around in time to witness a brief
scuffle. The big boy in the poncho and fedora managed to pry the pistol away from Dennis. He pointed
the gun at Hannah and she noted the steadiness of
his hand—his aim would be surer than the bumbling
skinny boy's by a good margin. She stared at the barrel of the gun and her lips curled backward to reveal
gritted teeth, through which a low, snakelike hiss emanated. She remembered a time not so long ago when
she'd trembled in terror at the sight of another gun
aimed directly at her head.

Tremendous anger burned within her, boiling just
on the edge of explosion. She wouldn't be a pleading, helpless victim again. Not like last time. Not
ever.

When she at last regained enough self-control to
speak, her voice exuded a potent level of malice that
clearly unnerved Dennis and his tubby friend.
"What's with the gun, boys?" She made a *tsk-tsk*
sound and shook her head in disapproval. "Sort of

blows the hippie image, don't you think? I've known some for-real pacifists in my time, guys, and they don't tend to be gun-toting types. So tell me the truth—are you guys just poseurs? Playing a role until graduation, when you'll move on to real jobs and adult life? Hmm, am I close?"

The big boy started to squeeze the trigger. "No. And shut up."

But then his eyes went wide and the hand holding the gun went limp. Hannah puzzled over this for a moment—until she heard something stirring behind her. Then she chuckled. "Okay, new rules—boys against girls. Ready to play?"

Hannah felt Constance brush against her as she moved past her and wrapped a hand around the boy's hand, closing his fingers more firmly around the handle. His eyes glazed over as he stared in shock at the dead girl. He didn't seem to realize the danger he was in. Hannah supposed he was simply unable to accept that the friend he'd seen killed moments ago was up and moving around again. Also, it probably wouldn't occur to him to fear Constance, resurrected from the dead or not.

The girl smiled at him as she lifted his hand and twisted it so that the barrel of the gun was now aimed straight at his face. Only when she began to push the barrel toward his open mouth did he at last snap out of the trancelike state. He tried to wrench his hand free of her grasp, but she was stronger than him now. He tried to pull away from her, but she gripped the back of his neck and easily held him in place. Then she pushed the barrel into his mouth, until the trigger guard was pressing against his fluttering lower lip. She slipped a finger through the trigger guard, curling it around his own stubby finger.

Hannah's breathing grew shallow as she watched this transpire. Excitement swelled within her. This was what it must feel like to be a dirty old man in a raincoat watching hardcore porn in a booth in an adult bookstore.

The gun discharged a bullet that blew out the back of the big stoner boy's skull and rained blood and brains all over the dashboard. Constance roared like a lioness, yanked his head down, and plunged her mouth into the gaping red hole. She made hungry snorting sounds as she drank blood and devoured tissue. Hannah felt a slight pang of regret in not having made the kill herself, but that was tempered by the voyeuristic thrill of watching a newly resurrected person hungrily partake of human meat for the first time.

Lucy Diamond surged past her and hurried through the gap between the seats. Only then did Hannah see that the driver's side door stood wide open, pale moonlight reflecting on the smooth metal. Hannah got a glimpse of Lucy's ruined face and realized that if anyone had done that to her, she would've been forced to annihilate the person. Fortunately, Lucy, like all newly resurrected, was consumed with the burning, undeniable need to fill herself up with the warm blood and flesh of the living.

The girl with the mangled neck disappeared through the open door and chased a dim, receding figure down the street. Hannah saw a glint of swinging silver beyond where Constance was still feasting on her dead friend. She leaned forward and squinted, and saw that this was the ring of keys still dangling from the ignition. An idea so fun in a twisted way that it was almost diabolical came to her. She crawled through the seats and positioned herself behind the steering wheel.

The engine sputtered to life as she turned the ignition key. She stepped on the gas pedal, revved the engine, then put the old rust bucket in gear and pushed the accelerator all the way to the floor. The VW bus leaped forward and in moments was hurtling toward where Lucy Diamond had taken Dennis down. Constance yelped in surprise and tumbled backward. The dead boy thumped against the dashboard and slid sideways into the gearshift. Hannah was too riveted by the sight of Lucy straddling Dennis's twitching body to realize what was about to happen. In the same moment that the front of the van smashed into Lucy's back the gearshift was abruptly knocked into the parked position, and Hannah took her second flight through a windshield in one evening.

She hit the asphalt maybe a dozen yards beyond where the VW came to a grinding halt and skidded facedown across the rough surface for several more yards. The road abraded her chin and the palms of her outstretched hands, removing several layers of skin in the process.

She remained where she was for several moments, then groaned and slowly sat up. She put a hand to her chin and realized that her incredible luck had at last run out. Her perfect cheekbones and small, straight nose remained intact, but her chin was a shredded mess. Fury engulfed her and she started looking around for someone to take it out on, but no living people were left. Lucy Diamond lay motionless on the side of the road, her back grotesquely twisted like a pretzel. Dennis was nowhere in sight. Hannah assumed his body was trapped somewhere beneath the VW. And Constance had likely gone back to chowing down on the boy she'd killed.

She got to her feet and stood swaying in the middle of the road for a moment. Her gaze moved from the utterly still Lucy Diamond to the VW and back again. She knew she should return to the van at once, evict its remaining occupants, and drive hell-for-leather toward home. She'd made a mistake playing with the hippie children; she saw that now. She could hear the Deathbringer's low, insidious voice. He was many miles from this spot, but she could hear him nonetheless, that creaky, hair-tingling tone that was so like a whisper from the grave. She could almost feel his cold breath sighing against her ear. She shuddered.

He would be unhappy with her should she fail in her assigned task. Which was an understatement. She had an idea the Deathbringer punished those who angered him via methods that made any physical punishment or torture ever designed by human minds seem like kindnesses by comparison.

Hannah sighed.

Lucy Diamond's eyes jittered in crushed sockets. She couldn't manipulate her extremities, but she was breathing. There was still a consciousness inhabiting that ruined shell. Hannah was tempted to spend a bit of time taunting the mangled wreck of a girl. But there was no time for any more trivial amusements. So she did as her new master instructed, returning to the VW bus and sliding again into the driver's seat. She frowned at an odd mixture of noises coming from the back of the van and turned in her seat to see what was going on.

Hannah, who had indulged in more than her share of sick and twisted pleasures this night, was surprised to find herself taken aback by the sight that greeted her. The dead boy was flat on his back, with his pants tugged down around his ankles. Constance, her long skirt hitched up above her waist, straddled his groin, bucking violently. The boy, despite missing most of his brain, had joined the ranks of the resurrected at some point during Hannah's close encounter with the pavement. A thick stream of drool dripped from one corner of his mouth and a steady moan that never once shifted pitch issued from his throat. He looked and sounded like a lobotomized mental patient.

Hannah frowned. By all rights her level of brain function should be the same as this poor kid's. They'd both had their brain pans emptied by large caliber bullets, after all. But Hannah supposed she must be a special case. The Deathbringer had worked some other kind of magic on her, something that had been only for her and none of the rest of the resurrected people. Unlike this boy, who, after all, had merely been a traveler unlucky enough to be passing through Dandridge at the precise wrong instant.

She decided against taking the time to disengage them, figuring they were too occupied with their carnal interlude to bother interfering with her. So she faced the road again and put the VW bus back in gear. The vehicle moved forward, but something she couldn't see seemed to be impeding its progress. Then there was a loud *thump-thump* sound as the bus bounced over Dennis's body. She glanced at the rearview mirror (long ago detached and held in place now with a mass of rubber bands) and caught a quick glimpse of the body and a dark smear on the road that clearly indicated where the bus had dragged it before it came loose.

The engine rattled and coughed as the bus picked up speed. The impact and violent shifting of gears hadn't done the old thing any favors. The rattling grew louder still as the speedometer crept past forty, and now it sounded like a jackhammer tearing through concrete. The bus was in its death throes.

Hannah could only hope it would hang on long enough to get her home.

CHAPTER THIRTY-TWO

One moment there was nothing. The world was a void. Just pure blackness. And in the next moment Mike O'Bannon was conscious again, his abrupt return to the world marked by an enormous throbbing pain that engulfed his head and seemed to extend partially down his spine.

Then came the mother of all paradigm shifts. The last thing he remembered was sprinting through the shattered rear door and in the same moment hearing Erin's scream. Then the world went away. And now it was back. Except that now he was sitting in a chair at the kitchen table. Except that "sitting" wasn't quite the right word, because it implied an action taken of one's own volition, as if he'd merely felt a tad woozy and had decided to sit down. This was clearly not the case. He was a prisoner, bound to the chair with cables and duct tape. Seated across from him was Avery, who appeared to be in precisely the same predicament. He was aware of another presence to his left, and, with a groan triggered by a fresh flare of pain that sizzled down his spine, he turned his head and saw what had become of Erin.

She smiled. The movement of her facial muscles caused the flesh beneath her chin to move, which caused the hideous gash in her throat to pucker in a manner resembling a second, bloated smile.

"Hey, sweetie, I missed you." Her new voice was low and ragged, nothing like the lilting, girlish voice he'd known. Hearing it almost made the revelation of Erin's death easier to bear. The glaring difference allowed him to believe this thing next to him wasn't really Erin at all, was just some demon inhabiting the shell formerly occupied by the second greatest love of his life.

Unexpected tears welled in his eyes.

He thought, *Easier to bear, my ass.*

He was startled by the strength of emotions he now felt. This grief was real and strong, and was almost as shattering as Hannah's loss. But as he thought about it he realized this feeling shouldn't come as a shock. In a lifetime, a human being will only know a small, finite number of people who care deeply for them. Whatever their differences, Erin had been one of a small and now rapidly dwindling group.

A disconcertingly sincere expression of concern formed on Erin's face. "Don't be sad, baby. You'll be dead soon, one way or another." The frown morphed slightly, becoming a tentative smile at the edges. "And when you've come over to our side, we can be together again. Won't that be nice?"

Mike's first thought was that part of him did want

to embrace that surrender. It would be so much easier than continuing to struggle. Not only that, but he had a feeling that humanity's imminent struggle against this death plague would be a losing fight. So there was something alluring about going over to the team with momentum on its side. But these thoughts were fleeting, weak impulses flickering through his mind in a moment of despair. *I'm going to fight,* he thought. *Until I draw my final breath, I'll fight this with everything I have.*

He forced his gaze away from Erin and looked at Avery, who was awake but didn't seem all there. Unlike Erin, however, he was clearly alive. Even in the absence of obviously fatal wounds, it was easy to tell the difference between the living and resurrected people. There were subtle indicators in the eyes and skin tone. But the biggest thing was the feral, bloodthirsty leer on the face of every resurrected person. Avery didn't have that, but he looked dazed. He was staring in a vague way at an indeterminate spot on the tablecloth.

"Avery."

No reaction. So Mike pitched his voice a notch louder: "Avery!"

At last, a reaction. Avery blinked a few times and lifted his gaze. He squinted at the man sitting across from him. "Mike?"

Mike sighed. "Thank God. You looked like you were out for the duration."

Avery shrugged. "No. I'm back now. Like it matters, since we're well and truly fucked. Until just a minute ago, bud, I thought you were brain-dead or something."

"I'm lucky I'm not, I guess. Do you know what happened? Did that girl do all this?"

A look of pain mixed with shame crossed Avery's face. "Yeah, she did. She's a fucking psycho, man. I'm really fucking sorry, I had no idea I was bringing a crazy person into your house."

Mike grunted. "Blame yourself later if you have to. I don't, just for the record. Right now, it's irrelevant. All that matters is finding a way out of this nightmare."

Avery heaved a big sigh. "There's something else you should know about Melinda. She . . ." He sighed again, hesitating.

Mike frowned when Avery failed to complete the thought. "She what?" He made a sound of exasperation. "Come on, Ave, we don't have forever here. If this is something I need to know, spit it out."

Avery cleared his throat and looked Mike in the eye. "All right, then. She says she killed Hannah. And, Mike, I'm sorry, but I believe her. She knows things only the killer could know."

Mike didn't say anything at first. For several moments he was barely able to think in a coherent way. What Avery was saying was just too bizarre. The notion that Hannah's murderer was somewhere in this house *right now,* failed to compute. That she'd wound up here via random circumstance was too wild an event to be true coincidence. He experienced a disconcerting sense of being a pawn on a celestial chess board, a thing being manipulated by gods. It was an unsettling notion and he didn't much care for it. He didn't like to think that his beloved Hannah's murder had just been the opening gambit in a fucking *game*.

He drew in a deep breath and tried to still the roiling, colliding thoughts. He needed to focus, narrow things down to what was most important just in this moment. He released the breath and met Avery's gaze again.

"Where is she?"

Avery opened his mouth to reply, but it snapped shut in the next moment, silenced by a sound of heels clicking on the floor tiles. Mike looked over Avery's shoulder and saw Melinda enter the kitchen with the axe propped lazily over a shoulder. She'd changed clothes again at some point and was back in the gutter punk-slut attire she'd been wearing the first time he saw her. Except that now she was wearing a bra pinched from Hannah's wardrobe. It was a bit big on her.

She reached the table and her eyes went wide with delight when she saw that he was conscious again. "Hey, stud. Good to see you back. Thought you were a goner." She sensed the rage boiling within him and smiled. Her gaze went to Avery before coming back to him. "I guess Avery, otherwise known now as 'my bitch,' told you I killed Hannah."

Mike didn't say anything. He clenched his teeth and air hissed in and out of his nostrils. He wanted to explode out of the chair and rip that goddamned axe from her hands and use it to split her hateful, smirking face right down the middle.

Her smirk became a grin. She was delighting in his helpless rage. "Aw, that's cute. Stud-boy wants to avenge wifey-poo." She breathed a mocking sigh and fluttered her eyelids. "Poor, deary me, I am *so* afraid."

She laughed.

Erin made a sound like air escaping through a faulty valve. Mike recognized it as a sputtering growl a moment later. Then she was thrashing against her bonds so violently that Mike briefly forgot all thoughts of revenge (or anything else). She clearly possessed strength many times greater than what she'd been capable of in life. There was a prolonged ripping sound—the sound of a lengthy strip of duct tape being torn loose. Something (coaxial cables, as he soon realized) struck the floor and her hands emerged from the rear of the chair. A few ragged pieces of duct tape still clung to her skin, but she was partially free now. She went to work on the cables and tape wound around her waist.

Melinda's eyes went wide with shocked alarm. Fear paralyzed her for a moment and Mike derived some small satisfaction from seeing the smug look vanish from her face. But the moment of panic passed and the girl's eyes took on a predatory gleam again. She raised the axe and moved quickly into position behind Erin. Mike made a desperate attempt to rock his own chair over and throw himself in her path, but only managed to make the chair's legs creak. He turned his head as far to the left as possible, hoping to see Erin burst free in time to ward off the axe blow and rip the girl's throat out. His heart sank when he saw that she'd never be able to shake loose the remaining bonds in time to do anything but remain a sitting target.

Melinda raised the axe still higher. Her nostrils flared and surprisingly well-defined muscles stood out in her slim neck and shoulders. She looked as if she meant to slam the blade of the axe through the crown of Erin's skull. Another fraction of a second longer and that may have happened.

Mike sensed a new presence in the kitchen. He tried turning his head still farther to the left, but his spine and neck screamed in pain and shook with the strain. There was an impression of rapid movement, something that made Mike think of a poisonous snake springing out of its coiled position to sink fangs full of venom into unprotected flesh. Something whistled through the air and struck something else.

A knife glanced off Melinda's right shoulder, carving a groove in the flesh before it went spinning away. The axe clattered to the floor and she fell against the table. She slid forward and leaned over Avery, a fluttering hand groping for his shoulder. She was dazed and weakened by pain, but her head snapped up at the sound of booted feet clomping in an unhurried way across the floor tiles. She glared at something beyond Mike's right shoulder. But despite her fierce expression, it was clear that whatever she was seeing frightened her. She backed away from the table and knelt to pick up her assailant's knife. She waved the bloody wedge of steel at her approaching adversary.

But he kept coming, so she moved into position behind Avery, apparently meaning to use him as a human shield. She pulled his head back and pressed the blade against his throat.

"Stop right there or I'll kill him."

A man moved into Mike's field of vision. He frowned. He'd never seen the guy before. He looked to be in his fifties, with long, graying hair pulled back in a ponytail.

His flesh looked weathered, as if he'd spent most of his life in a tropical climate. He wore a heavy brown jacket with fringe over a plain white shirt. The jacket was an odd choice of attire considering the season. Something in his flinty dark eyes bespoke intelligence and unwavering surety of purpose.

He kept advancing on Melinda in his unhurried but inexorable way, and when he spoke, his baritone voice was full of undeniable authority. "Kill him and you die. I'm allowing you just one opportunity to surrender. There will be no negotiation. Lay the knife on the table and step back."

But Melinda stayed where she was. "Who the hell are you?"

The man's hard expression remained unreadable as he said, "Broderick Hawthorne. I am an agent of the Guardians."

Melinda scowled. "The fuck? Is that supposed to mean anything to me?" She relinquished her hold on Avery and stepped back, brandishing the knife. "Hell, I don't care who you are—keep coming at me and I'll gut you. I've killed a whole bunch of people tonight and one more ain't gonna bother me none."

Hawthorne's gaze went briefly to the table. He afforded Avery, Mike, and Erin (who, apparently riveted by this mysterious stranger, had ceased working at her remaining bonds) a momentary appraisal before shifting his attention back to Melinda.

"I assume the woman at the table is one of your many victims."

Melinda snorted. "Hell, yeah." She shuffled back another step. Blood from her nicked shoulder trickled down her pale flesh, and she seemed unsteady on her feet. "You just keep coming, fucker, and I'll cut your throat, too."

"I don't think so." He moved another calm step

forward, the heel of his heavy boot making that starkly loud sound again. "And your window of opportunity has closed."

He moved with a speed Mike wouldn't have imagined he possessed, closing the remaining gap between himself and Melinda in less than the space of an eyeblink. He did something with his hands that happened so fast Mike saw only a quick blur of flesh. Then the knife was out of Melinda's hands. It was still spinning across the floor as Hawthorne secured the girl by wrenching an arm behind her back and clamping a big hand around her throat.

She struggled in his grasp, her little body thrashing like that of a wildly misbehaving child in the grip of a determined parent's arm in a supermarket checkout line. But her efforts not only failed to break Hawthorne's hold on her, they produced no noticeable results at all. The man remained implacable, as unmoving as a statue in the face of a hurricane gale. Then, at last, Melinda surrendered to the undeniable and sagged in Hawthorne's grip. She seemed to retreat into herself. Her eyes glazed and she started muttering like a mentally ill homeless person on a street corner.

Hawthorne looked at Mike. Mike, who rarely in his life had ever felt intimidated by other men, shuddered at the scrutiny. The man's eyes were like a dark glimpse into something ancient, yet ageless. He was a man, yes, but clearly he was no normal man.

Then Mike flashed back to something the man had said, something about the "Guardians," and he remembered something.

"My God." His mouth dropped open. He stared disbelievingly at Hawthorne for a moment before he was able to will his mouth to close. "The e-mail. That Web site. You're from *that* Guardians."

Hawthorne nodded. "I am."

Mike frowned. "But . . . I only sent that message a little while ago. Surely your organization isn't based nearby. I'm sorry, but that would be one wild coincidence too many for me."

"Nothing that's happened here tonight is coincidence." The hard tone of his voice shifted a bit, becoming marginally warmer and less militaristic. "And you are right. The Guardians have outposts all over the world, but none in your area. I am from the Mexico branch, and I was already en route to your town before you sent your message."

Mike squinted. "You don't look Mexican."

"It is not the nation of my birth, but that's not important." His tone had sharpened again. "I'll tell you all you need to know soon, but I need some answers from you first. Firstly, the book. Do you have it?"

Mike sighed. "I've spent the last little while unconscious, but as far as I know it's still in my living room."

Hawthorne's posture changed then, became more relaxed. "Excellent. Now tell me, that woman next to you, was she a friend?"

Mike glanced at Erin. Her gaze was still riveted to Hawthorne. Interesting. He'd yet to see any other resurrected person be so still. Usually they were manic, driven mad with the need to devour living flesh. He felt a fresh surge of regret and pain as he looked at her, and he had tears in his eyes when he looked at Hawthorne again.

"Yes," he said in a voice thick with emotion. "I even loved her once."

Hawthorne frowned. "This woman . . ." The furrow in his brow deepened. "How long has she been dead?"

Mike shrugged. "I don't know. Happened while I was out." He looked at Avery. "What would you say, Ave?"

Avery sighed. "I don't know. I've been nothing but scared shitless since I came to, so it's hard to judge time. But . . . I'd say no more than a half hour."

Again, Hawthorne's demeanor changed significantly. He seemed to relax again. "Then she is not the Prime." Something like a smile flickered at the edges of his mouth. "And I shall grant you a favor."

Mike frowned as he watched the man put his mouth to Melinda's ear and whisper something. He couldn't make out what Hawthorne was saying, but something about it startled the girl, snapping her out of passive mode. Her eyes widened and her mouth opened to emit a single panicked word she wasn't actually able to verbalize. But Mike could tell the word was, "No."

But then her eyes rolled back and her body went slack. The girl was dead weight in Hawthorne's arms, and he gently guided her to the floor. Then he stood up and stepped back. "Should be just a moment. . . ."

Mike shook his head. "What are you talking about? *What* should be just a moment?"

Hawthorne appeared not to have heard him. His gaze remained on the girl's prone, unconscious form. Mike was about to make a louder demand for information when he heard Erin gasp. He looked at her and saw that she had gone rigid in the chair, her spine straight and her head snapped back, her eyes unnaturally wide and seemingly every muscle and bone outlined against her flesh. She looked like a condemned woman strapped to an electric chair, with thousands of volts ripping through her body.

Another gasp made him look at Melinda again. She was conscious again and was sitting upright. She was panting like a runner at the end of a sprint. Her gaze settled on him and he felt a chill go through him. There was something different about her now. The mad gleam was gone from her eyes. He began to have a vague inkling what had happened and he didn't know whether to feel grateful, horrified, or some mixture of both.

Then her eyes flicked to the right and went wide with shock.

And her mouth opened to emit a piercing scream.

CHAPTER THIRTY-THREE

Hawthorne experienced only a small degree of satisfaction upon realizing the transference spell had been successful. Explanations would be insisted upon, and there simply was no time to supply them. The body formerly inhabited by the consciousness of Erin renewed its efforts to free itself of its remaining bonds. Soon she was able to cast aside the last length of cable, and she stood up and kicked the chair away.

She bared her teeth and growled at him like a rabid dog.

Hawthorne held her gaze and strove to show none of the fear or anxiety he was feeling. His voice was steady as he issued his instructions to her: "You didn't listen to me before. If you wish to survive, you must listen to me now. Your only hope is to leave now through that door and never return." He indicated the shattered rear door with a nod. "Should you decide instead to war with me or to attack these people, I'll have no choice but to eradicate this last vestige of pseudo-life I've allowed you. Go now and meet your fate elsewhere. Or perish now."

The woman made a growling sound again, but something in her demeanor changed subtly and Hawthorne knew his words had penetrated. She was of course furious and full of murderous intent, but she also appeared to sense the truth of what he was saying.

She turned and dashed through the rear door, disappearing into the night. He heard a faint rattling sound and knew she was scaling the chain-link fence that bordered the back yard. Hawthorne, who had more than enough complications to deal with, breathed a sigh of relief.

He retrieved his knife and went to work freeing the men of their bonds. They stood and stretched, working out the kinks in muscle and bone. Both men winced upon gently probing various spots on their heads.

Hawthorne made eye contact with the man who'd contacted the Guardians. "You are Mike O'Bannon." His gaze flicked briefly to the other man. "And you are . . . ?"

"Avery Starke."

The man was staring at the young woman on the floor, who was still in a sitting position. She was examining herself with eyes misty with emotion and wide with disbelief. Aware, at last, of the scrutiny, she looked at each of the men in turn before letting her gaze settle on Hawthorne.

"What the hell did you do to me?"

Hawthorne sighed. In his head, the ticking of a clock toward a still unknown hour of doom continued. He wanted only to secure the book. But he decided to spare a few precious moments for further elucidation. "A simple transference spell. When the specimen is extremely fresh, as was the case here, it is possible to switch souls, or rather that nebulous collection of brain energy composing unique identities. I had only attempted it once before. That time it did not work out. This time it did."

He then became unable to stand the delay any longer. He spun away from their confused expressions and exited the kitchen. A quick process of deduction by way of elimination led him to what was clearly the living room. His breath caught in his throat and his heart seemed to stop for a moment as his eyes found *Invocations of the Reaper*. He swallowed hard as he stared at the ancient cover. He was familiar with the book through secondhand description and knowledge handed down through the ages, but this was the first time he'd set eyes on an actual copy of the book. The Guardians possessed just one of the few remaining copies and that was hidden away in a remote and heavily guarded vault. Eldritch had on occasion dropped hints about the Himalayas, but that could have been careful misdirection. Despite Hawthorne's status as a trusted agent of the organization, he knew the ruling council's faith in him, or in any agent, only went so far. Anyone could potentially surrender to temptation and greed, so secrets were kept. Thus Hawthorne knew he was now the only human being outside of the high council (and the people in this house) to see the book in at least a century.

Setting aside the awe he felt in this moment, he reached into a jacket pocket and withdrew what looked like a folded black garbage bag. He sat before the book and heard the others entering the room. He glanced up to see them gathering around the coffee table. Mike O'Bannon was watching him closely and with great curiosity. The one called Avery only briefly glanced his way. He was too occupied with gaping at the body that now housed a consciousness clearly different in every way from the one it had been home to until just a few moments ago. Like Mike, the girl's attention was solely on Hawthorne, but he could tell her scrutiny had nothing to do with curiosity about the Deathbringer's book. She seemed angry to have been returned to life. Ah, well. There was nothing to be done, save killing her again, and that he would not do.

He unfolded the black square, revealing it to be a two-sided piece of pliable vinyl-like material, with pouches on each side. He slipped the forefingers of both hands into opposite ends of one pouch and stretched it wide. Then he slipped it over the front corner of the book and let the pouch snap shut. Next he flipped the book over and repeated the process with the back cover.

He let out a big sigh and closed his eyes in silent, grateful prayer for a moment. Then he got to his feet and tucked the book under an arm. "I know you're all confused." He met and held the girl's gaze for a long moment. "One of you more so than the rest, perhaps. But you must trust me when I say there is no time to explain. Not now. We must leave this place immediately. Together. The fate of the world depends upon it."

Avery at last looked at him directly. "You're kidding? The fate of the world? How fucking stupid do—"

Hawthorne was grateful when Mike hushed him: "Avery, shut up. I don't know what's going on any more than you, but we're going to trust this man. And we're going to do what he says."

Avery's face twisted in an expression of incredulity and he looked ready to argue further, but Mike silenced him with a glare so severe it might even momentarily have ruffled Eldritch; Hawthorne just managed not to smile.

Mike looked his way again. "What now?"

That was a very good question. How to organize the exodus. He gave it a moment's thought and said, "I suppose it'd be best if we left in one vehicle."

Avery shook his head. "No. No fucking way. I'll go. I'll even follow you, because I don't trust you and mean to be there if Mike needs help. But no way am I riding in the same car as you. I mean, what the fuck are you, some kind of burnout hippie wizard or something?"

The girl spoke up now. "I don't trust him either. I'll ride with Avery."

"Whoa, whoa, whoa." Avery held up a hand and backed away from all of them. "Before I agree to anything like that, I just want one thing straight." He leveled an index finger at the girl. "This . . . this person, used to be a crazy girl, but now she's Erin. Is that right?" He shook his head at the insanity of the idea. "I can't buy that, sorry."

The girl said, "I'm Erin. I dated Mike in college. We used to like to go to the University Center on Fridays and play pool and watch a movie in the Student Union."

A sad smile touched Mike's lips. "Avery, this is Erin. There's no question about it."

Avery's incredulous look slipped considerably. "Well . . ." He sighed. "I guess I'll take your word for it. I still want to know how a crazy thing like that can happen." He looked again at Hawthorne. "And you still didn't answer my question—what are you?"

Hawthorne resisted an impulse to slap the man silent. He was nearly out of patience. "You could call me a wizard, of sorts. I have learned skills most men never learn. But I *am* a man. A human being. But that is all I have time to tell you. Now we leave. Quickly gather what you need and follow me. My car, a Firebird, is parked two houses down. I'll be waiting there for you, Mr. O'Bannon."

And with that he left the living room and passed through the foyer on his way to the front door. He paused with his hand on the doorknob and afforded them a last backward glance. "What I said before wasn't exaggeration. The fate of the world depends on what we do tonight. On whether we have the courage to do what must be done."

There. Let them stew on that for a time.

Then he pulled the door open and stepped into the night.

CHAPTER THIRTY-FOUR

Hannah sensed something wasn't right as soon as she turned down the street leading to her home. Dire knowledge of something askew settled into her bones like a debilitating disease, briefly robbing her of the superhuman strength and energy she'd possessed since her resurrection. The feeling was born of fear. She did not want to disappoint the Deathbringer. There was nothing in the natural world that could frighten or intimidate her. But the thought of facing the Deathbringer's wrath made her go gooey inside, like the way she'd felt at a long ago school dance, when the most handsome boy in her class had asked her to dance with him as Nazareth's "Love Hurts" played over the gymnasium speakers. But there'd been a pleasant side to that feeling, a warm, giddy side. Here there was only stark, stomach-knotting terror.

She experienced an unexpected moment of melancholy at the human memory. The old emotions touched her and even made her eyes mist over. Then primal anger cut through the feeling. She was human no longer and had no time for such weaknesses. The rattling VW bus rolled to a lurching halt outside her home. A police cruiser and a car she didn't recognize, a Neon of indeterminate color in the darkness, were the only vehicles parked outside the house.

She stared at the house and sensed the emptiness. She sat in absolute stillness for a time; then rage contorted her features. She screamed and banged her hands repeatedly against the steering wheel. Then she went still again and stared out the window. There was something here, after all. Not a human presence, but something.

Something nearby.

A whiff of something faintly familiar filled her nostrils. Like everything else, her sense of smell was greatly enhanced. She hadn't yet pinpointed what was familiar about the smell, but it stirred something primal within her. She felt angry without knowing why. Not knowing what else to do just yet, she opened the VW's door and stepped down onto the street.

She scanned the yard and looked to her left and right.

Nothing.

She moved into the yard, continuing to scan the area around her. The VW's door opened again and the dead hippie kids joined her in the yard. She ignored them. They were of no consequence now—they were stupid and easily dealt with if necessary. Her body tensed. Whatever the alien presence was, it was closer now. Every one of her senses was on full alert, straining to discern the slightest indication of where the intruder was.

The smell was stronger now, as was her adverse re-action to it—it was as if her nostrils had been stuffed full of shit.

Then she smiled.

"Erin!" she called, her voice like an explosion in the otherwise silent night. "Come on out and play, you bitch! I'll teach you to keep your hands off my man. You whore. I'm not even a day in the ground, and already you're on the make. Come out, you pa-thetic cunt."

She stood in the middle of the yard and waited, knowing the woman would come. Sometime during the night she'd been killed. And now she was one of the resurrected people. She would be consumed with a thirst for violence. She would not shy away from this conflict.

Hannah ached for her to emerge from the darkness.

Ached to rip her to shreds, limb by fucking limb.

Melinda hunkered down behind a row of shrubberies that lined the front of the house next to the one where Hannah stood calling for Erin. She peered be-tween two of the shrubs and saw the woman she'd killed less than two weeks ago. It was disconcerting to see her back in this place, standing on the front lawn of the house that had been her home, her slice of dream suburbia, before a punk chick with a gun came along and blew the dream to pieces, turning it into a bloodstained nightmare.

Melinda shuddered as she recalled the liberating thrill that had sizzled through her as she'd watched the life blip out of the woman's eyes. She'd never felt so powerful, so like a god. Aside from her ability to manipulate stupid boys—which, after all, was a skill any girl with smarts could learn—she'd never felt very powerful before then. Hers had been a life lived on society's margins. She'd raised herself, basically, surviving to near adulthood despite her worthless mother's near nonexistent ability to provide food and reliable shelter. Realizing that she could decide to snuff out a life if she so chose, like, yes, a god, was the greatest thing that had ever happened to her.

But things had changed.

Death, for one thing, no longer meant what it once had. Before tonight, so Melinda believed, death was the end. Turn out the lights and say good night forever. It wasn't something reversible, something you could come back from, like a fractured limb or a hernia operation. It was the big snuff-out. The endless sleep. And Melinda had never believed in heaven, God, or any form of afterlife beyond existence on this grubby planet. So killing a person meant something. It was a thing no one could reverse. It excited her to think that by slitting a throat and bleeding a person to death she had ultimate control over that person's fate.

Except that now here was irrefutable proof that she'd understood nothing. The dead weren't staying dead. Here was her first victim, reanimated and out for blood. Until just moments ago, she would've considered that the most fucked-up and upsetting thing in her world. But she'd been expelled from her own body, and her consciousness now occupied the body of another of her victims. This constituted a mindfuck of epic proportions. She'd been alive, fully and truly alive, in those moments before that seedy old hippie dude had done his hoodoo magic on her. Then there'd been a blank moment, a moment of seeming nonexistence, and then she'd been back.

But different.

In every messed-up sense of the word. It meant she was dead now, for one thing. A resurrected person. And her new body was some ten years older than the one she'd called home for seventeen years. It wasn't nearly as sleek or as athletic as that young body had been. She recalled finding Erin attractive before, but she felt only repulsion now that the body was her own. It wasn't fat by any means, not by normal standards, but was plumper through the hips and thighs than she'd been used to. The physical differences were annoying enough, but the biggest problem she had with the new body was the big horizontal gash across its throat. The feel of cool air passing through the slit disturbed her, as did the way it felt like a golf ball embedded with tiny metal spikes was sliding down her gullet every time she had to swallow. Killing Erin had been fun, but now she was thinking she'd been a tad too hasty.

She snorted. *Fucking hindsight.*

In the yard next door, Hannah heard the sound and her head snapped to the right. Melinda sat very still as she watched the other woman's gaze slowly sweep the yard before going to the line of shrubberies. Then her head stopped turning and she could feel Hannah's gaze burning through the darkness.

Hannah smiled. "Peek-a-boo, I see you."

Melinda shuddered.

Dealing with this bitch wouldn't be easy. Even Melinda, who had only the vaguest inkling as to the reasons behind the rise of the dead, knew enough to discern that there was something that separated Hannah from the rest of the resurrected people. She was stronger, faster, and smarter than any of them. But Melinda wasn't afraid. She was surprised to realize she actually relished the prospect of the imminent conflict.

She stood up and pushed through the bushes to stand in the yard next to Hannah's home. "Hello, Hannah."

Hannah snarled. "You sound like you've been gargling with battery acid." Then the snarl became a leering smile. "Whoever killed you damn near took your head off, I see." She began to walk in Melinda's direction. "But I'm glad you're more or less intact. I'm gonna finish the job myself."

She crossed the green strip of yard that separated the two driveways and was less than ten yards from her quarry when Melinda chose to say something that brought her to an immediate, surprised halt.

"On your knees, bitch!"

The ragged voice that emerged from her body's torn throat was very different from the one that had issued the command to Hannah the first time, but the cadence was the same. The curled lip, demented Elvis sneer was the same. Hannah drew in an audibly astonished breath. At least for a moment, she no longer seemed so intimidating. Indeed, for one shining moment she looked every bit as terrified and helpless as she had that glorious afternoon flat on her back in her kitchen.

Melinda smiled. She raised a hand and curled in the bottom three fingers, pointing the forefinger like the barrel of a gun. "Look at me, bitch."

A few moments went by before Hannah remembered to breathe. Her eyes narrowed to slits and she studied Melinda's eyes for a time. She frowned, apparently detecting something inexplicable there.

Hannah's mouth opened. "You . . ." Then she shook her head. "No. It can't be. You didn't kill me. I remember that sneaky, snotty little cunt. A fucking teenager. A skinny skank." Her brow crinkled and she took another tentative step forward. "Unless . . . you bitch."

Melinda chuckled. "Unless what?"

A low rumble issued from the back of Hannah's throat, like the warning growl of a Rottweiler defending its territory. She moved another slow step toward Melinda. And yet another. Her head down in the posture of that same agitated guard dog.

Her voice was low and gritty and something about it was suggestive of the ticking of a time bomb. She was going to explode—the only question was when. "Goddamn you. I've killed a bunch of people tonight, Erin. But I've got an excuse. Some weird black magic resurrected me and turned me into a bloodthirsty monster." She said the last word with some difficulty. "But you . . . well, you were just a soulless psycho all along, weren't you? You never could stand that Mike moved on with his life instead of pining over you. So you obsessed over it. And you paid that little girl to kill me."

Melinda didn't realize she was retreating until her right foot went into a grass-covered hole, causing her to lose her balance and topple backward. Her rear end hit the ground hard and the force of impact caused her torso to snap backward, hitting the back of her head on a rock. A gash opened there and blood soiled the ground. Her vision blurred and the pain rendered thinking impossible for a moment. When she could see again, Hannah was standing over her. Melinda went still and stared up at her, struck by the strange reversal. Ten days ago she'd stood over Hannah the way the woman was standing over her now, and she felt at least an echo of the way Hannah must have felt then. She was afraid. But she also knew she wasn't as helpless as Hannah had been then.

But Hannah acted with shocking swiftness, shifting position and driving the heel of a shoe into Melinda's shredded throat. The pressure there was immense and increased exponentially by the moment. The pain was astonishing. Her throat was being crushed. She grabbed at Hannah's leg, digging her unnaturally strong fingers into toned calf muscle as she worked to dislodge the devastating weight. She tore open fabric and pushed sharp nails through flesh, eliciting a howl from her tormentor.

Still Hannah didn't budge. She pressed her foot down harder, and harder still, grunting like a woman straining to win a tug-of-war. There was a crunching sound as something gave way and Melinda would have screamed had she been capable of doing so. Hannah's determined sneer gave way to a grin as she realized the tide was turning in her favor, and she started moving her foot in a grinding motion that resulted in more sounds of crunching and ripping.

Then Melinda knew something fundamental had changed. She felt different. Less complete. Hannah ceased working at her throat and knelt next to her. That horrible grin mocked her, made her want to get up and run far away. But then Hannah was reaching out to her; was, it appeared, moving to stroke her hair and comfort her. A false perception, as it turned out.

Hannah gripped a handful of Melinda's hair and

lifted her severed head off the ground. She lifted her arm to its fullest extension and grinned at her trophy. Melinda felt drugged now, as if she were seeing everything through a marijuana haze. Only that high was usually more pleasant than this hopeless, gray feeling.

She saw her body lying on the ground. Erin's body, she remembered. It'd never truly belonged to her. The now ruined shell had just been a spiritual weigh station of sorts, a temporary place to hang out on the way to somewhere else. It was still animated and was trying to get to its feet. Melinda hoped it would get up and rip Hannah's shining-with-madness eyeballs out of her head. But a fresh dose of despair followed this thought. She knew Hannah was too strong. Too special. As she always had been. And just when she believed she could feel no worse, a disturbing thought occurred to her, the possibility that this was some grisly brand of divine retribution. Which, of course, caused her to think of her lifelong denial of things divine or spiritual. What if she'd been wrong all along? What if there were other places beyond this world?

If hell is real, she thought, *how could I not wind up there?*

Had she been capable of it, she might have cried.

And just when she imagined the worst was over, Hannah revealed that this was not the case. She lowered her arm and smiled at Melinda's slack, drooling features. She cooed to the head as she would to a crying baby.

"Guess what, sweetie? Hannah's hungry again."

She cackled.

Melinda managed to slowly open her mouth in a

silent scream as she felt Hannah's finger push into her eye socket. The scream that was not would have become a tortured wail in the next moment, when she felt the woman's finger curl around the stalk of her right eye. She felt the stalk stretch and snap as the eye came out of the socket with a wet plop.

Her remaining eye watched in abject, despairing horror as Hannah popped the eye into her mouth and slowly chewed it, clearly savoring the taste and feel of the orb. Then Hannah's throat expanded as the masticated tissue passed through it.

Hannah belched.

And Melinda experienced a sense of gratitude as she felt the woman's finger pushing into her left eye socket. At least now she would see no more of the horror surrounding her. Her time of misery, mercifully, was at an end. Then the world went dark and she heard Hannah chewing again.

It's over, she thought. *It's finally over.*

But it wasn't.

She heard Hannah swallow again, and belch again—and then the awful woman took her head in both hands and began to squeeze. *This* pain, the agony caused by the crushing of her skull and the compression of her brain, *this* was the worst pain she'd ever experienced.

And it went on for quite a while.

Hannah tossed aside the pulped head of her adversary and lifted her nose to analyze the various scents swirling in the air, specifically those generated by the live human beings who'd fled this place moments before her arrival. Two were instantly familiar and unsurprising. These were the scents her sharpened sense of smell identified as uniquely associated with Mike and her brother, Avery. A third scent was completely unfamiliar, but something about it was suggestive of an older male. The remaining scent trace was familiar, and when she identified it, her rage was stoked anew, and driven to a level even beyond what she'd experienced while grinding Erin's throat to dust beneath her heel.

She turned and walked to the edge of the street, sniffing at the air like a police dog on the trail of escaped criminals. She faced east and drew in a lungful of air through her nostrils. The pungent scent of her killer filled her like a deadly gas and she expelled the breath quickly.

She stared down the empty street and whispered, "Molly."

Then she ran back to the VW bus, climbed inside, and slid in behind the steering wheel. She turned the key in the ignition and heard a grinding noise. She screamed in frustration and banged the steering wheel with the base of a fist.

She went still.

Something was coming.

Her eyes flicked left and saw twin points of light approaching from the rear. Grinning, she got out of the VW and stood in the middle of the street. The car, an ugly beige Oldsmobile nearly as old as she was, came to a slow, shuddering stop, and its elderly male driver poked his head through an open window.

"Please get out of the road, young lady."

Hannah smiled. "Okay."

She then moved so fast she must have looked like a fast-forwarded image on a videotape or disc. There was no time for the old duffer to react. One moment

Hannah was blocking his way. The next she was next to the car, reaching through the open window and pulling him out.

She snapped the man's neck and tossed him aside.

Then, stationed behind the big old steering wheel, she put the musty-smelling car in gear and drove off to face her destiny.

CHAPTER THIRTY-FIVE

The Deathbringer touched Hannah's mind. In a diluted way, because she was the Prime, he could feel what she felt, see what she saw. He wished the connection was stronger, so that he might know precisely what had transpired, but what he was able to detect was worrisome. The book had eluded her grasp, a serious setback. In order to complete the invocation circle and weave the delicate magic necessary to accomplish his goals, it was imperative that the Prime reclaim the book from the reader of the original invocation. And only by closing the invocation circle could the dark magic currently wreaking such havoc throughout Dandridge be made powerful enough to send into the wider world.

As troubling as this was, the Deathbringer still felt certain his goals would be accomplished. The Prime had resumed her pursuit of the book. She would be relentless in her quest. She would recover the book.

Then she would meet with the Deathbringer at the appointed place at the appointed hour. At which the final reading from the book, the last Invocation to Conflict, would occur.

And humanity's death knell would begin to toll.

The Deathbringer walked slowly down the wide aisle of the auditorium, occasionally glancing left and right at the rows of seats filled by his people, his devoted acolytes, the resurrected people of Dandridge. They regarded him with the same reverence projected by devout Catholics in the presence of the Pope.

The adoration felt good. And it felt very strange. For centuries he'd existed as a lone, isolated entity, by necessity a creature of darkness and the shadows. Invisibility had been an integral part of his role in the scheme of things. He was one of the things children spoke of in whispers around summer campfires. He was the thing in the closet or under the bed, the thing that went bump in the night.

The bogeyman.

But that shadow existence was ending. As was the monolithic tyranny of the High Council of Reapers. Soon he and those like him would be free to emerge from darkness and hiding and hold sway over a world cleansed of the taint of humanity—and liberated from the yoke of the ruling power, from "God." He suspected a percentage of Reapers would resist and would fight to preserve the old, comfortable order. But he was certain a larger contingent would delight in the obvious turning of the tide and join him in his rebellion. But, always, no matter who adopted his cause, *he* would always be the movement's leader. The new God, one could say.

He crossed the floor in front of the stage, climbed

a short set of steps, and mounted the stage. He walked to the podium and stood with his head positioned behind a microphone, like a politician about to address an assembly.

But he would not speak to these people.

Not yet.

Not until after the Prime had recited the Invocation to Conflict. His thin, wormlike lips formed a slippery smile at the prospect, knowing his words would be the most inspirational any of these wretched creatures had ever heard.

He stood at the podium and observed the utterly silent congregation for a time, basking in the glow from the sea of rapturous smiles on the upturned faces of the resurrected people. He wondered if this was how Jesus had felt in the presence of true believers.

The thought was driven from his mind when the auditorium's front doors banged open and two resurrected people, big men in orange jumpsuits who'd been incarcerated at the local jail until earlier in the evening, entered with a screaming live woman. The female flailed and kicked at their legs, but the men were impervious to the blows. The resurrected people turned in their seats to study the source of the commotion. Some of them recognized the screaming woman. She was a forty-year-old hair stylist named Janine with big blond hair. Her captors steered her down the aisle, eventually having to drag her as she made herself go limp.

They reached the open floor area between the front row of seats and the stage and released her, depositing her in a heap near the stage. The men stepped back and the woman surged to her feet. Her body language indicated imminent flight, then her gaze happened upon the pale, angular wedge of face visible beneath the Deathbringer's tilted hat. She fell to her knees and stared helplessly up at him, her hands clasped in supplication.

The Deathbringer smiled again. "You insignificant thing. Your life has meant nothing until this point. But no more. You have a great role to play in the coming change." He lifted his arms and indicated the gathered crowd. "The world is being remade in our image. You will help it happen."

Tears leaked from the crinkled corners of the woman's bloodshot eyes.

The Deathbringer chuckled. "Yes. Your blood will fuel the Invocation to Conflict. Your death will help usher in the new age."

The woman shuddered and dropped her gaze. She wept silently.

The Deathbringer's gray, putrescent tongue emerged from the blackness of his mouth to slowly lick his upper lip.

He could taste it all now.

The blood.

The carnage.

The death.

And, most clearly, the glorious *change*.

CHAPTER THIRTY-SIX

Erin sat slumped in the passenger seat of Avery's Mustang, glumly watching the taillights of the strange old man's Firebird blink as its brake pedal was tapped. The car ahead of them slowed as they drove past a big Baptist church, and for a moment she was certain this was their destination. How fitting that would be, to have the big, final Good vs. Evil smackdown in a supposedly holy place.

But the Firebird accelerated and drove past the building and its vacant parking lot. She sighed and shook her head. "Where the hell are we going?"

Avery shrugged. "Like I know? We're just supposed to follow the guy. I get the feeling he's not even sure where he needs to go." He nodded. "Yeah, see, there go his taillights again. It's like he's looking for something, but he's not sure what."

Erin's laugh was devoid of humor. "Well, I don't know about you, but I'm so glad we've placed our fate in the hands of someone as whacked-out as that dude. So, okay, he's got some serious magic at his disposal." She grunted, and indicated her new body with a disgusted sweep of a hand. "Check me out, for instance. But he's like a cross between Timothy Leary and an old Indian medicine man. Which doesn't give me a lot of faith in his ability to save our asses."

Avery made a contemplative sound. Then he said, "You're right. But I can't think of too many other viable courses of action. In fact, I can't think of any at all."

Erin groaned. "So we're screwed."

"Unless this guy pulls some wild miracle out of his hat, then, yeah, I guess we are."

Erin sighed. She'd made the Timothy Leary reference for a reason. Everything that had happened tonight had a hallucinogenic quality, wilder by far than anything she'd experienced the two times she'd tried LSD, the drug popularized by the old acid guru and his counterculture cronies so long ago. The various encounters with resurrected dead had been bad enough, but this body switch was far too much of a mind-fuck.

She didn't miss the way she'd felt during her brief time as a resurrected person. Her humanity had deserted her. Though much of her rage and bloodthirst had been focused on Melinda, she'd known she wouldn't hesitate to eviscerate either Avery or Mike. She was grateful to be alive again, to have a human conscience again, but the knowledge that she'd have to spend the remainder of her life in a body formerly occupied by Hannah's killer sickened her. It was just so weird, and so wrong. The very worst part of the whole bizarre experience, however, was the quiet knowledge that another, more primal part of her, a part tucked away in the remotest reptilian recesses of her brain, was *glad* the switch had occurred.

She glanced down and studied her slim new body again. It was as if she'd taken her clunky old Neon down to a car dealership and traded it in for a sleek new luxury car. A Jaguar or a Lexus. And now that the body was her own, she had to admit that the long, shapely legs looked pretty hot encased in the black fishnets.

I'd fuck me, she thought, and was unable to stifle a nervous laugh. Frowning, Avery glanced at her. "You okay?"

Erin flashed a smile intended to be reassuring. "I'm fine. Just . . . scared."

Avery sighed and shifted his attention back to the Firebird, which was accelerating again after yet another aborted stop. "Fucking ditto. Scared shitless."

Erin continued to look at him, remembering the sexual tension she'd sensed between Avery and Melinda. It must be weird for him now, having the same body close to him and yet knowing it was off limits now. She felt bad for him. It was clear he was having a hard time not looking at her, even knowing, as he did now, that the body's former occupant had killed his beloved sister. She wished now she'd taken the time to change into more modest clothes before leaving Mike's place, but Hawthorne had insisted there was no time for anything other than gathering weapons and getting out.

Avery looked at her. "I think we're really stopping now."

The Mustang slowed as the Firebird drew to a stop near the town square. The Firebird's taillights flashed, then went dark. The car's doors opened and Hawthorne and Mike stepped out.

Avery steered the Mustang to a stop behind it and wrenched the gearshift into park.

He drew in a big breath, expelled it, and arched an eyebrow at Erin. "You ready for this?"

"No. But let's do it anyway."

Avery nodded. "Yeah."

They got out of the car.

Chapter Thirty-seven

Mike looked up and down Main Street, unable at first to pinpoint what was troubling him. The back of his neck tingled. He felt like he was being watched. But, aside from himself and his companions, there was no evidence of human activity in the vicinity. Still, something was off. Then he did note something peculiar—an unusual abundance of parked cars lining both sides of the street. Normally there would only be a few cars, if any, parked here at this late hour. But tonight there were dozens.

He looked at Hawthorne over the roof of the Firebird. "These cars . . ."

Hawthorne nodded. "There is a gathering nearby. The Rogue is readying his forces, preparing for the Invocation to Conflict." His gaze ranged over the green expanse of the square itself, lingering first at the gazebo and adjacent bandstand, then moving to the large cascading water fountain at the center of the square. Beyond that, at the far edge of the square, stood city hall, and next to it the town meeting hall.

Hawthorne's gaze came back to Mike. "You have to realize something before we proceed, Mr. O'Bannon. Your town is beyond saving. Much of the populace, perhaps most of it, has already been sacrificed to advance the Rogue's cause. And most of those still alive will be dead before sunrise."

Mike frowned. "You paint a grim picture."

Hawthorne sighed. "It is more than a picture. It's how things are. And know this as well—we are all, you and I . . . ," he included Avery and Erin with a nod at the slowing Mustang, "all of us . . . doomed. We'll likely be dead very soon. But you must believe me when I say that our lives are worth sacrificing if we defeat the Rogue."

The prospect of imminent death instilled no fear in Mike. If he somehow survived, he'd still be facing a bleak future without his beloved Hannah, and that, as far as he was concerned, was as bad as death. Maybe worse. He held Hawthorne's gaze and dropped his voice to a whisper as the Mustang's engine shut off and its doors creaked open. "I understand that. I accept it. But my friends may not."

A subtle shift of his features conveyed Hawthorne's understanding.

He nodded.

The Mustang's doors thunked shut and Avery and Erin joined them curbside. Mike saw Avery's brow furrow as his gaze roved the length of the street, knowing the man's thoughts mirrored his own of a few moments ago.

Avery looked at him. "Weird. All these cars, no people. Where's the party? And why weren't we invited?"

Hawthorne's throat produced a sound somewhere between grunt and humorless laugh. "Oh, we've been invited. In a way. Not only that, but we are the guests of honor."

Avery smirked. "Yeah. If you've got a really fucked notion of the meanings of words like 'honor' and 'guests.'"

Erin coughed loudly in a pointed way. The men looked at her. "Fine. So we're here. Something big's about to happen." And now she did as the others had done, studying the empty street and rows of parked cars before again addressing Mike and Hawthorne. "A child could figure that out. But how do we stop it?"

Hawthorne's thin-lipped smile was enigmatic. Mike had tried again and again to get the man to answer the same question on the ride here. And again he didn't reply. Not verbally, that is. Not at first. Instead, he reached into an inner pocket of his jacket and removed a slim cylindrical object the color of polished nickel. It was perhaps eight inches long and approximately as thick as the average ink-pen. But its pointed tip looked sharper and more lethal than an ice pick.

He held it up for all to see clearly, turning it slowly in his fingers, like a cheerleader wielding a miniature baton. "With this," the older man said, his tone one of hushed reverence. "A most sacred artifact, a gift from the world's oldest living shaman."

Avery, Erin, and Mike exchanged confused and skeptical glances.

Avery grunted. "I think you got ripped off, dude. I could get you a whole bag of those from Office Depot for a buck-fifty."

Erin jabbed him with an elbow. "Hush." She

looked at Hawthorne. "How is that . . . whatever it is . . . supposed to work?"

Hawthorne shifted his fingers, gripping the blunt rear end of the object the way he would a kitchen utensil. Then he jabbed it at the air—a brutal thrust that made Mike's eyes blink more rapidly for a while. He could imagine the sharpened end penetrating flesh to skewer the heart of an ordinary man. But their adversary was not an ordinary man. If Mike understood what little Hawthorne had told him of the Rogue—and he believed he did—their quarry tonight was something like the mythical Grim Reaper, a supernatural being who harvested the souls (or "life energy," as Hawthorne insisted on calling it) of dying men and women.

He stroked his chin and sighed. "I've got to admit to some skepticism, too. I wouldn't want you poking me with that thing, but we're facing a thing you tell me is immortal, and which has the power to kill with a touch. If that's our secret weapon, I'm afraid I'm underwhelmed."

Hawthorne smiled. "Of course." He allowed them another moment to study the object, then returned it to his jacket pocket. "What you must do now is ignore the testimony of your eyes and trust in what I am about to tell you. What looks to you like an insignificant sliver of metal is much more than that. Forged in ancient fires, it is invested with a magic so powerful as to be toxic when administered in just the right way to creatures like the Rogue."

Mike grunted. "Magic. I should have known it'd be something to do with magic. We've got to succeed tonight, if only to force reality to revert to its usual rules." He waved the bloody axe clutched in his right hand. "I understand the cutting force of a blade. I understand the destructive power of a bullet. These are concrete, real world things. Magic is . . . fairy-tale stuff."

Avery laughed. "Some fucked-up fairy tale this is turning out to be."

Mike's brow furrowed. "Hold on . . . what do you mean, 'administered in just the right way'?"

Hawthorne's expression turned grim. "I mean that I have to get close enough to the Rogue to plunge the Finger of Odin through his black heart, while you read the Rites of Closure from *Invocations of the Reaper*."

Mike laughed and shook his head. "Wait, wait, wait. Let me see if I understand this correctly. While you're confronting the bad guy, I'll be . . . *reading?*"

Hawthorne nodded. "You will."

Erin said, "Is it because Mike read the spell that started all this?"

Hawthorne's smile made Mike think of a professor expressing pleasure in a particularly bright student's ability to deduce what everyone else had missed. "Yes, except that the Resurrection Invocation wasn't the true beginning of your town's season in hell. The Rogue had set things in motion before that."

Mike had an inkling of what he meant. He spoke through clenched teeth: "Hannah." Tears stung the corners of his eyes. "It started with Hannah."

Hawthorne's eyes reflected a deep inner sadness. "I'm afraid so."

Avery's face twisted in confusion. "What? How could that be?" His tone was different now. Gone was the sniping edge of the cynic. Grief and anger burned through in every word. "Are you saying the son of a bitch killed my sister?"

Hawthorne said, "The girl killed your sister. But the Rogue planted the seed. It was a simple matter to spark murderous rage in a vulnerable soul. He needed a victim and a grieving lover to read the invocation. He needed a Prime."

Mike seethed. He chewed his lower lip. "And Hannah's the Prime. What does that mean, exactly?"

Hawthorne hesitated a moment. Then he looked Mike in the eye and released a big breath. "In order to cause a mass resurrection of recent dead, the Prime first had to be successfully restored to life."

Mike felt something cold close around his heart. A sense of all-consuming dread descended. "Hannah's . . . alive?"

Hawthorne held his gaze. "In a sense. But she is not really the woman you knew. She exists now to serve the Rogue's dark schemes. She is as bloodthirsty and brutal as any of the resurrected people you've encountered tonight. In fact, she is far worse. The Prime becomes a sort of super . . . zombie, is the word you'd use. And I told a lie by omission a moment ago. You do have one more role to play in this drama, Mike O'Bannon."

A piercing coldness now pushed into Mike's heart. He could feel the last vestiges of hope, the last traces of warmth, draining from his soul. He swallowed hard and shook his head. Hawthorne's grizzled face blurred in a fresh welling of tears. "No. . . ."

Hawthorne at last looked away. His gaze went now to the town meeting hall on the opposite side of the square. "Yes. You have to kill her, Mr. O'Bannon.

That's how the circle closes for good. The elimination of the Prime. A task that must be performed by the reader of the original Invocation. Only then will the resurrected people of Dandridge be able to rest."

"Shit." Avery made a sound of disgust. "That's so fucking wrong. What kind of sick bastards came up with all this complicated hoodoo crap?"

Hawthorne's gaze was still locked on the meeting hall. "Time is short. We cannot hesitate. Set emotions aside for the greater good. The fate of the world and all that. But to answer your question . . ." And now he did look at Avery. Pain was etched in the lines of the man's face. "The dark magic contained in *Invocations of the Reaper* was conceived by a society of disgruntled Reapers many centuries ago. But none ever had the temerity to use it. Doing so would've constituted a direct challenge to the authority of God."

Avery shook his head. "Damn. This . . . Rogue . . . he must have some big-time set of cajones."

Hawthorne shook his head. "No. He is just insane."

"I can't kill Hannah." Mike made a despairing sound. "If she has to die again, someone else has got to do it. You can't ask me to kill the love of my life. That's just not fair."

"Fair has nothing to do with it, Mr. O'Bannon," Hawthorne said in a voice with an edge so sharp it made everyone else wince. "You *will* kill her. If anyone else does it, the resurrected people will not rest. I thought I'd made that clear. Enough of this chatter. We have work to do. I believe we'll find our quarry in that building there. I feel him, his presence."

And with that he set off across the street toward the town square.

Mike stared at the ground while Erin and Avery

exchanged troubled glances. The thought of killing Hannah—of taking off her head with his axe—filled him with the same kind of yawning hopelessness he'd felt in the first days after Hannah's murder. He really didn't think he could do it, regardless of the consequences. Until he thought of something that disturbed him even more than the prospect of the heinous duty assigned him by Hawthorne.

Avery cleared his throat. "Look . . . Mike . . . we don't have to do this. We don't know this guy. We've only got his word that any of this crazy shit is real. We could all just drive the hell away from here."

Mike looked at him. "No. The Hannah I knew, the one I loved with all my heart, wouldn't want to go on this way. She was a good person. . . ." His voice quavered a moment, but he quickly recovered and carried on. "She wouldn't want to hurt people, or cause anyone pain. She would hate to know she'd become a . . . monster." He needed another moment to steel himself yet again. "And regardless of what I think of that man"—he nodded in the direction of Hawthorne's receding back—"I believe him. Not because he's offered any proof. He hasn't. But I feel the truth of what he says in my bones."

There was a moment of heavy silence.

Then, very quietly, Erin said, "So do I."

Avery sighed. "Goddammit. Yeah, I guess I do, too. So let's get on with this."

Then, like a squad of soldiers en route to the front line of a battle, they crossed the street and hurried to catch up to their new leader.

CHAPTER THIRTY-EIGHT

Hannah spun the wheel of the Oldsmobile and its tires squealed as it went into a whiplash-inducing turn. The car's fishtailing rear end clipped the side of a parked Lexus, denting the door and shearing off a side mirror. The impact served to set her back on a more or less straight path down Main Street. She saw the town square coming up a few blocks to the left and knew her journey was almost at an end.

Then something familiar caught her eye, snapping her gaze to the right. She frowned at the unmistakable sight of her brother's vintage Mustang. The Grateful Dead stickers on the rear windshield left no room for doubt. She wondered what Avery was doing here, and was surprised to feel a slight ripple of sadness as it occurred to her how likely it was that she'd have to kill him sometime within the next few minutes. He was with Mike, the other man, and Molly, and they were in possession of the dark man's book.

She shook the feeling off. She knew the echo of emotion was only a kind of psychic residue. It would not deter her from doing what needed doing. Not wishing her quarry to know that she was on their trail yet, she drove two blocks past the square before parking in the middle of the street. Then she got out of the car and stood on the warm pavement for a moment and sniffed at the air.

Her gaze then went to the town meeting hall, which was partially obscured from this vantage point by a small grouping of trees.

She smiled. "Time to play."

She crossed to the other side of the street, walked the two blocks to the square, and stood on a sidewalk beneath a sodium lamp, listening to its soft buzzing and the fluttering of insects flitting about the bright globe. She closed her eyes and strove to make out other sounds and smells.

Her eyes snapped open. She peered into the darkness and could just make out the backs of four people nearing the other side of the square. She feared none of them, and was confident in her ability to take on all four at once, but she could feel the dark man's presence in her brain again, urging her to proceed with caution. And so she would—at least for now.

She moved onto a patch of green grass and ducked behind the gazebo. She was far enough away to be reasonably sure the humans couldn't hear her, but she didn't want one of them looking back suddenly and seeing her before she was ready for that to happen. So she watched them creep up to one of the hall's lit windows and peer inside, and she felt the sudden wave of unease that rolled off them all a moment later.

Hannah recalled her brief glimpse of the dark man's growing army of resurrected dead earlier in the evening. Surely it had swelled to several times that size since then. How hopeless they must feel looking at the force opposing them. Again, she experienced a tiny flutter of empathy, and again it evaporated like a tiny drop of dew beneath the blazing summer sun.

She watched them move to the side of the building. She tensed, knowing she would have to act soon, but not knowing precisely what she needed to do.

Then the dark man spoke in her head: "Go. Melt into the shadows along the edge of the square. They will not see you until it is too late. Get the book and kill your man. Bring the book to me. Your work is almost done."

Hannah did as bade, moving to the tree-lined far left edge of the square. She kicked her shoes off and moved lightly over soft grass. The shapes huddled against the side of the building grew more distinct. When she was less than fifty yards away, her sharpened vision was able to make them out perfectly. She seethed at the sight of Molly with her brother and Mike. Nothing about the body language or scents suggested they were uncomfortable in the girl's presence. Either they didn't know the girl was her murderer, or . . . no, that just couldn't be.

An echo of the girl's voice resonated in her mind: ". . . *Because it's fun. Because they dared me to . . .*"

Molly's enigmatic reply to Hannah's demand to know why the girl was about to kill her. Hannah hadn't had much time to ponder the question of who "they" had been. But the girl's presence here certainly suggested some things.

Things that made her angrier than ever. A part of

her rebelled at the thought that Mike had put Molly up to killing her. Hannah and Mike had been so much in love, surely he wouldn't have been carrying on a sleazy clandestine affair with Molly at the same time Hannah had been busy making their wedding plans. But a more pragmatic side of her knew that such things had been known to happen. Seemingly respectable men in picture-perfect lives had affairs with younger women all the time. Some of them even grew so attached to their mistresses that they were driven to kill (or have killed) the women they were married or engaged to. How many cases like that had she followed on the news over the years?

Too many to fucking count, that's how many.

Soon she neared the end of the line of trees bordering the side of the square. She remained standing in shadow a little while longer. The moment still wasn't quite right yet. Less than thirty yards from where she stood, the meddlesome quartet of doomed humans argued about how to proceed.

Hannah smiled.

In a moment she would come forward out of the shadows and provide the final answers to all their questions.

CHAPTER THIRTY-NINE

Avery heard voices buzzing around him like bees, but he failed to detect any meaning in their words. The sight of the town hall filled to bursting with so many of his fellow townsfolk had stunned him into near insensibility. He felt drugged, like he was mired in an acid-induced hallucination. And he had a feeling this perception was shared by many tonight. He yearned to wake up and discover that none of this insanity, including Hannah's murder, had actually happened, that, instead of being reality or drug-fueled hallucination, it had just been a really bad dream, perhaps sparked by too much booze and bad food.

He'd listened to Hawthorne's quick history of Reapers and Guardians as they'd crossed the square and had felt nothing but skepticism. At best. But now, even without glimpsing that creature, Avery felt its presence, too. It was as undeniable as a force of nature, like a blast of winter wind or the whirling, sucking force of a twister.

This acceptance caused him to snap back to the moment, to the reality of the enormous and nigh-fucking-impossible thing he and this small group of people were about to attempt.

A snippet of words acquired meaning and blared in his consciousness like a voice screeching through a bullhorn: ". . . There's no evidence of guards anywhere, so there's no reason to enter anywhere other than the rear entrance. The closer we can be to the Rogue when we get inside, the better. Otherwise we'll never have a chance to perform these so-called Rites of Closure. Which are too damned complicated, by the way. No way we'll have time to get it done before they take us down."

The speaker was Mike. Avery looked at him and opened his mouth to say something, but Hawthorne cut him off. "The Rites are very specific and can only be performed the way I've described. And we must succeed, otherwise the human race will be extinct within weeks."

This time Avery spoke up before anyone could voice yet another retort. "There aren't any guards because they're not trying to keep us out. And Mike's right. I don't care how determined you are. We can't win." He indicated the meeting hall with a wave of his hand. "Not with the whole goddamned town on that fucker's side." He looked at Hawthorne. "Assuming everything you've said is true, they're expecting us. Not only that, they want us here." He nodded at the vinyl-covered book clutched tightly by the older man. "They want that thing, and we've delivered it to them. We're so dead it's not even fuckin' funny."

He expected the old hippie (or shaman, or wizard, or whatever the hell he really was) to scoff and immediately reject his concerns, but the man said nothing for a while. He frowned and appeared to be mulling over what Avery had said. Avery felt a flush of triumph at that, but the feeling was tempered by a darker implication—that his protest had instilled real doubt in the man. Regardless of the terror he felt at the prospect of following through on Hawthorne's plan, instinct told him confrontation now would at least be better than turning tail and fleeing into the night. They might die here tonight, but wouldn't that be better than to run and die a coward's death a few weeks later?

Erin spoke up first. "My God, we've been so stupid. Avery's right. It's so obvious. They've known we were coming all along, and we've walked right into their trap." Her eyes went wide and flicked from Avery to Hawthorne to Mike, and back again. She moved a step backward, clearly anxious to put some distance between herself and the meeting hall. "We've got to get out of here."

Neither Hawthorne nor Mike said anything, but they didn't budge. Hawthorne's resolve clearly hadn't wavered, after all. And Mike, despite his concerns, just as clearly meant to see this thing through.

So Erin's panicked gaze locked on Avery. "Please, you've got to make them understand. They'll be committing suicide."

Avery sighed. "And I'll be standing with them." He shook his head and made a sound of disgust. "I hate it, but it's really the only way."

Erin's shiny gaze went back to the meeting hall and the expression that crossed her face then made Avery think of a lone solider peeking out of a foxhole to see a huge, advancing regiment of enemy troops. The renewed surge of fear drove her back another step or two, and Avery decided to do something about it before it overwhelmed her.

He held out a hand and moved toward her, meaning to draw her into a comforting embrace, but before he could reach her he saw a white shape emerge from the darkness and bear down on Erin like a racehorse thundering down a track. What Avery did next occurred out of pure instinct. He moved to intercede, placing himself between Erin and the oncoming threat in the last moment possible.

Before he recognized the shape, his instincts again told him something true—that those were the last moments of his life. He'd put himself in the way of death—a force as unstoppable as a runaway freight train. And just before that moment of impact, the shape's face became clear in the darkness and he welcomed his dead sister with open arms, knowing this was his fate, that this had always been his true role in the scheme of things. He wrapped his arms around her as she struck him and bore him to the ground. And as her teeth entered his flesh and drew blood, he smiled and whispered a last endearment in her ear: "*I love you, Hannah.*"

He heard a scream (Erin?) and the shouts of the men.

Then these sounds receded and everything went gray. Avery's last blurred view of the world was his sister's blood-smeared face seconds after ripping his throat out. Maybe it was only illusion, but he thought he saw tears in her eyes.

Then he was gone.

And when he woke up a moment later, he was different. He got to his feet and hurried to join his sister. The smell of warm human blood made him salivate as he ran faster than he ever had in life, even as a kid running through fields in summer.

The tears that came to his eyes then did nothing to alleviate the screaming thirst that consumed him.

CHAPTER FORTY

Mike somehow managed to remain upright and focused on his dwindling group's goals. This was a pure miracle, by his reckoning. He'd seen his dead fiancée come out of the darkness like a bullet fired from a gun. Only moments ago the possibility of seeing her again, even in reanimated form, had filled him with conflicted feelings. But no more. The thing inhabiting her body was not his fiancée. Not really. Or if there was something remaining of the woman he'd known, the dark magic at work tonight had perverted it, twisting it beyond recognition. The Hannah-thing was more like a savage, or even a rabid animal, than a human female. The way she'd taken Avery down like a tigress tackling prey on an African plain would haunt him the rest of his days—assuming, of course, he had days remaining beyond this one.

They rounded the building and stood panting under an awning at its rear entrance. Mike noticed something curious—the back door, which looked to be of the sort that would automatically lock upon being shut, had been propped open with a cinder block. Like the front of the building, the rear entrance was unguarded. These things did nothing to quell the unease within him. If anything, they served as confirmation of everything Avery had said prior to stepping between Hannah and Erin.

And just thinking of that sent a disquieting pang through Mike. He hadn't known the man once slated to become his brother-in-law very well, but he wouldn't have imagined the man capable of so singular an act of bravery. So now he felt as though he'd slighted Avery in some unspoken way. But he shook the feeling off. There would be time for emotions—and regrets—later, if they survived.

He looked at Hawthorne, who was moving cautiously toward the open door. "She'll be back here soon. In seconds, maybe. There anything else you need to tell us before we charge in there?"

Hawthorne glanced back at him. "Be very careful."

Mike's anxiety level soared again, now that the moment of truth was at hand. "I still don't see how I can read the Rites of Closure *and* manage to kill that thing pretending to be my wife. Can't Erin do the reading?"

Hawthorne shook his head. "No."

And then he slipped through the open doorway and was swallowed by darkness. Mike looked at Erin and saw the fear burning in her eyes. It was so strange to look into these strange eyes and see Erin there, but he did, plain as day. He was afraid for a number of very good reasons, but he was especially afraid for her. She had no role to play in this drama.

He made a silent vow then to do whatever he could to keep her safe, even at the risk of making a mess of Hawthorne's precious rituals. He reached for her hand and she allowed him to take it. It was good to feel this simple human warmth for one more moment. He knew it could well be the last such comfort he'd ever know.

She showed him a brave smile that belied the fear in her eyes. "I love you, Mike. I never stopped."

Mike looked within himself to see whether he could say the same. There'd been so much unnecessary drama in his relationship with Erin, and the love he'd felt for Hannah had eclipsed everything else so completely. But he was happy to provide an honest reply. "I love you, too." He released a breath he hadn't realized he'd been holding. Then he gave her a light, briefly lingering kiss on the mouth.

He sighed and stepped back. "Now we go."

She squeezed his hand. "Okay."

Hand in hand, they moved toward the door.

Mike's body tensed as he sensed something hurtling toward them from behind. They'd lingered too long here, paralyzed by emotion, rather than doing as they should've done and following Hawthorne recklessly into the breach. He cursed and whirled about in time to place the blade of the axe between Hannah and Erin. There'd been no time to deliver an actual blow, but just putting it in her path proved sufficient. Hannah slammed into the blade and it punched through her belly.

Hannah's forward motion came to an abrupt halt and she looked at Mike with a trembling face and tears in her eyes. It was a heartbreaking sight, and it nearly rendered him incapable of doing what he had to do. Then he gritted his teeth and yanked the axe blade out of her abdomen, twisting it as he did so and opening a huge gash that spilled intestines and other organs.

Mike moved away from her and gripped Erin by an arm. He steered her toward the door. "Go! Now!"

Hannah tore at the drooping lengths of intestine, yanking them from her body and flinging them into the darkness. Then, seemingly unaffected by the wound, she advanced again on Mike and Erin.

She sneered. "You slut." She looked at Mike. "You cheating asshole. I can't believe you wanted this . . ."—she pointed at Erin and seemed to have difficulty choosing an appropriate word—"*skank.* This filthy little skank. Over me. You son of a bitch, how could you?"

The last thing Mike wanted at this point was to engage this reanimated facsimile of his fiancée in conversation, but he felt compelled to refute what she was saying. "I didn't. No matter how this looks, I didn't. There's so much you don't know and I don't have time to explain it. I'm sorry."

Though he truly believed this thing wasn't his fiancée, at least not completely, the apology felt necessary. Because he'd decided to change course yet again. His first instinct had been to flee and avoid this unpleasantness, but that just couldn't happen. This was his one chance to deal with this phase of the Closure rituals before moving on to the next. So be it.

He leaped forward and brought the axe up from the ground in a golf swing–like arc. The blade pushed through the flesh beneath her jaw and lifted her off the ground. Then Mike wrenched the blade loose and saw blood cascade down the front of Hannah's funeral clothes. But Hannah came at him yet again. Erin screamed and tumbled backward. Her head struck the cinder block with a sickening crack, rendering her instantly unconscious.

But Mike was too busy with Hannah to help her. He warded her off with a couple of quick swings of the axe, one of which took off her left hand just above the wrist, but still she advanced. Mike moved through the door and into the dark hallway. Hannah, blinded by rage and an all-consuming need to get to him, tripped over the step leading up into the hallway and pitched forward. She rolled over and looked up in time to see the axe descending like the blade of a guillotine.

She opened her mouth to say something, but the blade fell through the opening and went all the way through her head, making a clanking sound as it struck the floor below her. She clawed at the axe handle even as Mike worked to finish the job of removing the top half of her head from her body. At last this was accomplished, and he sent the head skidding down the hallway with a hard kick.

Now in a state of frenzy, he raised the axe to finish what he'd started, but a strong hand gripped his shoulder and a sad voice spoke in his ear: "No. It's finished. Look."

Mike blinked.

He looked at Hannah's body. Her unmoving body.

He shrugged off Hawthorne's hand and turned to look at the man. "What happened? The rest of them I had to chop into little pieces."

Hawthorne tapped the side of his own head and nodded at the headless corpse. "The Prime, theoretically, is virtually invincible. With one exception. You awakened the Prime by reading from the book. Therefore only you could kill the Prime. Because of your unique connection to her, decapitation sufficed where it would not with other resurrected people."

Mike shook his head. "That's a bit of information I should've known beforehand, don't you think? Why didn't you tell me that?"

Hawthorne shrugged. "It slipped my mind."

The older man twisted the axe handle from Mike's hand and pushed the vinyl-covered book into its place. "It's done and you best forget it, for now. When we confront the Rogue you will need to read from the very last page of this book."

Mike flipped the book open and looked at the page in question. He saw two longish paragraphs written in an unfamiliar language. His brow furrowed as he looked at Hawthorne. "How am I supposed to read this?"

Hawthorne smiled. "Just start reading it. Remember the original Invocation? This will be the same. The words will take control of you and read themselves."

Mike shuddered at the memory. "I don't—"

"You have no choice."

Mike released a big breath and nodded. "I don't. Yeah. I know."

He glanced back through the open doorway and saw Erin lying on the concrete walkway. He made a move in that direction, but again Hawthorne stilled him with a firm hand on the shoulder.

"No."

Mike shot him a desperate, hopeless glance. "But she needs medical attention. She'll—"

Hawthorne's tone was firm. "No. There is no medical attention available. She's alive, and for now she's better off where she is, unconscious and out of the action." He steered Mike away from the open door. "Let's take this son of a bitch down."

Mike swallowed a lump in his throat and allowed Hawthorne to guide him deeper into the darkness.

CHAPTER FORTY-ONE

The huge sound Hawthorne's boots made clomping down the corridor unnerved him. The way the echo resonated in the empty darkness made him feel like he was taking a solitary midnight stroll through a haunted mausoleum. But he wasn't alone. O'Bannon, silent as a misbehaving schoolboy on his way to a meeting with the principal, was just a few feet behind him. And, somewhere beyond the end of this corridor, was an auditorium full of people awaiting their arrival.

Dead people. The first enlistees in the Rogue's army of dead.

They reached a point where the corridor veered to the right and turned in that direction. The end of the corridor, represented by a set of double doors with frosted glass windows, was just ahead.

Hawthorne stopped just short of the doors and waited for Mike to catch up with him. The younger man's face looked pale in the dim light coming through the opaque windows. He looked like a ghost. Hawthorne banished the thought. They were both likely to die within minutes, so it was useless to get distracted by what he knew to be falsely precognitive feelings.

He withdrew the Finger of Odin from his jacket pocket. "Open the book, Mr. O'Bannon."

Mike released a shuddery breath and glanced down at the book. He frowned at it. "I'd really rather not." But he flipped the book open anyway and thumbed again to the very last page. He studied it a moment, probably failing to notice the way his fingers trembled slightly where they brushed the book's infernal pages. He summoned a weak smile. "But what the hell. Damn the torpedoes, and full speed ahead."

Hawthorne nodded. "Good. In a moment I'll open these doors and we'll go forth to meet whatever fate has in store for us. I want you to start reading that passage the precise *instant* the door opens. Follow me through the door and continue to read. Whatever happens, do not falter. Read it through to the end, even as the Rogue's minions are tearing you apart, if necessary." He paused. "Can you do that?"

Hawthorne was pleased to see the determination that shone in the man's eyes.

"Yes. I can. For Hannah. For Avery." He nodded at the double doors. "And for all those people, my friends and neighbors. I'll finish reading it with my dying breath if need be."

Hawthorne laid a hand on Mike's shoulder and felt the resolute strength there. He doubted he needed to tell the man successful completion of the task assigned to him would likely require just that.

He nodded. "You're a good man, Mike O'Bannon."
He sighed. "It's time."

Mike's gaze didn't waver. "I know."

Hawthorne knew the moment had come. To waste
another second thinking about it, or even discussing
it with O'Bannon, would be inviting disaster. So he
turned and threw open the door. The bright lights of
the auditorium made him blink faster for a moment,
but he was quickly able to assess the situation anyway. The door they'd come through was to the left of
the stage. The Rogue was waiting for them at a
podium on the stage. The dark man turned in a non-
chalant way to leer at the intruders. His face, which
looked like white parchment paper stretched over a
centuries old skull, was just visible beneath the tilted
brim of his hat. Dangling from the creature's elon-
gated neck was the black amulet worn by all Reapers,
the enchanted stone that protected the wearer from
the ravages of aging—but not, apparently, from a
good, prolonged thwacking with the ugly stick.

In the floor area in front of the stage was a blond
woman bound with chains, lying in the middle of a
pentagram drawn in her own blood. She was alive,
but just barely. Her bare white flesh was smeared
here and there with blood. She looked like an es-
capee from some sadistic serial killer's dank cellar.

The Prime.

Every Blood Invocation required one, and she was
the Prime for this one, the final step. Hawthorne felt
a twinge of sorrow. He could not save her. A rescue
attempt here didn't even rank on his list of priorities.
Now was the time to shunt aside things like compas-
sion and do the hard thing that needed doing. As he
moved to the front of the stage, he heard Mike's

voice reciting the Rites of Closure. He sounded as he likely had when reading the original Invocation, like a conduit for some other spirit or entity. His voice acquired a deeper resonance, like the voice of an imprisoned demon emerging from the darkest recesses of a sealed cave.

He hurried past the Prime, withdrawing his hand from his jacket pocket as he neared the short set of steps at the other side of the stage. He glanced back at the rows of seated resurrected dead and felt a new sense of unease come over him. He'd expected to see the Rogue's army swarming toward them. He'd been prepared to see brave Mike O'Bannon ripped to shreds while he made his desperate attempt to get to the Rogue and deliver a killing blow with the shaman's gift.

He scurried up the steps and mounted the stage, continuing unimpeded on a direct line to the Deathbringer. He had a moment to reflect on that other man's talk of being steered into a trap. Hawthorne, of course, had known enough to know the truth of this. Their quarry had drawn them to this place, had welcomed this confrontation. No question of that. What he hadn't expected at all was the way things had unraveled to this point. They were encountering no resistance at all.

But there was no time to consider the fresh implications and questions. No time to retreat and devise an alternate plan of attack. For good or ill, he and O'Bannon were stuck with the already decided upon course of action.

The Deathbringer turned to face Hawthorne as he drew near. A jolt of terror went through him upon seeing that white wedge of leering face so close-up.

But he gritted his teeth and managed to keep moving forward. He shifted his grip on the Finger of Odin and raised his hand high over his head. The Death-bringer held his head up and his arms out, like a father welcoming a child home from school.

Doubt consumed Hawthorne now. He wanted to scream. Something was wrong. He didn't know what, but he knew *something* was. He heard O'Bannon finish reading the Invocation, heard that ancient voice fall silent, and knew as clearly as he'd ever known anything that he was seconds away from death. He was doomed and all his efforts—for reasons inexplicable—had been for nothing. Still, he went ahead and did what he'd come here to do. It wasn't like he had a lot of other options.

His hand came down in a vicious arc and the Finger of Odin slammed into the Deathbringer's chest, impaling his black heart straight through its middle.

Erin came to in time to see Avery standing over her. Her first instinct was to reach for him. She needed help. Probably needed stitches in the back of her head, from the feel of it. Then the world came into crisper focus and she saw the tattered flesh where the formerly smooth expanse of his throat had been. And she remembered how he'd saved her life by stepping in front of the thing that had come flying at her from the darkness.

He didn't look too interested in saving her from anything now. He growled like a wild animal, making some of the ribbons of torn flesh jiggle in a way that made her stomach lurch. He pounced on her and might have ripped her throat out, but a combination of instinct and adrenaline saved her this time. She seized the cinder block that had knocked her unconscious and swung it in a hard enough sideways arc that it knocked his jaw askew, making his head look like something from a surrealist painting. Seeing that happen to Avery hurt, but she refused to let that stop her. She raised the cinder block overhead and brought it down in a devastating blow that staved in the back of Avery's head, making it look like a bloody mop. He fell to the ground next to her and pawed feebly at her chest. She swatted the grasping hand aside and rolled away from him.

She got to her feet and staggered backward a few steps to lean against the rear entrance. She felt woozy again, but, determined not to slip back into unconsciousness, she bit her lower lip and drew blood. She watched Avery struggle to get off the ground, but she no longer considered him a source of concern. He was still functional, somewhat, but the blow to his brain had damaged him in some fundamental way. This surprised her, as all the evidence she'd seen so far indicated the resurrected people were virtually indestructible, unstoppable. Maybe the change had something to do with something that had happened while she was unconscious.

Maybe this Deathbringer asshole was dead now.

She glanced around her and realized for the first time that Mike and the old man were gone. Of course. Either they'd assumed the blow to her head had killed her or they had been too occupied with accomplishing their goals to help her. She felt a twinge of self-pity at the thought but banished it immediately. They'd been right to continue on with their mission.

But she was back in the game now, and was determined to offer whatever help she could. She had a feeling Mike and the old man would need some. The door had swung shut when she'd picked up the cinder block and it refused to budge when she pushed the lock bar. She made a sound of frustration and backed away from the door. She looked down at Avery, who'd managed to get to his hands and knees. She stomped on the pulped back of his skull and drove him to the ground again. He struck the cinder block and rolled off it onto his back.

Erin picked up the cinder block, turned, and faced the door. She planted her feet and rotated at the waist as she whipped her arms around and flung the big block of concrete with all her might. It struck the right window dead-center and a shower of glass rained down in the hallway. She knocked away the larger remaining shards of glass and hauled herself through the new opening.

She stood in the hallway for a moment as she tried to get her bearings. She could see that the stretch of corridor to her right ended abruptly and led to nowhere, which meant there was just one way to go.

So she turned to the left and started that way. Her foot struck a previously unnoticed impediment, something that felt solid but yielding. She leaned in for a closer look and gasped at the sight of Hannah's decapitated and disemboweled body. Tears sprung to her eyes at the knowledge that this could only be Mike's grim handiwork. Hawthorne had said only he could kill the Prime, and apparently he had done just that. It was a positive development for their side, but she couldn't help but ache for Mike.

She heaved a heavy sigh, then stepped over the corpse and hurried on down the hall.

* * *

Hawthorne felt something like an electric jolt in that moment of impact. The shock of it sent him tumbling backward. He hit the stage hard and stared up at the Deathbringer in helpless horror. His eyes widened at the sight of a buzzing ball of white light that appeared at the spot where the Finger of Odin had entered the creature's body. It was intensely bright, so much so that he had to hold his arm up to shield his eyes. The ball of light crackled and sent out hundreds of bright little electric arms that crawled over the Deathbringer's body, weaving a cloak of brilliant light that overwhelmed all that darkness. The Reaper's face changed, too, becoming fuller and less like the countenance of a leering ghoul.

The brilliant light burned a few degrees brighter, then began to lessen. Soon, the Deathbringer's true form became clear again. The black cloak and the tilted black fedora covering the face of Death appeared through the shimmering light. And that grin, with those rows of razor teeth, was the same as before. But there was no denying that something fundamental had changed. And not for the better. Far from killing him, the Finger of Odin had only served to make him more powerful.

Hawthorne wanted to scream. He felt helpless, paralyzed on the spot. And completely without a clue as to what to do next. His mind could hardly credit the notion, but it was impossible to deny the reality before him. The Deathbringer was a bigger threat than ever. It might even be that he was truly invincible now. Which could only mean that he'd been betrayed somewhere along the line. Eldritch, at the very least, had to have known what would really happen when the Finger of Odin penetrated the Death-bringer's heart. And it was all too easy now to imagine that he'd been serving a false cause all along, that he'd been a pawn manipulated by forces far greater than he could ever comprehend.

Apparently, however, he had some small measure of fight left in him, because he'd at least managed to get moving again. It would be futile, of course, but he'd rather die fighting this obscenity than fall at its feet and plead for mercy. He scooted backward a bit and got to his feet.

The Deathbringer stayed where he was, showing him a glowing grin.

Hawthorne looked at Mike, who was clutching the book and staring entranced at the Deathbringer. He looked like a kid watching a Fourth of July fireworks display. Hawthorne jumped off the stage and tore the book out of his grasp.

There was an abrupt change in the atmosphere inside the auditorium. There was grumbling from the crowd of resurrected dead. The Deathbringer was still a shimmering figure, but the light was ringed now by a black aura. Hawthorne didn't need anyone to tell him the obvious—that the Deathbringer did *not* want him to have possession of this book. Not anymore. In his hands, it was dangerous in some way. Either because of some Invocation he could conceivably read to reverse this (which didn't seem likely, as he'd never be able to figure out which one) or because of concern for the safety of the book.

That had to be it.

And if not, well, the whole world was fucked anyway.

Whatever window of opportunity he had here was

damn near shut. The Deathbringer had moved to the edge of the stage. He was glowing brighter now. And that black halo looked more malignant than ever. Hawthorne didn't know what the hell that meant, but it couldn't be good.

The resurrected people were rising from their seats. Hawthorne didn't wait to be swarmed. Nor did he try to get Mike to snap out of his trance. He had to get away from here and destroy the book. So he returned the way he'd come, dashing around the stage and lowering his shoulder like a running back to crash through the double doors. The doors flew open and he ran headlong into Erin. As they tumbled to the floor in a confusion of intertwined limbs, the book flew from his hands and went sliding down the polished hallway tiles like a puck skidding down an ice rink.

Hawthorne saw it swallowed by the darkness as his arm hit the floor at a bad angle and snapped with sickening ease. It wasn't a clean break, either. He fell over, twisting the limb again and causing the bone to break through the skin. He bit back a scream and heaved himself into a sitting position. He could hear footsteps closing in from the auditorium. He looked at Erin and saw her watching him in an expression that was equal parts befuddlement and abject terror.

He opened his mouth and released a helpless whimper. Then he made himself say what he needed to say. "Everything was a lie. We were betrayed." He nodded to indicate the area of the hallway where the book would be. "Get the book. Get out of here. Destroy it. Burn it. I don't care how you do it, but destroy it completely. Go! *Now!*"

Erin looked into his eyes and appeared to see the

desperate conviction there. She nodded once and got to her feet. She wobbled for the first step or two, then moved with a quickness that momentarily gladdened Hawthorne's despairing heart.

The darkness swallowed her.

A heartbeat later he heard her footsteps stop.

Then she continued on, and soon was gone.

He smiled. He laughed. She had the book! *Thank God,* he thought. *She has the book!*

Then the hallway was filled with resurrected dead.

Soon he felt their teeth on his skin, felt their fetid breath. The breath of the dead. He felt their grasping hands tearing at him. He felt his flesh give way, his warm blood spill into cold, yearning mouths. He screamed at the searing agony, but, absurdly, he never stopped smiling.

His last thought as a living man was a prayer for the girl.

Then he awoke and faced the Deathbringer. The army of dead moved aside to admit him. Hawthorne looked up at his new god and smiled again. The two men, one dead, one immortal, shared a silent communion. The Deathbringer allowed him a look into the howling chasm of his own mind, and Hawthorne saw that Eldritch had been in league with the Rogue all along. He'd known the Finger of Odin wasn't an instrument of death, but was instead a key to almost unlimited power. He saw the great lengths Eldritch had gone to in order to conceal the unholy alliance. Crafty, behind-the-scenes machinations he'd worked at until near the very end, with an assassination attempt on the Prime that had been conceived to fail. Layers and layers of misdirection and obfuscation. His reward would be to become an immortal himself.

But Hawthorne saw something else, and this caused him to laugh. The Deathbringer meant to betray Eldritch as completely as the old wizard had betrayed his colleagues.

In exchange for this glimpse of the truth, Hawthorne told the Deathbringer about the girl, and about the frenzied instructions he'd given her.

The Deathbringer's everpresent leering grin faded.

He snarled.

And he gripped Hawthorne's head and twisted it off.

The Deathbringer's mouth opened to emit a scream that filled the hallway and rocked the building on its foundations. Then he tossed the old man's head aside and hurried down the hallway, with his army of dead following in his wake.

The only sounds in the auditorium now were those of Mike's own breath puffing in and out, and a steady sobbing from somewhere nearby. He'd lost focus somewhere along the way, had lost his slippery grip on this increasingly absurd and warped version of reality, and only now was he becoming aware of the world around him again.

He blinked and saw the nude hairdresser lying bound in the middle of the crudely sketched pentagram. *Her blood,* he thought. Someone had drawn the infernal symbol with the woman's freshly spilled blood. She was the source of the sobbing. Beyond her was the now empty stage. He spied a darkened spot on the stage, a rough black oval. It looked like a flash burn. Of course. Some kind of brilliant electrical field had engulfed the Deathbringer upon being stabbed with the Finger of Odin. There'd been enough voltage there to burn every death row prisoner in America to a crisp. Mike couldn't fathom why the fucker hadn't been reduced to a pile of ashes on the spot. To the contrary, the thing had been made stronger.

Belatedly, he realized that must have been the plan all along. Someone else's plan, that is. It was obvious that Hawthorne had been played like a sucker by somebody. With great clarity, Mike recalled the look of horror and astonishment on the older man's face as he'd gaped at his unnaturally energized adversary. The next thing he knew Hawthorne was twisting the book from his grip and running away. Things had gone a bit fuzzy after that, and Mike had no idea what had happened to the man.

He glanced behind him and saw that the auditorium was empty. At some point during that gray time the Deathbringer's army had departed. He assumed it'd been a very abrupt event. Whatever had happened had been urgent enough to cause hundreds of resurrected dead to flee this place without taking time to kill the last two live (and quite vulnerable) humans. The strange turn of events likely had something to do with Hawthorne and the book. He'd gotten out of here with it, and the Deathbringer wanted—perhaps desperately *needed*—it back.

Whatever. It was out of his hands now. He couldn't hope to intercede on Hawthorne's behalf even if he'd felt motivated to do so. There was just one dilemma remaining. He was alive. Somehow. Everyone he'd ever loved, everything he'd ever cared about, was all gone. But he couldn't just remain here on the floor, unmoving, waiting to succumb to starvation or whatever other grim fate awaited. Damned if he could think of a compelling reason to carry on from here, other than lack of anything else to do.

He looked at the chained woman. "Your name's Janine, right? You used to do my old girlfriend's hair."

She sniffled. "Erin?"

Mike nodded. "Yeah." But he didn't want to think about Erin, not with that awful sound of her skull striking the cinder block still so fresh in his mind. He chuckled. "It's so strange."

The woman sniffled. "Wha . . . what?"

Mike got to his feet and shook the last bit of fog from his head. He looked at the woman. The pentagram. And at the axe with which he'd chopped off the top of his dead fiancée's head. It lay at the front of the stage, where Hawthorne had discarded it prior to attacking the dark man with the Finger of Odin. Mike walked past the woman and picked it up by the handle.

He faced the bewildered woman again. "Just the mixture of various belief systems. Odin was a Norse god. I know because there was this goofy rock band a long time ago that took his name, which prompted me to look up the real deal." He nodded at the pentagram. "Which doesn't really seem to mesh with the Satanic symbolism on display here."

The look on the woman's wide-eyed, mascara-streaked face made it plain she thought he was insane. "I . . . don't . . ."

Mike shook his head. "I know. It's okay. Tell me something, Janine. Are you a very religious woman?"

The mention of religion had the curious effect of calming Janine immediately. She nodded. "Yes, sir. I am."

"Are you Catholic, any chance?"

Another nod. "Yes."

Mike smiled. "Which sort of puts you in a minority here in Baptist country, eh?"

This elicited a trembly smile. "Yes." She sniffled again and the smile broadened a bit. "A papist, some of the old-timers call me."

Mike's smile took on a sympathetic tint. "I was raised Catholic, myself. I'm second-generation Irish-American, but for at least a hundred years before that my ancestors lived in Northern Ireland. I'm well acquainted with that kind of prejudice. My grandfather could tell you stories that'd curl your hair."

Janine made a sound that was almost a laugh. It pierced Mike's heart.

He moved closer to her, swinging the axe at his side like a baseball player approaching the plate. "But back to the point." He nodded again at the pentagram. "Do you believe in the devil, Janine? In the literal hell, as in the lake of fire and the place where evil souls spend eternity in torment?"

Janine's expression sobered. "I do, Officer O'Bannon."

He sighed. "This is just supposition on my part, understand, but I think your beliefs made you more susceptible to the Deathbringer's dark magic. That's why he bled you and drew that fucking symbol with your blood."

She was frowning now. "I don't understand."

Mike nodded, affirming something to himself. "And I'd be willing to bet Hawthorne was descended from a line of believers in the old gods." He laughed without humor. "Finger of Odin my fucking ass."

Janine's frown deepened. She looked frightened now. She had a right to be.

"I need you to be honest with me about something, Janine." He came to a halt next to her. His grip on the axe handle tightened. "Did the dark man perform some kind of ritual before my friend and I got here?" He swallowed hard. "Do you recall the word 'prime' being used at any point?"

Her expression had been a combination of puzzlement and terror, but it changed abruptly, giving way to a spark of recognition. "Yes! That's what he called me. He said it over and over. I didn't understand any of it."

Mike closed his eyes.

He tried to come up with a compelling reason not to do what he knew he must. But he came up empty. Tears dribbled from the corners of his clenched-shut eyelids.

Janine's voice was weak and clouded with fear and confusion. "Officer . . . Mike . . . what's wrong?"

Mike willed his eyes open and summoned his sunniest smile. It felt like a grotesque mask, a false image of good will. "Nothing's wrong, Janine. Everything's right with the world and this is all just a bad dream."

Janine finally smiled again. She closed her eyes and sighed. "Thank God."

Mike lifted the axe over his head and brought it down quickly, muttering his own silent prayer of thanks to God for causing the woman to close her eyes and allow her this moment of near-grace while he performed what he knew to be a mercy killing.

But Janine's eyes fluttered open an instant before the blade sliced through her throat. Mike screamed as the axe struck the floor beneath her twitching body. He released the axe handle and sank to his knees.

He rode a flood of tears to the cold floor.

* * *

The Deathbringer felt something *tug* at him. It was the way a dog must feel when its owner snaps its leash to restrain it. It was a powerful sensation that brought him to a sudden stop near the center of the town square. Only a significant effort of will prevented him from toppling into the cascading water fountain. The feeling came again and he realized that he felt . . . *diminished.* He was still several times more powerful than he had been before tonight, but the backward shift was dramatic enough to be undeniable. He made himself concentrate and focus his energies. He sent out a psychic feeler and was unsurprised at the dead space it encountered.

He loosed a cry of rage that seemed to explode in the Dandridge sky like an incoming missile. The sound was so mammoth, so consciousness-obliterating in its sheer volume, that it caused the hundreds or resurrected dead to fall to the ground and lie there howling like babies deprived of their food.

The Prime!

Somehow the loathsome creature had been eliminated. Another landscape-flattening scream tore out of him and he staggered closer to the fountain. The Prime. The Invocation to Conflict and the intricate series of steps necessary to make it work. All for nothing. The second Prime had to live through to the end of the closing rituals and now that could not happen. All because he'd been foolish enough to believe he was invincible. He tried to imagine what fatal flaw in his meticulously devised schemes could possibly have been overlooked.

The answer came.

And he derived only minimal comfort in knowing

that the Invocation's undoing was unrelated to any fault in his plans. In his desperation to retrieve the book, he'd failed to account for the original Prime's lover. He cursed himself again. One (or several) of his resurrected faithful should've been directed to kill the man the instant he was finished reading his part of the Invocation.

Now the thing he'd dreamed of for so long could not happen. The ruling power could not be summoned. The swift elimination of human beings as the world's dominant species would not occur. He couldn't fathom how this had happened. How all his careful planning had been for naught. Then an awful possibility occurred to him. That this blown opportunity was his fault. He'd been too proud. Had been blinded by his ego. Too dismissive of the very real threat presented by determined humans. And the ultimate result of this stupidity was the worst part of the whole disaster—he'd exposed himself. The ruling power would be aware of the botched Invocation to Conflict. His mind reeled at the prospect of facing the power's judgment.

No!

His only hope was to regain possession of the book and perform a protective invocation, some bit of cloaking magic sturdy enough to buy him time. If he could do that, he could move to another corner of the world and try again. Only this time he would get it right. This time—

He gasped.

Something cold lanced him. It felt like he'd been stabbed with a blade made of ice. Then he felt something *moving* inside him. He glanced down and saw a length of something black and cancerous emerge from his chest. It popped free and clattered on the concrete. He stared uncomprehendingly at the strange object for a time, then awareness of what had happened made him sway on his feet again.

It was the so-called "Finger of Odin." A false name bestowed upon it by Eldritch, who'd known the Norse god's name would speak to Hawthorne, instill within him a false sense of confidence. It was actually a bolt of solidified ichor, the blood of a divine being, converted by dark alchemy to function as a power amplifier. But now it was as useless as a blown fuse. He kicked it and sent it skittering over the concrete and into the grass beyond.

Then he looked into the street and saw the girl. The vulnerable one he'd manipulated and sent to kill the original Prime. Somehow Hawthorne had persuaded her to act against him. But this was only because she didn't know he was her true benefactor. He was the one who'd freed the monster lurking within her, a dark and wondrous gift he knew she cherished. The relief he felt was immense, almost staggeringly so. He would survive the night, even go on to flourish elsewhere, despite his stupidity. All because of this one sublimely serendipitous moment.

He felt almost serene. He was steady on his feet again as he reached out to touch her mind. But that calm feeling vanished when he encountered resistance. He frowned and pushed harder, concentrating the full energy of his ancient Reaper's mind. But the effort was futile. He may as well have been pushing against a brick wall. For a moment he was immobilized by his confusion.

This just couldn't be. He'd gained access to a door within the girl's mind. A door that, once opened, could never be closed to him again. Which could only mean that another consciousness now resided in the girl's brain. Somehow she'd been displaced. He gathered every remaining reserve of psychic energy available to him and cast a wider net. This time he found the girl's mind and entered through the door he'd created. And he immediately retreated, recoiling from the howling pain there. She was still conscious somewhere, some crushed bit of her, but she was far away from here and less than useless to him now. Before he retreated, he saw enough to know Hawthorne was to blame, and he wished now he'd kept the man alive so that he might torture him and make him pay an appropriate price for his interference.

The figure in the street, the stranger inhabiting the girl's body, appeared confused. He had to get to her. Had to kill her and reclaim the book. He felt himself growing weaker. He'd expended too much energy working to bring about the Invocation to Conflict. And with the ichor bolt prematurely expended, he had nothing to fall back on. He moved away from the fountain and began walking toward the street, feeling a horrible weariness in his legs, a human frailty he'd not had to endure for so many centuries.

Before he could get very far, the faint figure turned and darted down the street.

He screamed again and hurried after her.

Standing in the street, Erin felt like a claustrophobic stuffed into a crawl space. She didn't know where to go, or how to go about getting herself there once she'd figured it out. She'd peeked through the windows of Avery's Mustang, hoping to see his keys dangling from the ignition. Not there. She'd then glanced into Hawthorne's Firebird. Again, no keys. Seeing this filled her with a senseless fury at the dead men. Why had they taken their goddamned keys with them? There was no one left to steal their fucking cars.

She shuddered as the truth of that hit her. As the enormity of it hit her. Dandridge was just a big open-air tomb now. There was a real possibility—perhaps even a probability at this point—that she was the lone remaining live human within the town's borders.

The realization made her feel desperately alone and terrified. The feeling deserted her in the next moment. A sound immense enough to dwarf that of a jet's engine filled the air and made her drop to her knees. She dropped the book and clamped her hands over her ears. She moaned and felt hot tears spilling down her cheeks. Then the sound abruptly ended.

She picked up the book with trembling hands. Then she rose to stand on wobbly feet, and her gaze went back to the town square. The creature Hawthorne had interchangeably called the "Rogue" and the "Deathbringer" was there. And he was lost and flailing, like a child wandering in a dark and frightening forest at night. Seeing him in this weakened state was astounding. He didn't seem as fearsome as she'd imagined. But Erin knew this was only because of whatever Mike and Hawthorne had accomplished in the meeting hall before the Deathbringer overwhelmed them. They were both surely dead now, but she believed they'd dealt the Deathbringer a devastating blow.

Oh, Mike . . .

Her heart ached at the thought of the terror and

pain he must have known in his last moments.

I love you, sweetie, she thought. *Forever. . . .*

Her resolve stiffened. No way could she allow his sacrifice to have been in vain. She saw the Deathbringer begin to move across the square again, and a sense of urgency sizzled through her like lightning.

She glanced down the street and saw, parked in the middle of the street two blocks down, a big old car with its driver's side door wide open. It beckoned to her the way a neon sign hanging over a bar door calls to an alcoholic. She kicked off Melinda's stupid heels and took off barefoot down the street. She heard another scream, though it was really more like a wail of distress, and knew the time was short. The Deathbringer would not rest until he had her. Until he had the book.

The keys better damn well be in the ignition, otherwise she—and, who knew, maybe the whole damned world—was fucked. Her legs pumped harder and the car drew nearer. She sensed the presence of the Deathbringer behind her. He'd rallied himself, and was in the street now and closing the gap between them. She heard distant rumblings. The voices of the dead. His resurrected people. They were coming to his aid. A whimper escaped her lips. The car—a dilapidated Oldsmobile—was still a block away. Soon the Deathbringer would be upon her. And he would have the book. And his swarming minions would have her. She could feel their hunger, their relentless need to taste warm human blood, and she was the last such morsel in the vicinity.

Erin pushed herself harder. She was glad now, very glad, for this younger, more athletic body. Her old one wouldn't have taken her so far so soon. She would probably be dead by now.

She slipped through the open door and landed behind the steering wheel. She dropped the book on the passenger seat and her hand went to the ignition, where it closed around a ring full of keys. A feeling of elation seized her as she twisted the key in the ignition and the engine rumbled to life. It wasn't the smoothest-running thing she'd ever heard, but she couldn't imagine a sweeter sound.

The Deathbringer screamed again as she put the car in gear and stomped on the gas pedal. The sound buffeted her mind like a high, whistling wind, but she kept her foot pressed down and the awful noise soon diminished as she zoomed through an intersection and down to the end of Main Street, where she made a sharp right turn and sped away from the center of town.

She remembered to breathe again about a mile later. She glanced in the rearview mirror, fully expecting to see a convoy of dead people speeding after her in cars and pick-ups. But she only saw an empty street. Still, she didn't let up on the gas until she was entirely out of the town proper and moving through a residential area. To her right loomed one of Dandridge's three major apartment complexes. To her left was a Quik Stop convenience store. It was lit up like a theatre on the night of a big Hollywood premier. But there were no cars in the lot and the store looked empty.

Erin's bare foot tromped the brake pedal and the Oldsmobile squealed to a stop in the street. She turned the wheel hard to the left and zoomed across the road. She had no idea whether the store was locked up and didn't wish to waste any time finding out, so she kept her foot on the gas pedal as the store's entrance loomed. Then she closed her eyes and braced for impact. She felt the car shudder and heard a shower of glass. Her eyes snapped open and she saw the Oldsmobile's front end plow into an aisle of snack food and drinks. Its engine was now sputtering and steam was emerging from beneath the hood. She grabbed the book and got out of the car. Stepping carefully around shards of glass, she made her way to the checkout counter. She selected a disposable lighter from a display stand and hurried back through the ruined entrance.

The sense of urgency gripping her was still strong. She had no illusions of safety. The Deathbringer and his army might still be coming. Were *probably* still coming. So she ran across the parking lot to the nearest gas pump, where she removed a nozzle from its hook and flipped up the switch. Praying the pump wasn't set for pre-pay only, she stripped the vinyl (or whatever the hell it actually was—the material felt strange to the touch) cover off the book and let it fall to the ground. The book landed on its spine and fell open near the middle. The pages ruffled in the light breeze.

Erin said a final prayer and aimed the gas nozzle at the book.

Then she squeezed the handle and gas came forth like water from a hose. Tears of joy and relief sprang to her eyes. She held the handle and doused the book completely. For the hell of it, she splashed the discarded cover with gas, too. Then she flicked the switch back down and returned the nozzle to its hook.

She stood panting there a moment longer, listening to the thudding of her own heart and straining to hear the approach of the Deathbringer's army. At first she heard nothing. Then there was a growing buzz, the droning sound of many engines drawing near.

Erin knelt next to the book. She flicked the lighter and applied the tongue of flame to the gas-soaked pages. There was a *whoomphf* and an explosion of hot air that propelled her away from the book. The heat singed the back of her hand, but she didn't catch fire. She sat back on her ass and saw flames consume the book and its cover. She laughed. Tears flowed like bitter wine.

And now she discerned another sound in the distance. The droning buzz gave way to a succession of more discordant noises. She puzzled over it a moment, then realized it was the sound of dozens of vehicles crashing into each other.

Erin sat entranced by the fire a moment longer, then realized the danger she was in. She got to her feet and ran from the parking lot. She had no idea whether she'd splashed around enough fuel to risk igniting the underground tanks, but she saw no point in sticking around to find out. She crossed the street to the apartment complex, where she began a systematic search of all the cars parked in its lot. One of them, she knew, would have keys dangling from the ignition, left behind by someone in a hurry. She would take that car and drive far away from this place. Hundreds of miles. Maybe thousands. Then, in someplace completely different from her home, maybe an isolated town on a high desert plain, she would stop and try to think about how to go about making a new life for herself.

She struck pay dirt with just the third car she checked. A red Honda Accord with Mardi Gras beads dangling from the rearview mirror. A chick's car, she could tell right away. She said a prayer for the mystery woman (who, like everyone else in Dandridge, was probably dead), then got in the car and began her long journey.

The Deathbringer watched that portion of his faithful that hadn't been able to find cars fall to the ground and knew the fight was over. The girl had destroyed the book. He couldn't fathom it. Only minutes had passed. Yet somehow she'd conceived of a way to eliminate the source of the powerful magic that had made his grand scheme seem possible.

He raged inwardly another moment longer, felt the bitterness fill his veins like poison, then something changed within him. This was the end. The *real* end. And at last he saw the true reason for all his scheming. Beneath the thirst for power was a plainer, more melancholy reality. He was just tired of this existence. For the first time in a very long time he thought of his long-dead family. And weariness settled over him like a blanket draped gently about the shoulders of a sick child.

Nickolai, he thought. *My name is Nickolai. Not Reaper. Not Deathbringer.*

Nickolai.

He was surprised to find a dormant trace of the man he'd been within him. That part of him awakened now and felt horror at what he'd become, at what he'd done to this town. Thousands of innocents dead. For nothing.

And he knew now that he no longer wanted the power he'd so craved.

He just wanted to rest.

At last.

Forever.

He realized then that he wasn't completely without power. It remained within his ability to make this final thing happen. He raised a hand to the black amulet dangling around his neck. His long, tapered fingers—so alien to the eyes of Nickolai—closed around the smooth, cold stone.

The Deathbringer—Nickolai—breathed one last sigh.

Then he gathered the last of his strength and pulled hard, snapping the amulet's chain. He opened his hand and looked at the stone. An R for Reaper was etched into its surface. As long as the stone touched his flesh, he could live forever. The ruling power would take it from him soon, he knew.

But he didn't want it to come to that.

He'd lived too long in the service of . . . whoever, or whatever, the ruling power was.

He opened his hand, tilted it, and watched the stone fall to the pavement and bounce away. The change happened immediately. For one shining moment he was completely human again, and he knew an instant of pure happiness. Then the accelerated decomposition began. He felt his flesh rot and his organs liquefy. His eyes turned to mush and the world disappeared. His bones twisted and snapped. All of this happened too fast for there to be any real pain. His decaying body pitched to the ground. And his last conscious feelings as he struck the pavement were overwhelming sorrow and regret.

Soon all that remained of the Deathbringer was a mound of ash amid a pile of black clothes. A breeze came along and stirred some of the debris, lifting it and casting it to the wind.

For a time Dandridge was still and silent, a ghost town.

Then there was a big boom, an explosion on the outskirts of town. A fire at a convenience store raged out of control and spread over much of the area. By the time fire departments from neighboring counties arrived to quell it, an apartment complex and a portion of nearby forest had burned. A frantic search for local authorities lead to the first of many grisly discoveries. In the months to follow, there would be numerous investigations. In the end, most would conclude that an act of biological terrorism was to blame for the eradication of an entire small town's population. Some gas or nerve agent that had driven them all mad and made them kill each other in a blood-thirsty frenzy. No one knew what had really happened. The government scientists who examined the dead *knew* terrorism wasn't to blame, but they could come up with no other explanation. Certain shadowy elements in the intelligence community were more than happy to propagate the terrorism theory. It served their purposes very well.

EPILOGUE

Mike heard the convenience store explosion. He'd heard another explosion earlier. The scream of the Deathbringer. But this was something else. The sound roused him, allowed him to emerge from the lake of grief and self-pity he'd been wallowing in, and he got to his feet. He walked calmly down the aisle between the rows of seats, pushed open the front entrance, and stepped outside.

He looked beyond the water fountain at the center of the square and spied a familiar dark figure standing in the middle of Main Street. His grip tightened around the axe handle and he began to move in that direction. He supposed it wasn't possible that he could kill a creature like the Deathbringer with a simple physical tool like the axe, but that didn't deter Mike. He meant to continue this struggle down to the final beat of his broken heart.

But there was something curious in the posture of

his adversary. Something that made him move with caution rather than the abrupt charge into the breach he'd planned. It took him a moment to recognize what it was he saw in the creature now, and when he did he found it simultaneously astonishing and obvious.

The Deathbringer was a defeated thing.

And he knew it.

Mike knew he should feel elation at this knowledge. But all he felt was emptiness.

The Deathbringer was defeated, sure. And the wider world was safe again, at least from this threat. But Hannah was still gone. He'd mutilated her beautiful body with this very axe. Everyone else he'd known, his friends, family, colleagues, neighbors, all of them were gone. The only world that had ever mattered to him, this idyllic town of his birth and childhood, was a barren place, populated only by ghosts now.

He flipped the axe aside and continued on toward the Deathbringer. He watched the thing tear something from its throat and look at it a moment before allowing it to fall to the street. Mike watched the creature's rapid disintegration with only mild interest, knowing that the process was but a coda, a denouement. The real end for the Deathbringer had already occurred, brought about by some unseen event. Perhaps something to do with the explosion. Or maybe it was something internal, an inner reckoning.

Whatever the case, Mike didn't care. He knew he had no role left to play in this drama. It was all over but the sighing. By the time he reached the street, the Deathbringer was a pile of ash, as inconsequential as a cloud of dust or a passing daydream.

Mike's gaze was drawn to something in the street. He moved away from the Deathbringer's paltry remains and scooped up the smooth black stone. He frowned, and turned it over in his hands, puzzling over it. The etched R made it clear this was the thing the creature had removed from around its neck.

Reaper.

With the tip of his forefinger, he traced the deep groove of the gothic letter and felt a strange coldness penetrate him to the core. Then he heard the sound of boot heels clacking on the pavement and his head snapped up.

His heart almost stopped. It was the Deathbringer. Except . . . it wasn't. It was someone like the Deathbringer. Another Reaper, this one come to collect the soul of its colleague, no doubt. Mike didn't move. His heart fell back into its normal rhythm. He wasn't afraid of anything anymore. Especially not death.

The Reaper stopped at the pile of empty clothes. He studied the swirling pile of ash a moment, then spoke. "What will you do now, Michael O'Bannon?"

The voice was similar to that of the Deathbringer's, creaky and thick with the decay of centuries. It was the voice of the grave. Not so long ago—just hours ago, actually—Mike would've found the sound unnerving. Extremely. But now it didn't bother him.

Strange.

He shrugged. "I don't know. Kill myself. There's nothing to live for. My world is gone."

The Reaper turned to face him. "There is something to live for." He nodded at the amulet in Mike's hand. "The Reaper who wreaked such havoc here left us prematurely. Usually the job is . . . well, forever.

And we only recruit new Reapers as the world's population rises." The Reaper smiled. The expression wasn't quite as hideous as the Deathbringer's leering grin, but it wasn't pretty, either. He had the same wormy lips, the same crowded rows of razor-sharp teeth. The same bizarre angles that made his face look like a white wedge of sculpted porcelain.

Mike massaged the amulet with the base of his thumb. "What's this got to do with me?"

The Reaper said, "Everything. Always there has been a balance, a delicate pattern of threads linking the world of the living and the one beyond. Disturbing that balance is dangerous to all living things in all the worlds."

Awareness of what the creature was implying caused just the smallest pang of regret somewhere inside Mike, because he knew he was about to leave the human world behind. He would not turn down the Reaper's offer. The way he saw it, he would be accepting a sacred duty. The thought of leaving behind all the simple joys (and heartbreaks, don't forget those) made him grieve briefly for his lost life.

He looked the Reaper in the eye. "You need me to restore the balance."

"Yes."

Mike nodded. "Okay."

The Reaper smiled.

And took Mike by the hand.

Had anyone been there to witness the event, they would have seen two men standing in an oddly intimate pose.

Then they would have seen the men blink out of existence.

Gone to who knows where.

341

The ether, maybe.
Or the graveyard of lost souls.

In a while the sound of sirens would pierce the Dandridge night.

But for now Dandridge was quiet. Soft, swirling breezes ruffled the leaves of trees in the town square and brushed the lips of the dead like the final, bittersweet farewell of a thousand lost loves.

☐ **YES!**

Sign me up for the Leisure Horror Book Club and send
my FREE BOOKS! If I choose to stay in the club, I will
pay only $8.50* each month, a savings of $7.48!

NAME: _____

ADDRESS: _____

TELEPHONE: _____

EMAIL: _____

☐ I want to pay by credit card.

☐ **VISA**   ☐ **MasterCard**   ☐ **DISCOVER**

ACCOUNT #: _____

EXPIRATION DATE: _____

SIGNATURE: _____

Mail this page along with $2.00 shipping and handling to:
Leisure Horror Book Club
PO Box 6640
Wayne, PA 19087
Or fax (must include credit card information) to:
610-995-9274
You can also sign up online at **www.dorchesterpub.com**.
*Plus $2.00 for shipping. Offer open to residents of the U.S. and Canada only.
Canadian residents please call 1-800-481-9191 for pricing information.
If under 18, a parent or guardian must sign. Terms, prices and conditions subject to
change. Subscription subject to acceptance. Dorchester Publishing reserves the right
to reject any order or cancel any subscription.

GET FREE BOOKS!

You can have the best fiction delivered to your door for less than what you'd pay in a bookstore or online. Sign up for one of our book clubs today, and we'll send you *FREE* BOOKS* just for trying it out... **with no obligation to buy, ever!**

As a member of the Leisure Horror Book Club, you'll receive books by authors such as **RICHARD LAYMON, JACK KETCHUM, JOHN SKIPP, BRIAN KEENE** and many more.

As a book club member you also receive the following special benefits:
- **30% off all orders!**
- **Exclusive access to special discounts!**
- **Convenient home delivery and 10 days to return any books you don't want to keep.**

Visit **www.dorchesterpub.com** or call **1-800-481-9191**

There is no minimum number of books to buy, and you may cancel membership at any time.
*Please include $2.00 for shipping and handling.